Paula
Edgington

Payback Time

Payback Time
By Paula Edgington

First Published 2007

ISBN 978-1-84753-450-7

Acknowledgement

I would like to thank everyone who has supported me in the writing of Payback Time. Particularly Michael Yates of the Hemsworth writers group, and Ken Anderson for his advice and patience in the layout design and production of the book.

Prologue

The huge white articulated lorry with *Transportes Routiers* emblazoned on its side in red lettering crawled along the M62 from Manchester towards Leeds. It had come up the country from Dover to deliver some gym equipment in Manchester and was then crossing the country to deliver some more in Leeds. Before that it had driven the length of France on the A9 and had originated near the Mediterranean coast of France. The number 34 at the end of the registration plate showed that it came from the department of Herault.

The driver was now on the highest motorway in England and although it was dark, Christian Dubois could sense the bleakness of Saddleworth Moor as it stretched away around him into the night. Strange shapes seemed silhouetted in the landscape. He wasn't sure if they were part of the hillside or part of his imagination. He was aware that this was the very area where Myra Hindley and Ian Brady had buried their child murder victims. As the wind whistled around outside the cab of his lorry, a shiver ran down his spine. A shower of rain splattered on to his windscreen startling him, the glittering diamonds of rain slanted across in the headlight's beam. He reached down to flick on the windscreen wipers and turn up the heater. An ambulance sped past him creating a light spray, its blue light pulsating in the darkness.

Other than this and the occasional delivery lorry for one of the supermarket chains, there was very little traffic on the road tonight. His headlights picked out a blue and white sign on the edge of the carriageway for the next service station at Hartshead Moor. Not much further now thank goodness, it had been a long drive and he was feeling tired.

He rubbed his eyes, blinked hard, and tried to focus on the road. The lights of the service station came into view ahead of him and the slip road markers rumbled under the wheels of the lorry. Christian followed the directions on the signs which separated cars and lorries into different areas of the car park. He rolled the wagon gently to a stop on the area of the car park designated for lorries and parked slightly away from the other vehicles which were obviously here for an overnight stop, the cabs were in darkness and their curtains tightly closed against the night. Some stood with their rear doors fastened open to show they were unloaded and not a potential target for hijackers.

He parked away from them partly because he didn't want to disturb the other drivers and also because he wanted his lorry to be parked where it could easily be picked out by someone looking for him. He'd been instructed by his boss, that as the building in Leeds where he was to deliver the weight lifting machines was somewhat difficult to find because of the one way system, someone would meet him at the service station and he could then follow them for the remainder of the journey. It seemed a bit of an odd arrangement. Surely with his satellite navigation system he should be able to find the place. He was being well paid for the job; they shouldn't feel the need to send someone out in the night to help him to find the way. In fact now he came to think of it, he was being *very* well paid for a simple delivery of gym equipment.

He shrugged off the sudden feeling of apprehension. He was getting on a bit and although he no longer enjoyed the long drives outside France, if he could make a little extra money here and there, so much the better. It didn't always do to be difficult or to ask too many questions. If he did they'd soon find someone else to take his place. A younger man would jump at the job. He had made good time on the drive it was only 5 a.m. and he was half an hour early for the meeting. Looking in the driver's mirror he was always surprised by the sallow and lined face which looked back at him. His eyes were still the bright blue of a man 30 years younger. The rest of his face was that of a man not far off retirement. He ran a hand over the grey stubbled chin. Mon dieu, he desperately needed a wash and a shave. He decided he had plenty of time to walk inside and get a coffee and a sandwich. British motorway food had improved in recent years he thought, as well as the general standard of cleanliness and presentation.

He let himself gingerly down from the cab, flexed his knees which were stiff, stretched his arms, pulled on his baseball cap, zipped up his navy blue fleece jacket and crossed to the café. He felt in his trouser pocket for some change and pulled out a hand full of Euros. Pushing them back in he reached into the other pocket where he found his sterling. Inside the service station he selected a cheese and pickle sandwich and a coffee served in a disposable cup with a lid to take out. A haggard looking middle aged woman who was wiping down tables had dropped her damp, grubby cloth and came across to the till to take his money. He was glad that she didn't have to handle his food. Dubois handed her a £5 note and pocketed the few coins he was given in return. Back in his cab he took a bite from the sandwich, chewed it in anticipation for a couple of seconds and then opened it to inspect the contents. He'd never get used to what the English described as bread and as for what they called cheese, well….. He took another bite and shook his head. No good, he couldn't possibly eat it. Lowering the window, he threw it hard into the bushes. Let the birds have it - if they would. He sipped from the paper cup, the coffee wasn't bad he had to concede, and turned the radio on. It was playing something soothing to help the insomniacs. He tuned it to another station. Still fairly quiet, but at least the music had a bit of a beat. He was feeling very tired now and hoped the music would help him stay awake, he wound down the window for a bit and felt a blast of cold air, just another driver breaking a long and monotonous journey. He looked up as a white van drove in to the car park. The police vehicle pulled up and dimmed its lights; the two officers got out and crossed to the café. Christian peered through the dark. It was a Police Collision Investigation Vehicle. It was only when he let out a sigh of relief, he realised how tense he was.

He looked at his watch and reached down to pull his mobile phone from beneath his seat, he punched in the number he'd been given and waited whilst the call connected.

It rang twice and a voice said, "Is that Chris?"

"Yes, it's me" replied Dubois.

"Look to your left" the voice instructed him. "Can you see me?"

Christian looked across the car park to his left and saw a white transit van parked in the shadows which flashed its headlights twice. "I see you, what's your name please?" asked Christian.

"Wait until I set off, and then follow me. Stay close" replied the voice.

"OK" replied Christian but he may as well not have bothered. The line had gone dead. He looked at the phone in surprise as if it would provide an explanation. Turning it off, he put it back under the seat. He started the engine of the huge lorry, rolled it back on to the motorway and followed the taillights of the white transit van towards Leeds.

One

She'd been very deeply asleep. It was a dream of swimming deep underwater, surrounded by a dark glassy greenness and a persistent ringing in her ears. She began to panic, she couldn't get her breath, it was becoming darker, perhaps she was too deep. As she struck out with powerful strokes towards the surface of the sea and of consciousness, the ringing in her ears became rhythmic. She shook her head to try and clear it of the irritating noise, and in doing so awoke to the unrelenting tone of the bedside telephone. The green figures of the digital clock on the bedside table showed 1.58 a.m. as DCI Kate Peace reached out into the darkness to pick up the handset. Her first fumbling attempt sent it clattering to the wooden floorboards. "Oh shit!" She fumbled in the gap between the bed and the bedside cabinet, for the switch of the lamp and having successfully located it, rolled over the edge of the bed to pick up the handset from where it had come to rest, in a pool of light, against the wardrobe door. She pressed the green button to accept the call.

"Hello, Kate Peace here" she mumbled automatically as she struggled to sound alert.

"Hello, Inspector Peace, I'm in Seacroft, I'm afraid we need you down here straightaway" It was the voice of Detective Sergeant Phil Simpson. He sounded grim.

Just what you didn't need at this godforsaken hour, she thought. Ok, er… what's happened?" asked Kate, yawning and forcing her eyes to stay open. Having already freed herself from the tangle of bedding and thrown back the duvet, she swung her legs over the edge of the bed into the chill air of the old farmhouse, and wriggled into a pair of black cotton knickers. Holding the phone in one hand she grabbed a pair of grey wool trousers which were hanging over the back of a nearby chair. Struggling into them one handed she wobbled slightly as she felt around underneath the chair with her foot trying to locate the black leather slip on shoes she wore to work. She had one on but had to crouch down to see the other one. She retrieved it from under the dressing table.

"There's been a shooting down here. I'm at the Rose and Crown just off the ring road. Two young males have been found in the car park. One's dead and the other one they've just taken away in the ambulance. He didn't look good I'm afraid. He was gasping like a fish, the paramedics were shaking their heads, they didn't look too optimistic" said Phil Simpson. "Oh, and I've sent George Offord and a uniform down to the hospital with the ambulance to keep an eye on things down there"

Kate reached into the second drawer down and dragged out a long sleeved black stretch t-shirt. No one was going to be looking to see what she was wearing at this hour. She kicked a pair of grey jersey, jogging bottoms out of her way and under the bed. She wouldn't be needing them for a while. There'd be no time for jogging tomorrow morning, or for the foreseeable future. No-one on a murder investigation team has time for their hobbies, even family life takes a back seat as Kate had found to the cost of her marriage.

"OK, Don't worry, I'm on my way" Kate assured Simpson. "And Phil, can you make sure someone's called Dr. Manby, and the forensics team, and the photographer? We're going to need all of them out there. And get the area taped off will you; don't let anyone near the body. If there is any evidence at the scene get it into marked envelopes. We don't want any problems later with the chain of evidence. You know the script." Kate knew that Phil would be irritated by her reminders but was conscious that a woman in what was still seen to be a man's job couldn't afford to let any slip ups happen, however small, even if they were committed by someone else. Ultimately she'd be held responsible.

"Don't worry, I've arranged it. They're already all on the way" he sounded a bit miffed.

"Ok, well I'm on my way too now. So just hold the fort until I get there. I should be with you in about twenty minutes or probably less. There shouldn't be anything on the road at this hour of the morning" Replacing the handset of the phone in its stand, she paused just long enough to pull a brush through her dark brown shoulder length bob a couple of times, before securing her hair firmly in a business-like knot at the nape of her neck with a black velvet scrunchie. She then dashed across the landing to the bathroom. Forcing her eyes to stay open she looked at herself briefly in the mirror as she passed. Not a pretty sight. As might be expected, she looked like she'd just rolled out of bed. She slicked on a token gesture of clear lip gloss. A compromise between not completely neglecting her appearance, and not giving anyone the excuse to say she'd found it more important to spend time on her make-up than getting to the crime scene. Never mind, it would have to do. She turned and tripped over a pair of trainers left on the bathroom floor the evening before. "Damn" she muttered and grabbed at the door jamb to stop herself falling. She dashed down the oak staircase of the old farmhouse, slipping into a ¾ length waterproof jacket which hung from the oak newel post as she passed, and winding a cashmere scarf round her neck a couple of times before picking up her black leather shoulder bag from the table in the hallway. Bending briefly, she patted the head of the dozing golden retriever who opened one eye as she passed the kitchen door. Turning back she flicked on the light switch and ran into the kitchen, where she deposited her bag on the pine table and crossed to the cupboard below the Belfast sink. Reaching into the large paper sack she put a couple of scoops of food into the dog's metal dish and refilled his water bowl.

"I might not be back for breakfast Jasper old boy, so don't wait up for me"

She smiled down at the sleepy dog that had already closed his eyes again. Kate acknowledged this as a sign of his age, in his younger days he would have been unable to resist the sound of food landing in his dish. If she was delayed, as she often was, she knew that she could call and leave a message later for Betty, her neighbour, who would pop round at breakfast time after milking and let the old dog out for his constitutional.

Kate felt among the detritus in her bag for the car keys and let herself out of the house. The Yale lock on the heavy door snicked sharply behind her. A blast of icy wind hit her as she crossed the yard clicking the remote control on her key fob as she ran towards the car to get out of the cold. The car's interior light came on in welcome and Kate reached for the door handle. She settled herself behind the wheel, turned the key in the ignition and was rewarded by the throaty purr of the Audi as it sprang to life. She twisted the control of the car's heater to its highest setting, flicked on the headlights, and pressed the Coldplay "Parachutes" CD in to the car's player. It was too cold to drive with the car's window open, so this should help wake her up. It had been a Christmas present from her teenage nephew Charles. She wasn't sure if it was to her taste but was flattered to think that Charles thought she was still of an age to appreciate it. Swinging the silver Audi in a wide arc, she crunched across the gravel driveway, the headlights picking out the dry stone wall of the farmyard as she passed through the open five barred gate and onto the single track road down to the village and then on towards Leeds. She reached into the glove compartment for a cereal bar and a bottle of mineral water which she kept a ready stock of for such situations.

What remained of the night would be tiring hungry work.

*   *   *

Kate stopped at the bottom of the residential road, bringing the car to a halt and parking up under an orange streetlight. She was glad to see that the blue-and-white crime-scene tape was already in place preventing her or anyone else getting any closer to the scene.

A young uniformed police constable stepped out into the road barring her way. His pimply and abnormally white face suggested that he was perhaps called to the scene first and had found the body. "I'm sorry, madam the road is closed until further notice" he said hands behind his back, feet apart, and skinny chest thrust forward assertively. "If you turn round and go back to the roundabout and take the third exit….." he said, starting to give her an alternative route into the town.

She wound down the car window "It's ok" she replied cutting him off in mid sentence. Climbing out of the car, she fished in her handbag for her ID card and held it out for the young PC to inspect.

"Sorry Ma'am" said the young PC shamefacedly.

Kate smiled thinly, slamming the car door, and stepped past him dismissively, ducking to get underneath the taut blue and white plastic tape.

She turned and flicked the remote locking system of the Audi, its indicators flashing back at her in response. Walking round the side of the pub and into the car park at the rear she could immediately see the tall slim figure of Phil Simpson, the collar of his beige Mac turned up and buttons fastened up to the neck in attempt to keep out the cold. He stood with Dr. Manby, the Home Office pathologist, their heads together in conversation. They turned towards her as they heard her approach.

"Hi Kate" said the genial Dr Manby. Little seemed to ruffle him. Certainly not being called from his bed in the small hours of a freezing February Sunday morning. Impeccably dressed, in a dark jacket, white shirt, and sporting a bow tie, he looked like he'd just come from the theatre or a smart restaurant. Now semi-retired and living in the smart area of Roundhay, he'd been able to steal a march on Kate and had had twenty minutes start.

"Hello Doctor, so what can you tell us?" She knew that at this stage the Doctor would be unlikely to commit himself to anything specific or even remotely helpful, but went through the motions out of politeness. It was all part of the game they played. There was a similar conversation at every crime scene. It felt like a rehearsal for a school play.

"One white male, probably early to mid twenties and he's dead"

"Is that it?" she tried to inject a note of surprise into her question, as if she'd expected more. Although they could all see that the body in front of them was as dead as a door post, it wasn't official until it was confirmed by the doctor.

"No, he died from gunshot wounds. That's it. At the moment" replied Manby with a satisfied air.

Kate feigned disappointment, but knew better than to press for more information at this stage. They were both playing their parts well.

"You can be moving him as soon as they've finished taking the pictures Kate. I'm away back home for a couple of hours sleep; I've seen as much as I need to for now. I'll see the laddie later on this morning" The Doctor waved a goodbye to Kate and strode away, hands in pockets, into the remainder of the night.

Jason Young, the crime scene photographer rubbed his hands together and blew on them in a bid to keep the circulation moving. The bright arc lights which had been set up to enable him to take his photographs gave the scene an air of a film set, and the body that of an actor posed as if to shock. When some one called "cut" he'd get to his feet laughing and walk away. The body on the ground however had taken a real bullet to the centre of the chest and lay ignominiously on his back between a pile of overflowing black refuse sacks and stack of empty plastic beer crates. He'd only be leaving the scene in a body bag. In life he had been a good looking young man. He was broad shouldered and well muscled. But had high cheek bones, and fine facial features. He wore navy blue track suit bottoms and a hooded sweatshirt, on his feet were top of the range Nike trainers. The reflective silver logo glittered in the arc lights. His sweatshirt was partially unzipped and underneath it he wore the fashion equivalent of an old mans string vest in bright yellow, except that it was now for the most part stained blood red. He obviously took pride in his appearance and like a lot of youngsters felt it more important to look good than keep warm.

Kate stood back, turned up her collar and thrust her hands deep into the pockets of her jacket whilst Jason Young the photographer finished taking his pictures of the scene. The camera flashed and whined. Jason walked round the body and took several shots from the opposite side. He then crossed to the black canvas hold all which he'd placed on top of an empty grey metal beer barrel which was awaiting collection by John Smith's brewery. Reaching into the bag, he pulled out a video camera. He walked around the body filming it from all directions, close up and then further back, then turning and filming a broad sweep of the pub car park and the rear of the premises.

Finally he straightened up and turned to Kate, hands on hips. His highlighted hair, golden tan and straight white teeth made him look more like a top salon hairdresser than a top flight photographer "OK, that's me finished" said Jason. "You can let the space men at him now"

Jason was referring to the scene of crime forensic team who waited patiently in their all-in-one disposable hooded, white paper suits, which would ensure that they did not contaminate the area. Pulling their masks into position and donning latex gloves, they moved forward. They worked to the strict belief that at a crime scene everyone brought something and took something away. That was how the perpetrator was caught. They didn't want to contaminate the area by leaving any fibres or hairs from themselves.

Before she gave the order for them to start work, Kate studied the body for some time, liking to get a feel for how the victim might have been in life. "Ok, you can start now" she told the forensic team. She turned to Phil Simpson and asked; "Were there any witnesses?"

"Well, no-one we've spoken to admits to having seen anything but it's that sort of area where they wouldn't have noticed the Pope in his golf buggy if they thought it would keep us off their backs. An old lady across the road who says she couldn't sleep heard what she thought was a car door slamming and looked out as a car drove away at speed. Of course, she didn't know the make or model only that it was a dark coloured car, very fast and very noisy."

"Did you see anything else?"

"A group of kids who were larking about in the churchyard reckon they looked over the wall as a blue car drove by, but it's difficult to know whether or not to believe them, they're so full of whatever this week's offer of cheap lager is from Tesco they don't know whether they're on this earth or Fullers. Anyway we've taken their names and addresses and can follow them up later But I don't think they'll be able to tell us anything useful."

"Well *I* can tell you who he is…"

Kate spun round at the woman's voice behind her shoulder. "And you are?" she asked.

"I'm the landlady, love. Noreen Game. Game by name, and game by nature, so they say" She exhaled a long breath of cigarette smoke and laughed into the night air. Her dry peroxide hair stood out like a crazy halo illuminated by the sharp lighting of the crime scene photographer. "And that" she said pointing to the body in the parking space, with her cigarette, "Is Leon Edwards……. bastard."

Kate looked across at Phil and raised her eyebrows as Noreen Game continued to study the body impassively.

Abruptly, Noreen Game turned on her white stiletto heels, grinding the deposited tab end underfoot and walked unsteadily towards the rear door of the pub, calling over her shoulder, "So, does anyone want a drink? It's on the house" as she disappeared inside.

Two

THE large dark blue Vauxhall Omega car followed the same route which the ambulance had taken through the night streets of Leeds a few minutes previously. There were few about in the streets now, either traffic or people. The occasional straggler climbed into a taxi and was whisked homewards. Roller blinds were being secured over the windows of fast food outlets, a marked police car patrolled the city streets, no more than a representational presence. The flashing blue light on the ambulance had been merely a formality, unnecessary on the virtually clear roads. The Vauxhall pulled into the forecourt of the hospital and parked up in one of the three spaces clearly marked "No Parking" by the entrance.

Detective Sergeant George Offord walked through the automatic glass doors and into the reception area of the hospital. He made his way across to the large circular desk in the centre of which the staff were standing. Although it meant that enquirers could approach from any direction, it was a wonder the staff behind it didn't get dizzy. At this time of the night there were only two people manning the desk using a couple of phones and with one computer screen switched on which was currently swirling with the blue and white hospital logo pattern of the screensaver.

He approached the desk, fastening the middle button of his tweed jacket, and dusted some stray cigarette ash from his sleeve. He reached into the inside jacket pocket for his ID card and palmed it ready for inspection.

As soon as he saw it one of the men wearing the light blue shirt and navy sweater of the porter's uniform picked up the phone and quickly said a few words which Offord couldn't quite catch. With a sideways movement of his head, he motioned George across to a double door, above which was a sign reading Accident and Emergency Department. "Over there mate, they're expecting you"

"Cheers" George nodded his thanks and putting his card back in his pocket, he crossed the general waiting area towards the Accident and Emergency Department. He passed through the door where a tired looking young nurse waited to show him through to a room with a sign on the door which read 'Doctor's Office'. She stood aside, pushing the door open for him to squeeze his bulk through.

Approaching retirement George was of the old school but becoming increasingly aware of how the years of snatched meals of pork pies and Cornish pasties washed down with a few beers had taken their toll on his figure and, as there was always some busy body trying to tell him, on his health.

Behind the desk in the small windowless office was seated a young Doctor, bespectacled and with dark, wavy hair, wearing a long white coat and with a stethoscope slung round his neck. He rose to his feet, leaned anxiously across the desk and shook George's proffered hand. "Good morning Inspector. I imagine you're here about the guy they've just brought in from the shooting" It was a statement rather than a question.

"Detective Sergeant." corrected Offord "Yes, how is he, able to talk to us yet?"

"Take a seat" the doctor offered.

George unbuttoned his jacket and settled himself at the opposite side of the desk

"At the moment he's still unconscious I'm afraid. They've got him down in Resus. And obviously are doing everything they can for him but it doesn't look good. At this stage we just can't tell. In the long term, and by that I mean over the next hour or so we'll know what the chances really are." he twiddled a pencil nervously.

"Oh hell, we really need to talk to him as soon as possible. At the moment we've no idea who's behind this. He's the best chance we've got. You know the other lad who was with him died? Shot dead at the scene"

"Yes, so I gather. Pretty ghastly, but as I say, I don't think you realise, at the moment we just don't know what sort of recovery, if any, he might make" said the young doctor helplessly.

George almost felt sorry for him. He was clearly out of depth, pushed in to do the talking whilst someone more senior was fighting for the shooting victim's life. Or so it was to be hoped. "No point in me hanging around then at the moment, but I'll be leaving a uniformed officer here to keep a guard on him"

The Doctor's eyebrows rose almost comically on receiving this information.

"But as I say," George couldn't resist poking a bit of fun at the young man's formal attitude, "At the moment *we* just don't know who's behind this shooting, and when they realise that he's still alive they might want to have another go. You know, try and finish him off."

The Doctor stopped twiddling his pencil, placed it carefully on the desk in front of him and looked at George over the top of his tortoiseshell framed glasses, and then took them off altogether, rubbing his eyes. Without the glasses he just looked young and shocked. "You don't think any one would try anything here in the hospital?" he asked in a whisper.

Offord shrugged his shoulders. "Who can say? Anything's possible, we don't know what this is about, who they are, or how desperate"

"I think I'd better inform security"

"Might not be a bad idea" Offord stood up and pushed his chair back from the desk, reaching out to shake the young man's hand. "Anyway I'll be off now. Can I take your name, in case I need to speak to you again?"

"Oh, yes of course, sorry, I'm Richard Turnbull" the Doctor replied distractedly, still visibly shocked at the possibility of armed gangsters round every corner.

Offord made a note of this piece of information. And then gave a parting quip. "Right Doctor, I'll bid you good night. I should get yourself a quick cuppa." Doctor Turnbull looked up at George clearly uncomprehending. "But you'd better be sharp lad, someone will know who he is and it can't be long before the grieving relatives roll up and you've them to deal with"

Without waiting for a reply Offord turned smartly and walked out of the stuffy office. He made his way out of the hospital and across the car park to where the unmarked police car remained parked in one of the ambulance bays. He squeezed himself back into the driver's seat and looked across at PC Murray.

"Murray, they're still working on him at the moment. So get yourself in there lad. I want you outside the door of that room. And make sure you stay close to him. Like a monkey on a stick" Offord looked at his watch, it was almost 4 am. "I'll have two more lads down here to relieve you by six, don't worry, you won't be late off duty."

PC Murray nodded in acknowledgement of his instructions and stepped out of the car. "Like a monkey on a stick indeed!" he thought. Smoothing back his straw coloured hair, and positioning his peaked cap to best advantage the young PC pulled back his broad shoulders, fastened the silver tunic buttons, pulled straight his jacket and marched into the hospital. Perhaps there'd be some nice sympathetic young nurse who could provide him with a cup of tea and a biscuit or two during his vigil.

Offord reversed the car out of its space and set off for the police station. Perhaps he could get hold of bacon butty and a pot of tea in the police canteen before he met up with Kate Peace and the rest of the team to discuss how the investigation would progress. These meetings always bored him. George saw himself very much of a 'hands on' policeman, and would much rather be out and about at ground level, questioning people. He reached into his jacket pocket and felt around for the couple of unwrapped Rennies he knew were there. He popped them both into his mouth together. He straightened himself as much as he could within the confines of his seat belt and gave a loud and satisfying belch. Perhaps he'd not bother with the bacon sandwich after all, but a mug of tea would go down well, all the same. George Offord backed carefully out of the parking space and accelerated swiftly through the hospital gates, driving the short distance through the streets to Millgarth Police Station.

*   *   *

Kate Peace and Phil Simpson followed Noreen Game through the back door of the pub and into the bar. She was standing behind the bar with her back to them and jabbed twice with her glass at the optic, dispensing herself a double gin which she place on the bar and splashed a token drop of tonic water into. She took a swift mouthful and turned to Kate and Phil. "What's yours then?" she asked.

"Er, half a bitter for me," said Phil looking across at Kate to see if this was acceptable. Kate nodded almost imperceptibly. They needed to look friendly and approachable. The woman clearly needed a drink and they would get more out of her if she felt at ease and the interview was on a more informal basis.

"And for you?" she asked Kate.

"I'll have the same as you, but make it a single, please." Noreen Game served the drinks, and Kate was thankful to see, was more generous with the tonic water in Kate's drink, sloshing a good amount into the glass and an even greater amount over the surface of the bar, than she had been with her own. She came round from behind the bar and heaved herself onto a high barstool, hampered by her short, tight, black Lycra skirt. After a couple of failed attempts with her lighter she managed to light a cigarette and took a long drag from it.

Kate took a sip of the gin, careful to turn the glass so that a smudge of coral lipstick which remained from a previous customer faced away from her. "So, Noreen what can you tell us about what happened here tonight?"

Phil Simpson discreetly pulled his note book from his pocket, clicked out the point of his biro and prepared to take notes from the conversation.

"Nothing really - they were in here most of the night, they arrived about half past nine or quarter to ten..."

Kate cut her off. "Who were *they* Noreen?" she prompted.

Noreen Game looked up from her glass. "Leon Edwards and Eliot Nelson"

"Was there anyone else with them?" enquired Kate.

"No-one that I could see. They were sitting over there together in that corner near to the bandit." Noreen pointed across the room with her cigarette. "They had a few lagers apiece, chatted, and made a few calls on their mobiles. Then about half past one I think it was, some guy came in and went across to them. They stood up and left their drinks and all went out the back door to the car park"

"Did you know him, this man who came in and talked to them?"

"No, I've never seen him before"

"What did he look like?"

"I don't know. I only really saw the back of him"

"Did you notice what he was wearing?"

"A dark coloured tracksuit. Blue or black, and the hood up over a baseball cap. I remember the peak stuck out from under the hood"

"Do you think that they knew him?"

"Oh yes. He walked up to Eliot and slapped him on the back. You know in fun, said 'Hi, how're you doing' or something like that"

"What did he look like, Noreen, tall, small, fat, thin?"

"Just ordinary....err tallish, slim. Like I said, tracksuit bottoms, hooded sweatshirt"

"Black, white?"

"White I think, Yes, I saw a bit of his face as he walked in He had a scarf round his mouth. I thought perhaps it must be cold outside"

"What happened next?" prompted Kate.

"They all walked out the back together, and then there were these loud bangs, I told myself it was a car backfiring but I think I knew it wasn't. I ran to the back door just as a car was pulling away, a blue saloon I think, with a spoiler on the boot. I saw them on the ground and came back in and called 999" Noreen Game's voice trailed away, she gulped another mouthful of gin and hurriedly brushed a tear from her cheek.

"It's OK Noreen, you've had a shock. It's not a pretty sight out there" said Kate passing the other woman a paper tissue from her bag. "Sorry to keep pushing you Noreen, but it sounds to me like you didn't have much time for Leon Edwards."

"I know you shouldn't speak ill of the dead and all that...... He is, isn't he? I mean they haven't moved him"

"Yes Noreen, I'm afraid he is dead"

"Well you might as well know now, there's no point beating about the bush, I hated him - my Jade thought the sun shone out his arse, listens to his so called music all the time. Do you know what he calls himself? Leeds' white rapper! Huh I ask you! What a prick! And the mess she's in...."

Phil scribbled frantically. Kate tried not to look puzzled but nodded, encouraging Noreen to go on.

"I can't prove it, any of it, but I'm sure it was him got her using the gear. She won't hear a word against him, of course. And he has the bloody cheek to come in here, and sit in front of me, in my bar, as if butter wouldn't melt in his mouth... Well, if you ask me, he got what was coming to him!" Noreen sniffed and took another gulp of gin.

"Was Jade Leon's girlfriend Noreen?" asked Kate.

"No, Jade is Eliot's girlfriend… though God only knows who that baby of her's belongs to because it doesn't look like him. But they all love Leon the 'pop star' No Leon's got some stuck- up piece - Carla I think she's called, a model or some such I hear. Bloody model air- fix more like!" Noreen seemed to run out of steam.

"We'll need to talk to Jade, Noreen, where can we find her?" asked Phil.

Noreen's head snapped up at the sound of his voice as if she'd forgotten he was there.

Kate took the opportunity to tip her barely touched gin into Noreen's almost empty glass.

"Over there, in the tower blocks" Noreen nodded across the room as if they could all see through the end wall of the bar. "Brookfield Mansion, Flat 52"

Kate waited for some scathing remark about the unlikely name for the concrete tower block, but none came.

"We'll leave it for now Noreen, thank you for your help; we'll probably need to get back to you later." Kate got to her feet.

Noreen drained the last of the gin which Kate had poured into her glass.

Phil stood slowly, draining the last of his beer and replaced his note book in his inside jacket pocket, nodding a brief goodbye to Noreen Game as he followed Kate from the pub.

"Well, Phil," said Kate "What do you make of that?"

Phil smiled into the darkness and replied "Someone didn't like his music?"

"Oh very droll" said Kate as they reached their cars "See you back at the station"

*   *   *

"OK," said Kate as they took their seats around the Formica topped table in the squad room, "What we need to do next is get ourselves out there this afternoon and ask some questions. We need to know what's behind this, because so far I can't work it out. It's not a random shooting. Not even a drive by. Someone who they seem to have known walked into the Rose and

18

Crown and got them outside with the intention of them being shot down either by himself, or more likely by someone else, in cold blood."

"What makes you think there was some one else involved?" asked Phil, playing devil's advocate. The team often did this, bouncing ideas off one another.

"I know he could have been working alone, but can you imagine: you walk into a pub, get two guys out into the car park and then say to them 'Can you just wait here a minute whilst I nip to the car and get my gun?' And the one we saw, at least, was a fit looking young man. It would have to be a brave bloke to take two of them on single handed."

"Yeah, point taken" said Phil.

"And I don't know how they've got into something as serious as this. I've had a word with Jim downstairs, according to the computer, Nelson's got a bit of previous form. Taking and driving away cars as a juvenile. Later he was pulled in for possession of a controlled substance, but not with intent to supply. They couldn't make that stick. The amount he had could well have been for personal use. But he drives a flash motor, there's a nice Jeep Cherokee in the car park of the Rose and Crown which is registered in his name, so where's the money coming from for that? He's into something and we need to find out what. It looks like he might have been playing out of his league here. And the other lad, Edwards.... Nothing at all, he's clean as a whistle. I know Noreen thinks he's a bad 'un but he's either clean or damn clever."

George Offord straightened in his plastic chair. The hastily grabbed bacon sandwich which he'd succumbed to in the canteen was making its presence felt. There was a sharp pain in his right hand side. He was going to have to try to cut down. He patted his jacket pocket trying to locate his packet of Benson and Hedges and the green disposable lighter and then remembered he was in a no smoking zone. He wished to God Inspector Peace would get a move on; he was dying for a fag. He sighed loudly and looked at he door longingly.

Kate looked across at him and asked "Are you alright George. Not boring you am I?"

"Fine, I'm fine, it's just that these chairs aren't very comfortable." He straightened his back and altered his position slightly, emitting a quiet, gassy belch.

"Well I'm just about finished" replied Kate, "Phil this afternoon can you go and have a word with Jade Game? See what you can come up with. And find out where I can get hold of this Carla. George, will you check what's going on down at the hospital. If you can't talk to Nelson, then see if you can talk to the family? They may know something about his contacts or if he's been behaving any differently lately. I'll go and interview Carla when we track her down. DC's Rayner and Chatten can organise a house to house in the area of the Rose and Crown, and follow up the kids who were in the churchyard, see if they can come up with anything else" Kate rose to her feet looking at her watch. "But first I've got to get down to the Infirmary, I told Dr Manby I'd be down there in time to watch him perform the post-mortem" and having seen Manby at work before she knew that perform was the right word.

Three

Kate made her way unwillingly through the dimly lit cream painted corridors on the lower floors of the hospital towards the mortuary. She pushed open the opaque plastic swing doors and found herself in a small corridor which ran between a couple of offices. She pressed the bell on the wall for attention as requested by the sign and sat down to wait on the old wooden hard backed chair.

Dr Manby popped his head round the door. He was already dressed in his green surgical scrubs, covered with a disposable plastic apron and plastic shoes ready for the post mortem. Even the sight of this made Kate's imagination run riot and she felt a little queasy. Despite having been to several post mortems, it was still something she found unpleasant. She was coming to think that it wouldn't change and was something that she'd just have to get used to. Being a vegetarian, the chemical smell of cleanliness combined with the smell which reminded her of raw bloody liver made her heave.

"Kate my dear, do come through," said Dr Manby with a welcoming smile, holding the door for her to pass in front.

For all the world, thought Kate, as if she was entering a G.P's surgery not a butcher's shop. Kate walked into the room in front of Dr Manby and stood on the spot he suggested. This, she thought was probably the best place to get an unimpeded view of things, unfortunately.

Leon Edwards was laid on the metal table. He'd already been weighed, measured and photographed from every angle before Kate got there.

Dr Manby turned on his dictaphone and stood at the side of the table with his hands behind his back. He paced from the head of the table to the foot and back, nodding gravely to himself. Then he leaned forward and examined the hole in Leon Edwards' chest.

Did he enjoy playing this part? Kate wondered.

He stood up again and said, "Shot at fairly close range, probably from 3-4 yards away. Certainly no more." He pointed the area of entry in the centre of the chest. "See? here and here." He looked up at Kate waiting for her agreement.

"Yes" said Kate obediently, staring determinedly at an area somewhere above Dr. Manby's head.

"I'd say it was a sawn off shot gun. They're easier to carry about. Less obvious, Eh Kate?"

"Yes," replied Kate again. Perhaps if she thought about something else, it would take her mind off the awfulness of what was happening.

Dr. Manby turned and picked up a scalpel, which glinted as he held it to the light as if to check the cutting edge, and then bent to make the first cut in the Y-shaped incision before peeling back the flap of flesh.

Kate tried to study the opposite wall and compile a mental shopping list of what she needed to buy for tea. Perhaps not. She felt clammy and dizzy, her mouth filled with the salty taste that precedes vomiting. "No, I won't" she said to herself and concentrated on breathing in and out regularly and deeply, determined to stick it out. Think about something else, a holiday in the sun, she promptly felt hot and dizzy. Next years Christmas presents, she felt sick and clammy,....anything, anything.

Dr Manby's recital droned on in the background. Kate took a deep breath and breathed out very slowly whilst counting up to a hundred in her head. Someone had one told her it was difficult for your body to remain tense whilst breathing out. It seemed to work, so she did it again and then counted backwards from a hundred down to nought, trying not listen to the details and probable timing of Leon Edwards' last meal. She always thought kebabs most unpleasant things anyway, and this just served to confirm her opinion.

"OK," said Dr. Manby, after what seemed like an eternity, dropping the scalpel on to the metal trolley with a clink, peeling off the latex gloves with a thwack, and dropping them into the yellow clinical waste bin. His colleague started clearing away some of the equipment prior to reassembling Leon Edwards and stitching him up again.

"Well that's that then, eh, Kate? Didn't tell us anything we didn't already know, did it?"

Kate breathed a sigh of relief and felt her shoulders relax as the tension left her. "No, no, I suppose not" she said, forcing a smile "Well, um, thank you for letting me attend"

"Always a pleasure to see you my dear, any time, you know you're always welcome here" said Manby. He escorted Kate to the door. "I'll get the report typed up and fax it over to you" he called, his voice becoming necessarily louder.

Kate was already half way up the corridor, desperate for some fresh air.

Dr Manby smiled to himself and went back into the room.

*   *   *

Phil climbed the stairwell in Brookfield Mansion. As usual the lifts weren't working. The area smelt like a bad public toilet. He stepped carefully between the most dubious looking patches of unidentifiable deposits on the floor. Thankfully, Jade's flat was only on the fifth floor. He knocked at the door. And studied the graffiti on the opposite wall '*I woz 'ere. I don't know why*' and the details of a couple called Carl and Jodie who seemed to want to advertise their sexual prowess. As he expected, there was no reply. Cautiously he pushed open the letter box and called through it,

"Jade are you in there? Answer the door. It's the Police. We need to talk to you" Phil knew that by now Noreen would have been in touch with her daughter. He heard footsteps getting closer behind the door. The door opened and Phil held out his identification card. "Jade Game?" He looked at the large black circled eyes and pale pinched features of the girl in front of him.

"You'd better come in" replied Jade as she turned and walked away, leaving him to close the door and follow her. They walked down the dark windowless passage which had three doors, all leading off to the left. The first door was closed. Through the second Phil could see a small windowless bathroom which looked none to clean or tidy, damp towels lay on the stained carpet and dirty clothes overflowed the linen basket, it smelt of mould. The next door took them into the sitting room where the usual large screen television stood over near the window and a black leather three piece suite dominated the rest of the space, barely leaving room for the small fold away square wooden table and two chairs.

On one of these sat Noreen Game, elbow on the table, cigarette in one hand and a glass in the other, containing a gin and tonic if it held the contents of the two bottles which stood on the table next her.

A baby of indeterminate sex sat in a high chair and amused itself by rubbing a jam sandwich round the tray with the flat of its hand.. At least it looked well fed and cared for, if not particularly clean.

"Grab a pew then," said Noreen nodding towards the other flimsy chair across the table from her.

Phil sat down carefully on the folding seat. It didn't look very robust.

"Get him a coffee love" Noreen instructed Jade.

Phil thought that if the standards of cleanliness in the kitchen were anything like the bathroom he'd rather not risk it. "No, It's Ok Jade. I've just had a drink and I won't keep you long. There's just one or two quick questions we need to go through if that's alright?"

Jade didn't answer so he continued: "Jade you know what happened to Leon and Eliot last night?"

Jade still didn't respond.

"Answer the policeman!" said Noreen to her daughter, banging her hand on the rickety table. Gin sloshed over the rim of the glass and added to the other unidentifiable stains on the table top.

"Jade you know that Eliot is very ill?" said Phil.

Jade shook her blond hair back out of her eyes "Yeah, my mum said" she nodded across at Noreen.

"Do you know who might have done this?" Phil asked.

"Nope, how would I know?" Jade said sulkily.

"No ideas at all?" queried Phil disbelievingly.

"No! I told you" shouted Jade.

"OK so do you know *why* this might have happened?" asked Phil.

"No" Jade mumbled.

"Oh come on, Jade, you must have some idea. Leon Edwards is dead and Eliot could end up the same way," Phil said impatiently.

At this Jade looked up and again pushed her long blond hair back from her face, suddenly looking tired, no doubt not helped by the demands of her small child. "I've told you I don't know anything about what they were doing. You wanna ask that stuck -up Carla bird what they were all doing, she was always with them, 'Cos I don't know alright? Ask no questions, you get no lies is what I always say."

Phil realised that Jade either truly didn't know anything or wasn't going to say so. He wondered if it was because her mother was there and decided to change tack.

"OK, Jade where was Eliot when he wasn't here?" He didn't really expect a useful answer.

"At work…. They both work, worked" Jade corrected herself "down the gym on Chapeltown Road"

"And Carla, where will I find her?"

"I dunno where she lives but she runs the hairdressers 'Cut'n Tan' It's the one in Roundhay."

Phil wrote all this down. There seemed little else to be gained from Jade at the moment. "I'll leave you for now then, but we will need to come and see you again at some point." Phil got up to leave. Noreen took a long slow drag on the cigarette and Phil realised he didn't have a clue what she was thinking. Jade was already on her way to the door as the baby threw the remaining portion of its sandwich onto the floor. Probably a good idea, thought Phil.

*   *   *

George parked his Vauxhall at the edge of the kerb outside the red brick semi- detached local authority house. He heaved himself out of the car and looked up and down the street. It looked quiet enough at the moment, and he hoped there wouldn't be too much missing from the car when he came back out. He took a quick drag from his cigarette dropped it on the path, ground it out with his heel and kicked it down a grate.

Number 41 Croft View wasn't the best kept house he'd seen. Someone had planted a privet hedge several years ago but the few remaining scraggy bushes had about had it. He picked his way up the garden path, dodging the old settee and a couple of rusty bikes. As he knocked hard at the door it opened and a small scruffy looking man with a defeated air stood aside, letting George into the square hallway. The living room was through the door directly ahead of him.

It was difficult to see at first in the dimly lit room for two reasons. Firstly, the thin curtains were drawn, this may have been as a mark of respect but George thought they were probably always kept closed. And secondly there was a thick fog of cigarette smoke. A small square table was pushed against one wall and three people sat around it, smoking and flicking cigarette ash in the general direction of the already overflowing glass ashtray. Some time in the past an attempt at house keeping had been made with a plastic wipe-clean cloth in a red and white check covering the table, but whoever had had the idea had long since given it up as a bad one. On the top the pattern was barely distinguishable under the stains left from the numerous empty beer cans and slops of coffee from the mismatched mugs which littered the surface.

A large woman sat on a plastic chair originally intended for use in the garden, her massive pendulous bosom wobbled freely under the baggy round necked tee shirt, her large thighs encased in black stretchy leggings bulged through the gap between the seat and the arms of the chair. For a brief moment George tried to imagine this unlikely couple on the job. She must have weighed at least 18 stones and he was probably about 8 stones wet through. No, it was too awful to contemplate. But they had had three sons. There was a great clatter as she tried to clear a space on the table top and several empty cans fell to the floor and rolled away. A further one must have been quite full as it landed on the grubby carpet with a loud thud and fizz as the contents spilled out.

"This 'ere's me son Daz, just got here from Manchester." she pointed across with her cigarette, at a young man with shoulder length, fair hair, green eyes and an olive complexion. "And me other son, Wayne, lives at 'ome with us"

Wayne too was probably fair but it was hard to be certain with his head shaved.

Daz didn't look up but had an air of disinterested arrogance, Wayne viciously ground out the cigarette he'd been smoking in the glass ashtray.

"I'm sorry we've had to meet under these circumstances" said George relieved that at least he hadn't had the job of breaking the news of Leon Edwards' death to his family.

The two brothers who, George guessed were both older than Leon, had the smug but cagey air found in those who had spent time as a guest of Her Majesty.

"And Leon's dad of course," Her way of introducing the beaten little man who stood in the doorway of the room.

George decided that it was Mrs. Edwards who wore the trousers in the house and decided to address himself to her. "Mrs. Edwards, we need all the help we can get to catch these people and I know this is a difficult time for you, but I need to ask you a few questions, is that OK?"

"I know you've your job to do and I'm happy to help, but our Leon was a good lad, never in any bother" she said.

George thought if only he'd had a fiver for every time he'd heard that one. "Does Leon live with you?"

No, he's doing well for 'imself our Leon, 'ad a job at the gym and did his D.J.ing on a night. Lived in Chapel Allerton" she said proudly with a nod of her head. As if living there could absolve him from any wrongdoing.

"Was Leon involved with any people who might have wanted to harm him?" George asked her.

"No, who'd want to hurt our Leon? He was a good lad."

Daz watched the exchange with narrowed eyes, which slid from one speaker to the other, it could have been the cigarette smoke but George didn't think so.

"Daz can you think of anyone who might have wanted to harm your brother?"

"No, I 'aven't a clue" he sounded bored "Don't live round here no more, do I, so I wouldn't know nuffink"

George knew when he was on a loser so switched tack.

"Wayne, did Leon ever say anything to you to make you think he was in any trouble?" asked George.

"Nah, Leon wouldn't upset anyone" said Wayne.

"Well he upset someone enough to shoot him didn't he?" George reminded them.

"Mistaken identity" said Wayne.

George chose to ignore this remark. "But he must have mixed with some funny customers in the club scene?" George suggested. "Drug dealers, users, and allsorts"

"Well, that's as maybe, but it doesn't mean that he knew them or they'd want to shoot him, does it?" Mrs. Edwards replied.

"No. No, I suppose not" sighed George. "You wouldn't have a key to his house by any chance would you?"

"Well, as it happens I do." Daz looked at her sharply but she didn't see it. This was obviously news to him. "He left me a key for emergencies. He once had his cards and keys taken out of his jacket pocket at one club. Stolen! Would you believe it? Some people don't care who they nick from!"

George struggled to follow this line of logic, if indeed there was one. "Do you think I could borrow them, I'll give you a receipt of course. We'll need to search the house, it may give us a lead."

"Ere, Wayne, pass us me bag from behind that chair." Mrs. Edwards duly foraged in the bottom of the plastic shopping bag. Pulling out old receipts, carrier bags, a couple of used paper tissues, and a string bag of the kind which stretched to take excess shopping when the first bag was full. Eventually she gave up and upended the lot onto the living room floor. "Ah, ere we are," she said proudly as a bunch of keys fell to the floor with a jingle. She picked them up and passed them to George.

"Thank you very much, Mrs. Edwards," he said wondering what the other keys were for. "I'm going to leave you this card with my number on it and if you think of anything at all, no matter how insignificant, er small," he corrected himself, "it may seem, you can reach me on this line."

She took the card from him and placed it in a prominent position in front of the clock on the mantelpiece. Mr. Edwards, with the look of a beaten dog, who hadn't uttered a word during the interview, opened the door for George to leave.

George stepped out onto the garden path, the fresh air coming as a relief to his stinging eyes, and negotiated his way round the old furniture. He was just about to get into the car when he looked down, stepped back and then made a quick circuit of the car. Mm, not too bad for this area. Only the four hub caps were missing. He drove from the Edwards' house down to the infirmary. He wanted to keep tabs on Eliot Nelson's condition. If he was to die as well, they'd be looking at a double murder investigation. He parked in one of the spaces in the car parking area for the general public and went into the hospital. The reception desk was much busier today. People asking for directions to the wards and queries about payment for car parking seemed to be the two most popular topics. George waved his card and one of the staff came forward to speak to him.

"I'm looking an E. Nelson, he was brought in during the early hours of this morning," George told the receptionist, a small thin faced man with beady eyes and a short thin nose, whose name was Simon Bird according to the identification card which hung round his neck on a piece of tape.

In a bird-like manner the receptionist tipped his head to one side and clicked the mouse on the computer screen to bring up the admissions page. "Intensive Care" he informed George. "If you follow the red line painted on the floor…"

"It's O.K. I've been there before" George cut him off in mid speech and set off heavy footed along the red line. When he reached the door to the unit he rang the bell on the wall for attention. It made no sound but must have registered somewhere as a nurse wearing a trousers and top of pale blue cotton came to the door.

"I've come to ask about a Mr. Nelson" he told her.

"Ah yes, his parents are at the bedside. I'll show you to Sister's office, it's a little more private and I'll ask them to come and speak to you for a few moments" she said "Would you please use the hand wash before you come in?" she asked, pointing to a plastic bottle of pink liquid, fitted with a pump dispenser. "Our patients are very vulnerable to infection"

George made a play of thoroughly disinfecting his hands to oblige her but secretly wondered looking at her delicate hands if she did the same, and if not what unmentionable germs lurked on the door handles after all the revolting messes that nurses had to touch in the course of a day. That in mind he tried hard not to touch anything himself, letting her walk in front and open all the doors. He'd read in the papers about the awful flesh eating germs you could pick up in hospital, never mind the more common things like sickness and diarrhoea viruses. He'd be glad when he was out of the place.

The Sister's Office was a small glass walled cubicle which looked out on to the dozen beds in the room, hardly private George thought. He watched as she approached the furthest bed where a middle aged couple sat one either side of the male form which was covered only by a cotton sheet, from which various tubes, which fluids into and out of the inert body and wires attached to a bank of machinery emerged. George didn't like hospital and had a horror of ever ending up in a place like this. Who would there be to sit at his bedside? He saw the couple stand, and the woman direct the man to take his seat again. She made her way across to the office. George stood and waited. He didn't want to take the seat behind the desk, he thought it seemed too intimidating. She pushed open the door slowly and lingered in the doorway unsure of what to do or say.

Mrs. Nelson?" he checked "Come in and sit down" going on to make all the correct noises of sympathy for her. He decided to opt for friendly informality and perched his bulk on the corner of the desk, palms downwards on his knees "How is your son?" a fair opening question to get the ball rolling he thought.

She looked across to the bed and pulled a crumpled paper tissue from up the sleeve of her pink cardigan, dabbing at tearless eyes, which had no tears left. "He's unconscious… won't be long though" she told George, searching his face anxiously.

Thank God, thought George, breaking into a smile. Perhaps he'll able to tell us something.

She took a deep and noisy breath in, and gathering herself, exhaled again and then continued "They've been very good, so kind to us, but we've agreed that they can turn the life support machine off. And then we'll sit with him till he's gone. The nurse said it wouldn't be long."

Four

Monday morning was bright and sunny, with a summer's blue sky and the odd scudding white cloud, but with a sharp freshness that reminded those who were brave enough to shed their winter coats in favour of lighter jackets that it was still only February and a frosty nip was in the air. It was a trick of a day.

Out at Kate's farmhouse a thin white line of snow could still be seen under the old hawthorn hedges around the orchard, where it was still too early in the year for the sun to get sufficient height in the sky to completely melt it away. Kate stood in front of the old pine wardrobe, with her index finger on her lower lip, both doors were wide open as she tried to decide what to wear. She ran her finger along the rails. What should it be? Cream blouse, or white? Her complexion she thought, taking a swift look in the mirror, was quite pale after the winter. Cream was probably more flattering at the moment. She put the cream blouse on the bed. Black skirt, or brown? She held them up in the air on the hangers and crossed to the cheval mirror holding each in front of her, in turn. Yes, she preferred the brown knee length one which was cut on the bias, she decided as she twisted from side to side studying her reflection. Now where were those beige suede knee high boots which went so well with it? She bent down and scrabbled in the bottom of her wardrobe. Shoes, and boots, bags, and belts, scarves and ….a hat! She pulled out the cream straw hat. It had a wide brim which sported a spray of three large pink Tea Roses and threw it across onto the bed in disgust. She couldn't even remember buying it. Perhaps someone had loaned it to her. It was awful. Whose wedding had it been for? The wardrobe really was in a mess, it was high time she had a good clear out and got rid of all the clothes she hadn't worn for a year, to the local Oxfam shop.

She straightened up suddenly, hitting her head on the shelf. For a second when she closed her eyes she saw whirling lights. What on earth was she doing? She was only getting ready for work for goodness sake. Ok, so she was meeting Phil Simpson for an early lunch to compare notes and see what they had so far. No, this was silly! But he was rather cute. She felt herself blush in recognition of her feelings. Quickly she gathered up the blouse, skirt, and boots and threw them back into the bottom of the wardrobe and closed the doors, turning her back to the wardrobe and leaning against the doors. She took a deep breath, "Right let's start again" she said to herself. Opening the doors she pulled out the serviceable charcoal grey two piece and the white blouse. Pushing the rejected skirt aside with her foot as if it were something distasteful, she found some practical black court shoes. "There, that's more like it" she said putting on the sensible outfit together with her professional woman expression.

Kate looked out of the bedroom window, as she brushed her hair into a sleek bob and then gave it a quick squirt of hair spray. The dark bibbed cock sparrows huddled grumpily together in the bare branches of the apple trees. On his own, below them, perched on the back of the wooden bench was the robin chirping merrily away. Kate had trained him to come into the kitchen window of the farmhouse, where she left him a few scraps on the sill. He would tilt his head and eye the old dog Jasper curiously before having his fill then taking himself back to the safety of the orchard.

It reminded Kate of the orchard at the vicarage where she had grown up. As a child she had loved playing in the orchard. It felt like a magical place, enclosed by a high limestone wall and reached by a high wooden gate with a heavy wrought iron handle. Kate imagined herself as Mary Lennox in the *Secret Garden*. Playing on the swing and in the small tree house which had been built for the sons of a former incumbent, and set high in the branches of one of the apple trees. She had thought the trees here in her own garden may have been used in the same way one day but she very much doubted it now. Where had the years gone? There'd been a time when she wondered if she and Keith would have a child but it had just never happened and they'd accepted that. She had been busy climbing the steep and often slippery ladder of success and Keith's time had been taken up with establishing his own I.T. company. Well, she thought they'd accepted it until he'd come home one day and, completely out of the blue, told her that he was leaving her for someone else. Laura, he'd said her name was. Someone he'd met in the course of his work. He seemed, once having started on the subject to want to tell her all about this woman. Kate, shocked by his attitude, didn't want to know what the woman was called or anything else about her. She was far too angry. Yet Keith, whilst making apologetic noises about how he had never intended this to happen, and how he still cared about Kate had seemed proud of himself, in a way. He'd then to her horror gone on to tell Kate that Laura was expecting his child. So that explained his smugness. And he'd seemed nothing short of amazed at Kate's total aversion to the whole scenario. So… that as they say, was that. There didn't seem to be anything else to be said. Finale! And oddly, Kate was surprised that after the initial breaking of the news that she wasn't more shocked by the sudden announcement. She felt, at first, a deep simmering rage, which she realised could have been completely self destructive and did her best to keep it in check. And for a while she'd become rather too fond off a few extra glasses of wine during the long evenings. But she realised that drinking, and certainly drinking alone wasn't the answer, and consigned the remaining bottles of wine to the dustbin.

Looking back of course, all the signs had been there if she'd chosen to see them. They were both so busy they could go days at a time without seeing one another. He had to work late and often at the other end of the country, so was away overnight. He seemed to spend ages in the study, on the phone discussing business, and then there'd been the sudden renewed interest in going to the gym before and after work. Which, at the time she congratulated him on, and even paid for his membership at a private gym in Harrogate as a birthday present. Fool! She cursed herself. Why was the wife always the last one to realise what was going on beneath her nose?

Well, there was no use crying over spilt milk as her mother would have said and she couldn't even plead she'd put her career on hold for him. It had happened a couple of years ago now and at last she found she could study it objectively without her feelings ricocheting from anger to a dull emptiness.

After a couple of counselling sessions she'd found it helpful, on the advice of her counsellor to deal with it by the method of compartmentalizing her feelings, and visualizing them as some unpleasant item which was being kept in a locked box. From time to time she would take it out, examine her feelings towards it and then return it to the box and lock it away. Lately though, when she had taken out the nasty object to observe it, it had to her delight, all but withered away.

Bright green daffodil shoots were just visible poking through the black earth beneath the gnarled trunk of the lilac bush. Kate loved this time of the year. Spring was approaching, a time of expectancy and new beginnings. She realised that she'd spent the last two years in a limbo. Occupying herself with work, work and more work. Perhaps now, it was time to put the past behind her and move forward.

*   *   *

She had arranged to meet Phil Simpson and George Offord at the Caraway, a Café which was in the back half of a health food shop. She walked through the Queen's Arcade, enjoying a quick look in the windows of the fashionable boutiques in the precinct as she dodged between the mid- morning shoppers. She crossed over Briggate and passed between two old buildings into a narrow cobbled alleyway and past the side of the City Varieties Theatre. It was like stepping back a hundred years. In the next courtyard was the health food shop and Caraway Café. She pushed open the door of the shop and above it a little bell tinkled.

"Can I help you?" asked the young woman, with her back to Kate, who had been arranging packets of dried beans on a shelf behind the counter. She turned round tucking a strand of her long strawberry blond hair behind her ears, the multitude of narrow bangles chinked together as they slid up and down her arm. "Oh Hi Kate, I didn't realise it was you. Long time no see"

"No thanks Em, I'm not shopping today. I'm just going through to the back. I'm meeting a couple of people for lunch." Kate replied. "Have they gone through, did you notice?"

"There was just a fat chap and a rather nice looking younger one with him. Are they the ones you are looking for?" Em smiled.

Kate laughed at the description. "Yes that sounds like them"

"They went in about five minutes ago. I had my eye on the young one, pity he's with you," laughed Em.

Kate felt herself colour slightly. "Em, they're my work colleagues! There only here *'with me'* as you put it, for a coffee and a sandwich. So you're in the clear from that point of view, I don't think he's spoken for, if you're interested"

Em studied Kate closely. " If you say so... anyway I'll let you get on. There's a delivery van just arrived from the flour mill" she looked over Kate's shoulder, "so I'll have to see to that now, but I'll try and catch up with you later, yeah?"

"Yes, that would be great." She had a lot of time for Em and considered her a very astute young woman. Her beautiful but dreamy appearance belied a sharp brain. Kate often wondered why Em worked as a shop assistant, she thought it was a waste. She had also helped Kate with one of her previous investigations. Kate could feel Em's eyes on her back as she made her way through to the café.

It was only 11.30 and apart from a couple of young mums who were fitting in a quick coffee and a piece of flapjack before going to collect their offspring from nursery, the three of them had the place to themselves. Kate was pleased to see that the two men had taken the table at the far end of the room which was partially screened by a waist high wooden partition covered by huge leafy green plants.

Kate crossed the stripped and waxed floor of the café and sat down at the round pine table, on the remaining empty chair between George and Phil. "Hello you two, are you both well?" She didn't wait for a reply, bending to place her bag under the chair and then looking round for the waitress.

A fresh faced girl with a small purple gemstone in her nostril and the clear skin of a vegetarian came out from the kitchen area and gave them each a menu, pointing out the "Today's Specials" listed on a blackboard on the wall.

Kate had picked the café as they did good vegetarian meals as well a selection of more ordinary food. So many places she had found, advertised their ability to provide vegetarian food, expecting a limp salad or cheese omelette to be greeted with enthusiasm. Kate asked for a black decaffeinated coffee to be brought whilst she studied the menu.

Phil Simpson said "Make that two"

The waitress looked at George. " Can I fetch you a drink sir ?"

George looked at them from under his eyebrows. "I'll have a proper coffee please"

"Of course, sir, Would that be espresso, filter or cappuccino?"

"Oh er , just a filter coffee will be fine."

"Of course, is that white or black sir?" asked the girl.

"White!" he snapped.

"Milk or cream?" the girl continued.

"Cream, and plenty of it! Really, this is like twenty bloody questions." George dropped the menu onto the table in exasperation.

The girl pursed her lips. "Thank you, sir, I'll fetch the drinks whilst you decide on your meals"

George looked miserably at Kate. The girl returned with the drinks. Kate glanced over the menu and said "I'll have the serve yourself salad buffet"

Phil looked up at the blackboard "And I think I'll have the cheese and leek pie with a jacket potato and side salad, please."

George ran his finger down the menu…. Aha!, at last something he recognised. A freshly grilled vegetarian bacon sandwich, surely that would be safe. He turned to the girl who stood with her pen poised above the little notebook. "And just a bacon sandwich for me please" he said with an air of triumph.

"Thank you, Sir" the girl made a note of it on the little pad. "Will that be in white, brown or granary?"

"White"

"And would you like bread or a roll?"

George almost choked on the mouthful of coffee he'd just taken. Was she having a joke at his expense, he wondered. "Any!" he yelled "I don't care!"

"Thank you, sir" said the girl as she reversed rapidly out of the room.

Kate stifled a laugh and took her deep wooden bowl across to the salad bar. Poor old George was like a fish out of water when faced with anything that wasn't from a frying pan or meat and two vege. and covered in gravy. Kate placed her bowl on the table whilst she looked over the buffet. Picking it up again she started by filling it with a bed of lettuce and then placed a large spoonful of the wild Camargue rice salad on top, selected some roasted yellow peppers and tomatoes and topped it with a couple of rounds of goats cheese, and balanced a freshly baked rosemary and olive bread roll on top of it. She returned to her seat just as the others were being served with their meals. It smelt marvellous. Even George managed to raise a smile.

"OK so what have we got so far?" she asked.

Phil began to relate his interview with Jade. "It isn't a great deal of help as far as finding out what might have been behind the shooting, Jade was doing a good impression of 'I know nothing' but at least we know where Carla works now. Also, that both of the shooting victims worked at the gym together. But I had a definite feeling that Jade knew more than she was saying. She seemed to be holding something back but I suppose it could have been that she didn't want to talk in front of Noreen" he said. "And I don't really know why Noreen was there. I know the Rose and Crown was out of commission while the forensics have been there, but it was almost as if she was there keeping an eye on Jade to make sure she didn't say the wrong thing."

"What's Jade like, Phil?" Kate asked.

"She's not the sharpest knife in the drawer, she really is the stereotypical unemployed, single, young mum. Probably spends most of the day smoking and flicking the TV channels between Jerry Springer and Jeremy Kyle. She looks a bit neglected, as if she lives on MacDonald's and washes it down with the odd bottle of Stella. The kiddie looks well enough though. And stuck up there in a high-rise flat, trying to live on benefits and with a small baby for company all day, well it's no wonder is it? …." Phil tailed off, leaving them to imagine the scene.

George then told them how he had spoken to both sets of parents. How he'd seen Mrs. Nelson at the hospital and how it had been decided to switch off the life support system. Kate already knew this, George had 'phoned her straight away to let her know, but until now Phil had been unaware. He then went on to tell them how he had been to visit Leon Edwards' family and had spoken to Leon's mother at their home in Seacroft. Leon hadn't lived with them for some time, so there was little to be learned from them about his day to day activities or contacts. By the time George got there the family had already been informed of Leon's death.

Thankfully for George, WPC Linda Capstick had been the one who had been given the task of breaking the news of Leon's death to his parents and then of accompanying them to identify the body down at the mortuary. Unfortunately for her, before deciding to join the Police Force, she'd spent a short time as a student nurse and cultivated a sympathetic manner which seemed to land her all the jobs which needed a gentle touch. George could see no injustice in this and still felt it was a woman's job to do the women and family bit. "You stick to what you're good at lass" he'd once said to her and been genuinely surprised at the way she'd received what he thought of as praise. He gave her a wide berth for a few days after.

"Good, so I'll go and pay Carla a call this afternoon, see if she can shed any light on things. I think you two should get back to the office and get all this down on paper" said Kate. "Phil I'd like you to meet up with me later, I'll ring you and let you know what time to be there when I've finished at the hairdressers and we'll both go down to the gym and find out what we can from them there. I know it's early doors, but have either of you any gut feelings yet about why these two have been killed, I know it's not quite your usual drive-by shooting, but it has the same sort of feeling"

"It's revenge for something, but the question is what?" said George.

"Most likely drugs… we're in the club land and dance scene. I wonder if they've been dealing drugs, something fairly small time and wanted to expand or tried to cut out the middle man. Both the Gym and nightclubs are good places to sell. Or if they've upset the supplier by messing with the product, cutting it with something else to make it go further maybe" said Phil.

"I hope they haven't messed about and created a bad batch" said Kate remembering what had happened a couple of years ago, and how the result had been a string of deaths from bad heroin. She looked at George who was busy wiping the remains of the bacon fat from his plate with the last morsel of bread. "And George, if you could draw up a plan for DC's Rayner and Chatten to do a house to house around the area of the Rose and Crown with a uniformed team tomorrow and then get the rest of the reports together we'll meet in the morning in my office at nine and go through it all."

George, mouth full, nodded, and chomped enthusiastically on his last piece of bread. The bacon sandwich hadn't been too bad after all. Not quite the usual taste. He wondered what a vegetarian pig looked like. Anyway it shouldn't take too long to get his reports written up and then once Phil was out of the way he'd probably have time for a couple of swift halves in the Nag's Head. It wasn't turning out to be a bad day after all.

Five

KATE parked the silver Audi just across the road from "Cut'n'Tan."
The beauty salon stood in a row of shops, with the usual Chinese
Takeaway, and newsagent, between a florist and a small computer accessories
store. Two bay trees stood in terracotta pots on the footpath at either side
of the entrance. There was a black metal canopy with "Cut'n Tan" painted
in gold lettering above the door. She crossed the road and walked into the
shop. Kate lingered for a moment at the reception desk studying the price
list, which was placed next to some photographs of models with intricate
and completely impractical hair styles. It wasn't cheap to have your hair
done here, she noted, and then addressed the only person working in the
salon.

"My name's Kate Peace, I've come to see Carla?" she said to the woman
styling the customer's hair.

"Hi, I'm Carla," the stylist answered her, "I'll be right with you, I won't
be a sec. Have a seat. Can we get you a coffee?" she asked as she finished
blow drying a customer's hair.

"No thanks. It's Ok" replied Kate, loosening her scarf.

She crossed the newly laid laminate wood floor and sat in a tobacco brown
leather bucket chair. The place seemed to be all leather, chrome, mirrors
and glass, illuminated by small spotlights. You could smell the leather of
the chair and the newness of the fittings and equipment. It must have cost

quite a bit to fit the salon out she thought. The local radio station played unobtrusively in the background, some discussion about traffic congestion in the city centre. Blonde hair carefully piled on her head to give a casual look, and light golden tan, Carla was a good advert for the business thought Kate. Picking up a copy of *Vogue* from the glass topped table next to her, she flicked idly through the pages of adverts for make- up and clothes, not taking them in but using it as an opportunity to study Carla carefully over the top of the magazine. She was an attractive girl, Kate decided, tall, slim, with high cheek bones and a slightly up-tilted nose and with a touch of the heroin- chic look about her. Her nails were painted a crushed raspberry colour which matched her lip gloss. Her carefully shadowed hazel eyes and dark eyebrows suggested that the blonde probably wasn't natural, but so well done that a man would never guess. The low cut, well fitting denim jeans exposed the top portion of a black Chinese design tattoo just above the waist band. Perhaps not quite as chic as she wanted to put over then, reflected Kate.

A young woman came into the shop, paused briefly at the reception desk and then asked to use a sun bed.

"Gina" called Carla "Can you come through and find Sue's jacket and then take this lady through to the sun bed suite?" Gina approached from behind a wooden bead curtain, the beads in her braided hair rattled against each other as she bent languidly folding a towel. She placed it next to the basin, drew herself up proudly, and went to speak with the two women at the reception desk. Kate thought that Gina had a look of Naomi Campbell, her complexion was flawless and her almond shaped prune dark eyes smouldered.

Carla gestured towards the curtain and said to Kate "Let's go through to the office"

The two customers eyed Kate curiously as she stood up. Kate was both older and better dressed than the usual clientele, they knew that there was something odd about her, but were not sure what. Kate was glad she decided not to send George or Phil. Totally different to each other in their manner and dress yet something about both of them still shouted *Police* the minute they walked in the door. Following Carla into the small but well equipped office she saw that it looked out over a sheltered sunny yard where wooden garden furniture provided somewhere for the girls to pop out and have a smoke.

"Nice place you've got here Carla" said Kate. "I think I'll change my mind about that coffee"

"No problem" said Carla picking up the phone and pressing an internal line. "Gina, can you bring us a couple of coffees love? Yes it is nice, we're lucky Mr. Johnson's just had it all refurbished. Looks good doesn't it?" said Carla in reply.

"Have you worked here long?" Kate asked .

"Only about six months, but I was at one of the other shops before."

"Oh, whereabouts"

"The one in Briggate" Carla said.

"Here you are. Two coffee" said Gina pushing open the door. She set the tray down on the table between them and left again.

"And you said shops… how many are there?"

"Four at the moment, and another due to open next month in Leeds. And I think there are a couple of shops in Manchester as well"

"I expect you know why I'm here?" asked Kate, sipping at her coffee.

Carla looked down and studied her perfectly manicured nails. Then she looked up at Kate her eyes welling with unshed tears.

"You've come to talk about Leon and Eliot haven't you?"

"Yes, that's right. We need to find out everything we can about Leon and Eliot to catch whoever did this" Kate told her. "Can I ask who told you about the shooting?"

"Jade 'phoned me yesterday and told me but I don't know anything. I can't think of anyone who'd do something like this"

If only she had a fiver for every time she'd heard that one Kate thought. "But Leon was your boyfriend, right?"

"What makes you think that? Oh, I get it. It was Jade's mum wasn't it? She's got a vivid imagination has Noreen. I'll give her that much"

"So, let me get this right. Leon didn't live with you and you're not Leon's girlfriend?"

"Well not exactly. I mean we all hang round together. You know, just good friends and all that. But I'm not his girlfriend. Listen, when Leon's playing his music he get's all these young girls hanging round, it drives him mad. I just go along and pretend we're an item. It keeps them away."

I bet it does thought Kate. She could imagine it would take someone with a lot of nerve to compete with Carla for looks.

"And Leon doesn't live with you then?"

"Good God, no! What gave you that idea?"

Kate was beginning to wonder that herself.

"No Leon shared a house with Eliot in Chapel Allerton, on Madeley Terrace. It's just behind the school" Carla told Kate.

"What's the number of the house?"

"Number 41."

Kate duly made a note of the address." And when was the last time you saw Leon?"

"Not this weekend, the weekend before. It was Friday night he was D.J. ing at 'Frankie's Bar' near the Merrion Centre"

"Did you notice anything or anyone out of the ordinary, Did you see Leon talking to anyone, or arguing with them whilst you were in the club?"

"No, it was just the usual clubbers out for a few drinks and a dance. I didn't see anything unusual at all."

"And you can't think of anyone who might have wanted to harm them. Anyone they've crossed lately?"

"No, but I'm not sure Leon would have talked to me about anything like that anyway, even if there was."

"But you didn't notice if he was acting oddly, if he was nervous or angry about anything?"

"No, he didn't seem any different at all....I still can't believe this has happened. They didn't have any enemies....they just liked going out and having a laugh, you know?"

"Well, I can assure you they did have an enemy or we wouldn't be sitting here now"

"Yes, I suppose you're right" she said thoughtfully.

"Well, thanks for the coffee Carla. If you do happen to think of anything that might help us. Or remember something out of the ordinary that's happened lately, it doesn't matter how small a detail you might think it is, you must let us know. We can decide if it's relevant or not." Kate passed Carla a card with her number on it "If I'm not there just leave a message with the officer that answers and I'll get back to you. OK?"

Standing, Carla took the card and slid it into the back pocket of her jeans. Picking up the phone she asked Gina to come and show Kate out.

"It's OK, I can see myself out" Kate said.

*   *   *

Kate had arranged to meet Phil outside the gym in Chapeltown. It was an uninspiring building with a sign over the door which read simply "Chapeltown Fitness Centre" It looked as if it could have originally been a Chapel and at some time in its more recent past according to a peeling sign to the right of the door reading "The Roxy" a cinema or bingo hall. He was standing on the corner, hands in the pockets of his beige Mac which flapped in the breeze as she parked in one of the half dozen marked out spaces on the forecourt of the gym. Close circuit TV cameras covered the forecourt and also the larger parking area to the rear of the building which had a large warehouse backing onto it.

They went in, and after showing their ID cards told the girl behind the desk that they needed to speak to whoever was in charge. She was a graceful, statuesque black girl, wearing a navy blue tracksuit with the fitness centre logo embroidered above her ample left breast. Phil tried hard not to stare but failed dismally. Her carefully straightened hair was streaked through with red and gathered into a high ponytail. She did not answer them but gestured towards a seating area with a coffee machine. She disappeared into the gym and came back moments later and showed them through to a room which said *Managers Office* on the door. She pointed to the two seats in front of the desk and then disappeared, closing the door behind her.

"Wow, what's she like" said Phil, loosening his tie slightly.

"Very odd" said Kate. "do you suppose she can't speak, or at least perhaps she can't speak English?"

A moment later a tall, muscular young man wearing the same uniform tracksuit as the girl came into the room and took the seat behind the desk.

"Hello, I'm Liam Nevin, the duty manager here today. What seems to be the problem?" He seemed quite edgy and fidgety, biting his nails and looking from one to the other of them with a nervous distracted air. He had a slightly unkempt and pasty look about him and clearly realised that they were police.

Kate introduced herself and Phil and said "We're here today as a result of receiving information that two young men, Leon Edwards and Eliot Nelson were employed here. Is that correct?" at the same time she showed him her ID card.

Liam Nevin chewed his nails with even greater concentration.

"Did you know them?" Kate asked.

"Well now, I don't know everyone who works here. We've a lot of part timers you know." answered Nevin.

"Did you know them?" persisted Kate.

"I've seen them around once or twice. You know, our shifts sometimes crossed over as they came on duty" Nevin started to look even more uncomfortable beads of sweat stood out on his forehead.

"When was the last time you saw either of them?

"Let me think, I think it was last week …or perhaps not. No, I don't think it was. Probably the week before"

"You must have some sort of records of who is on duty when. Get those out and we'll have a look at them, if you can't remember"

Nevin crossed to the grey metal filing cabinet pulling open the top drawer. "Here we are… No that's not it." he slammed the drawer closed and opened the next one down "Must be this one. No." He slammed it closed yet again and made a pretence of rifling about in the third drawer.

Kate crossed the floor silently, stood behind him and peered over his shoulder. The drawer was empty.

"Mr Nevin why do I get the feeling that you're not being completely straight with us?" Kate asked him.

Nevin slammed the drawer shut. "I haven't been here long and I'm not sure where the paperwork's kept." his hands fell limply to his side.

"Could it be that you don't keep any paperwork?" she asked him.

"No, I mean yes, I mean I'm sure there is paperwork and that somewhere, but I don't think it's kept on the premises" said Nevin feebly.

"Right, I've had enough of this messing around. I don't know what your game is here, but you're coming down to the station" said Kate in exasperation.

"Whoa.. Hang on a minute. I haven't done anything wrong. You can't do this" said Nevin backing into the filing cabinet with a crash.

"Well you're acting pretty strangely for someone who doesn't know anything. Phil give control a ring and ask them to send a car will you? Mr Nevin looks a bit warm, a little ride out in the fresh air might help him cool down a bit don't you think?" asked Kate. "We'll go over a few more questions down at the station"

Nevin sat down heavily behind the desk.

*   *   *

When George had got his reports copied and given instructions to the two DC's to start a house to house around the Rose and Crown the next day, he left the station and crossed the road going round the back of the Playhouse and towards the Nags Head. He pushed open the wooden swing doors and went up to the bar. The Nags Head was an old pub. Not quite spit and sawdust but certainly reminiscent of the post war era, having managed to avoid getting caught up the mass demolitions which had happened during the regeneration of the city centre. It was almost five o'clock and there'd be a mixture of people in there at that time of day. There was no jukebox or satellite television in the Nags Head. If you asked Wilf, the landlord, and he was in a good mood he would turn on the 14 inch colour portable television which stood at the end of the bar. There were one or two people just calling in for a quick drink on the way home from work. And one or two old regulars who'd be in there most of the afternoon sitting over a couple of halves and studying the form between nipping next door to William Hill's to put on the odd 50p bet.

It was two of these that George particularly wanted to catch if they were still there. Alf White, and Len Smith. George had known them both for donkey's years, in fact he'd been at school with Alf. Both Alf and Len had lost their jobs on the railway during Margaret Thatcher's shake up and disheartened by the whole sorry episode had shown no real inclination to work since. George didn't know how they made their money. Perhaps a bit of work on the black, nothing iffy he was sure. A days work for an old mate here and there on occasion, being paid cash in hand. They weren't grasses or coppers' narks in the accepted sense, but old mates who enjoyed a natter over a few free pints supplied of course by George who just liked to catch up on local gossip. It was amazing what these two either knew or overheard. They knew most of the shoplifters and pick-pockets who came in to the pub to sell the Mach3 razors they pinched from Superdrug or credit cards from someones handbag. They didn't want much. They'd be happy to raise a fiver to pay for the next hit. Then they went home and slept it off until they needed something else to sell for another fix and take to the streets again. What a life thought George.

He looked around the bar. Yes, there they were over by the window, each with half an inch of beer in the bottom of their glasses. Alf was just emptying a box of dominoes onto the table and turning them face down. George caught their eye and mimed someone lifting and drinking from a glass. The man on the right of the two gave George a thumbs up sign.

George stood at the bar, one foot on the brass rail and tried to find a clean drip mat to put his elbow on. Failing he put his hand back in his trouser pocket and studied the picture of the prize winning Tetley's dray horses which had pride of place in the centre of the wall, whilst he waited to be served "Three pints of Tetley's please" he said to the landlord, and then as an afterthought "And three packets of cheese and onion crisps as well"

"Right you are, coming up" said Wilf as he pulled on the repeatedly on the ceramic handle of the pump. No electric pumps here.

George paid for the drinks, placed the corners of the three packets of crisps between his front teeth, and wrapped his meaty hands round the three pints drawing them towards the edge of the bar, it wouldn't have been the thing to ask for a tray. He walked across to where Alf and Len were sitting and placed the three pints and the packets of crisps on the table.

"Now then lads, how's things?" George addressed them jointly looking from one to the other.

Alf took a gulp of his beer and set the glass down again on the cardboard drip mat, he rubbed his hands through his stubbly silver hair and said to George, "We're much the same, not a lot doing, do you fancy a game of doms?"

"I'll give this one a miss, but don't let me stop you" he pulled the top of one of the packet of crisps apart and slid the other two packets across the table to Len and Alf.

"Not got time eh? I reckon you'll be busy with this here shooting business won't you?"

"Yes, I can't say much but the official quote is that 'We are following several lines of enquiry at present'..." George replied.

Len wiped the back of his hand across his mouth to remove the froth from the beer and smirked. "By that you mean you buggers have no idea who did it!"

"Yes, something like that" admitted George popping another crisp into his mouth. "I don't suppose you've heard anything on the grapevine?" he looked from one to the other as he crunched.

Alf leaned forward making a show of looking around to see if anyone was listening, and then took a couple of gulps from his beer which were followed by a heavily pregnant silence giving import to the moment before he went on to say "Not really, but I can give you a tip...."

George leaned over the table too, reflecting Alf's wish for secrecy. "What's that then Alf?"

Alf lifted his index finger and tapped the side of his nose, and then gave the up turned dominoes on the table a couple of slow turns, nodded and said "Don't say I never pass on important information"

"Yes, Ok, get to the point for God's sake. What is it?" asked George tensely.

Alf put his hand up to the side of his face to prevent anyone overhearing and said "Little Miss, 2.30 at Wincanton tomorrow" Len and Alf burst into roars of laughter.

"Very good, you old sods! You nearly had me going there!" said George joining in.

*   *   *

Kate sat behind the small metal table which was bolted to the floor of the interview room and Phil sat on a straight backed chair just by the door. The custody officer brought Liam Nevin up from the cells where they'd kept him cooling his heels whilst they had a coffee in Kate's office and discussed how the interview would be run. Kate would ask the questions and signal to Phil if she wanted him to take over, but all in all they had no real reason at the stage to suspect Liam Nevin of being personally involved. It seemed that the gym wasn't keeping the books straight but at this stage Kate wasn't too concerned about that. Only if there was some connection to the murders of Leon Edwards and Eliot Nelson. It would be interesting though to see if he had any background information about them. He was certainly uncomfortable about something.

The custody officer led Liam Nevin along the corridor. He shambled into the room and looked round him at the beige walls with the small window set high in it. Without the overhead strip lighting it would have been gloomy, with it, it was glaringly bright and the grubby bleakness was accentuated.

Liam sat on the plastic chair facing Kate, and cast an uneasy look over his shoulder at Phil who sat making notes. There was no need for this as the interview would be taped, and Phil was in fact writing:

1. Don't forget to book the car in for a service.
2. Call at Marks and Spencer's for something for tea.
3. Drop suit in at the drycleaners.

When offered, Liam had refused the presence of a solicitor saying:

"I don't need one. I haven't done nowt"

So it was just the three of them.... cosy. Kate ran quickly through the speech about the time, date, and who was present, adding that Liam Nevin had refused the offer of the duty solicitor.

"Right Liam, so you're telling us that you didn't know the two men who were shot. But they worked at the same gym as you on a part-time basis. Is that correct.?"

"Yes" replied Liam

"Yes, what?" asked Kate.

"Yes, I did know them from work but not very well"

"And did you know them outside work? Did you ever meet them out of work, go out drinking with them or socialising anywhere else?" asked Kate.

"No, I knew them from work, alright, but we weren't what I'd call friends as such. We didn't go out together. I've been in places and seen them there, but not gone there with them you know."

"Whereabouts would this have been Liam?" giving him time to think had obviously made Liam decide to talk Kate decided. It often worked.

"Not this weekend, but last weekend. I went to the "Glasshouse" said Nevin "They were both there. Leon was playing the music and I bumped into Eliot at the bar."

"OK Liam, so try and think back to the night when you saw Eliot at The Glasshouse. Why did you go there specifically" asked Kate

"I went with some mates, because Leon was D.J. there that night, they like the music he plays"

"And do you like Leon's music Liam?"

"It's Ok. But it all sounds the same to me"

"Was it your idea or your friends, to go there?"

"I can't remember who of thought of it first. I think we were always going to go. We often go there on a Saturday"

"What just to listen to the music? What about women, were you on the pull?" Kate enquired, eyebrows raised.

"Yeah well if there were any decent women there we wouldn't have said no but that wasn't the main reason" Liam began to relax a bit as the talk moved away from the two victims.

"What about drugs then. The Glasshouse is a good place for scoring I hear?" Kate said.

"Now hold on a minute! I don't do drugs" Liam jumped to his feet, both hands palm down on the table top.

"Ok, calm down, I'm only asking"

Liam sat down again scowling.

Kate thought he was a bit jumpy perhaps there was something about the drugs assertion that worried Liam. "So you all went to listen to Leon and have a couple of drinks. Is that right?"

"Yes, that's right" Liam replied.

"Was it busy that night?"

"It was bloody heaving, Leon was getting pretty popular. People came from all over Yorkshire to listen to him." Liam told her.

"What sort of thing did he play?" asked Phil from behind him.

Liam looked round wondering where the conversation was going.

"Well he mixed a lot of his own music. It was different. That's why people liked it. You know mainly dance and techno" he said.

"Did you see anyone else there, anyone local that you know?" Kate suggested trying to jog his memory.

"Yeah, Carla was there with Liam, and I saw her later talking to Devon Johnson" answered Liam.

"And who is Devon Johnson?" asked Kate.

"Devon Johnson owns the gym" said Liam Nevin.

The name rang a quiet bell with Kate she made a mental note to pursue it later. "And you didn't see or hear anything that night that seemed unusual?"

"No, Eliot was saying that he might not be working at the gym much longer. He had a bit of a holiday planned, in France I think he said, and a job lined up down south when he came back but he didn't say what it was." Nevin told Kate.

"And what about Leon, did he have any plans for moving away?"

"I never heard him say so"

"That'll do for now Liam but we will want to talk to you again, so don't think of going anywhere without telling us. And if you do think of anything…. get in touch"

Kate gestured to the custody officer who was waiting just outside the door.

"So I can go?" the relief on Nevin's face was obvious.

"Yes, but don't go too far. We will want to talk to you again" said Kate as Nevin was led from the room. The door closed quietly behind him.

"So what do you make of all that Phil?"

"I don't think he's Mr. Squeaky Clean, I think he knows them better than he lets on, but he's giving us enough to keep us off his back for the moment. And I think the gym's not quite above board either. I wonder if the Drugs Squad have anything on them? It would be an ideal place to distribute from. I'll ask them to check, shall I?"

"Yes Phil, do that and I think we need to find out a bit more about this Devon Johnson character too. Have them put his name through the computer and see what comes up"

Kate looked at her watch. It was almost six o'clock. "I've had enough for today Phil. I'm off home for a long soak, a glass of wine and old film. I'll see you in the morning. My office at nine o'clock" said Kate as she lifted her jacket from the back of the metal framed chair and made for the door.

Six

Kate had been unable to sleep, spending a restless night tossing and turning as a jumble of confusing thoughts chased each other round inside her head and conspired to prevent her dropping off. She tried to get her thoughts in order and couldn't. The more she tried not to think about the case, the more fretful she felt. She watched as the numbers on the digital clock changed more and more slowly. In the end she gave it up as a bad job, threw off the duvet in a fit of annoyance, got up, had a shower and made herself a cup of coffee. She let Jasper out into the orchard where he wandered stiffly and aimlessly in the early morning light. Consequently she arrived at the station much earlier than she would usually have done. The cleaning ladies were just leaving as she trudged wearily up the steps to the main entrance. She almost collided with Gladys Oliver who, as she fastened her raincoat and, looking at the slanting rain, paused on the top step to pull a red paisley patterned head square from side pocket of her nylon shopping bag. It wouldn't completely protect her but might just save her hair a bit. She wanted to call into Sylvia's café for a quick pot of tea and a currant teacake and have a chat, before catching the number 15 bus to the Gala Bingo hall. She secured the head square firmly under her chin in a double knot. "Good morning Miss, we don't often see you, you're about bright and early today"

Kate squinted up at the clouds "Good morning Gladys. It's early certainly, but I'm not sure about the 'bright'"

"No you're right there Miss. But it's the early bird that catches the worm and all that. You have a good day" and nodded her greeting at Kate before marching off purposefully up the street.

Kate hoped she could catch a bit more than a worm.

Sitting at her desk, she started going through the reports they'd already gathered, trying to find some indication of where they should go next. She looked at the already mounting pile of paperwork. It was amazing how quickly it accumulated, but they had to move fast, doing as much as possible as quickly as possible. Everyone knew that the first 48 hours or so, of any serious case were the most important. Anything which a witness had seen was still fresh in their mind. On the top was Dr. Manby's post mortem report which had intrusively spewed itself from her fax machine. It didn't tell her anything new. She didn't want to go through the gory details again. Seeing it at first hand had been bad enough. She folded it in half, slipped it into a manilla envelope, sealed and labelled the flap for easy recognition and hoped that she wouldn't need personally to refer to it again. The interviews with both sets of parents hadn't really given them any pointers but that in itself wasn't unusual. How many parents of normal young men in their early twenties could honestly say that they knew exactly what their sons did every hour of the day. And these two didn't even live with their parents, so the chances were even slimmer. Jade seemed to be in the dark as to what Eliot was doing when he wasn't with her. Either she didn't want to know what he was doing, preferring to remain in ignorance if it was something shady, or he didn't want her to know what he was up to. And Noreen seemed to hate both the young men but had no firm knowledge with which to back it up. Which may, or may not have been significant. Kate admitted that she was puzzled by Carla, who lived in Roundhay, a nice area, and who had a good job at the salon. She didn't quite seem to fit into the picture at the moment, but who could tell. Both the young men had worked in the gym and been involved in the music and dance culture. This seemed to be the most likely lead at the moment. She wandered across to the window of her office which looked out on to one of the busy streets of the city centre. People were dashing through the rain to work. One woman jumped aside but was drenched as a double-decker bus hit a huge puddle at the kerbside. Turning back Kate crossed to the coffee maker, poured herself a cup and sat behind her desk contemplating the painting which hung on the opposite wall. She found that the abstract in hot swirling shades of orange, red, and gold usually helped her to think, but today her mind was a blank. At the moment she didn't know what was going on. It looked very much like a drugs related killing. The dance scene was notorious for its associated drugs culture. The use of Ecstasy and Amphetamines was well known and it was quite possible that the gym where Eliot Nelson and Leon Edwards had worked was being used as a distribution centre for drugs too. Body builders often took huge amounts of steroids to help bulk up muscle. "'Roid rage" was a recognized phenomenon. Could there be some sort of connection Kate wondered, between the drug crazed body builders and a drugs deal or double cross that had somehow gone wrong, resulting in the shootings? They'd visited the gym already, but perhaps they needed to talk to Mr. Johnson the owner. Johnson, hang on a minute. Kate rifled through the pile of sheets again. Yes, there it was on the report sheet for her visit to "Cut 'n' Tan" Carla had said her boss was called Mr. Johnson. A common enough name, it would probably be a coincidence but they'd better find out. She was glad she'd noticed that. It may be nothing but there again it was something else to look into and they were pretty short on leads at the moment...

She looked up at the wall clock, quarter to nine. The others would be in soon, then they could pool their findings and decide where to go next with the investigation. These sessions which allowed them to bounce ideas off one another often provided a new direction in which to go. Kate sorted her papers into order, liking to have the reports to hand in case she needed to refer to them during the meeting, and picked up the handwritten sheet of A4 which listed the points she wanted to cover with the team. They'd need to get hold of the phone records for both the men's mobiles and the land line to the house if there was one, and check them out, as well as any bank statements to see if there were any unaccounted for large sums of money moving in or out, which might provide a lead to the motive for their deaths. They'd have to search the house for any letters and speak to any friends or associates who had corresponded with them. This would be going on at the same time as the forensic and other investigations. There was a lot to co-ordinate, and all these possibilities had to be explored. Most of the information gleaned would be discarded, but processes had to be followed and all possibilities examined. You never knew what might come to light from the most unlikely sources. They would have to visit all the usual places and people which two twenty year olds might be expected to deal with. They'd have to visit the gyms and bars and follow up receipts from the music shops to the clothes stores. Despite what people thought, there was still a lot of boring slog and foot work, in modern day policing. It wasn't all action and excitement.

*   *   *

Phil Simpson, as she had expected, arrived promptly at two minutes to nine. A bit of a snappy dresser, he looked as usual, cool, calm and ready to face whatever the day might throw at him.

"Help yourself to a coffee Phil" said Kate waving him across to the coffee machine.

"Thanks" Phil picked up one of the white bone china mugs which were stacked in the chrome stand next to the coffee pot, poured himself a mug full, picked up two of the individual servings of cream and two paper sticks of brown sugar.

Next to arrive were the two young D.C.s Dave Chatten and Paul Rayner. Rayner was recently married and was expecting the birth of their child at any time. Chatten came across as a bit of a wide boy, still playing the field, She thought that each probably secretly envied the other, but that was life. People always thought the grass was greener on the other side of the fence. Her team were a real mixed bunch. And she thought that was a good thing. The greater variety of views and ideas put forward the better. Looking up at the clock as they came through the door, they apologised profusely for their lateness even though it was only one minute past nine by the clock on the wall. Kate deliberately kept the clock a couple of minutes fast. She felt it gave her the advantage of wrong footing those who cut it fine, and that it kept them on their toes. Also it helped make sure people were away promptly. She thought of it as the "going home clock". Not that she had anything to rush home for. Kate looked at her watch irritably. Where the hell was George? Well she wouldn't hang about. He must be somewhere en route, or he'd have phoned to let her know that he was going to be late. He was probably outside looking for a parking space.

"Morning, you two. Help yourselves to a drink"

"Morning Ma'am" they replied in stereo.

Kate arranged the pile of papers in front of her as Chatten and Rayner quickly took their seats "Ok everyone, if you've got your drinks sorted, and you're sitting comfortably, let's get down to business" She picked up the piece of A4 paper and was just about to speak. There was the sound of raised voices in the corridor and a thump as something heavy was dropped on to the floor.

"Sorry love, I didn't see you…" George's muffled voice could be heard. Sure enough a moment later he puffed in through the door. His suit looked crumpled and his tie was askew, but at least he'd made the effort to shave if the bloodied piece of tissue paper stuck to his chin was anything to go by.

"Sorry, I'm a bit late. I couldn't…."

Kate cut him off with a raised hand. "It's Ok George, just grab a coffee and pull up a pew." Secretly she was a bit put out but didn't want to make comment in front of his junior officers. That could wait until she saw him later.

There was a knock at the door and a flustered looking young woman from the admin team drew a sheet of paper from the stack of files she was still trying to rearrange after her collision in the corridor with George, and handed it to Phil, who thanked the woman and placed it in front of him on the table.

Kate ran first through the reports which George had compiled after he had interviewed both sets of parents. She then went on to detail the interviews at the hairdressing salon with Carla and the outcome of their visit to the gym and subsequent interview of Liam Nevin. Now all of the team were fully conversant with the information they'd collected so far.

"Phil is that anything useful that's just come in?"

"Could be. Looks like we've got the car they drove off in after the shooting. A dark blue Subaru Imprezza was found abandoned just off Scott Hall Road" Phil read from the piece of paper which had just been handed to him. "But I'm not sure it's going to help us much. It was reported stolen from Bradford last week. A car like that stands out, so a pound to a penny they've had it hidden in a lock- up somewhere"

"Who's the owner? Is there any connection there?" Kate asked.

"You're not going to believe this, what a classic." he laughed. "The car was owned by Millside Garage, the Subaru main dealers. Two blokes turned up and asked to take it for a test drive. There's been a spate of cars been pinched when people have taken them out on their own. At one time they just asked people to leave their own keys as security but they had a couple of cars pinched and were left holding the keys to another stolen vehicle, so the chap in the show room went with them, but they drove off down a back street in Manningham and told him they had a gun and to get out of the car. He didn't argue. They drove off and left him there. He had to ask a passing mini cab driver to call us"

"I don't blame him for not putting up a fight," Kate said "as it's turned out they were probably telling the truth. It could have been curtains for him too. Anyway arrange to have it brought it in and have the forensics go over it I don't expect they'll have left any traces but we can try. But if he was in the car with them for some time, he must have got a good look at them?"

"The description he gave was: Both Afro-Caribbean males, one wore sunglasses and a woolly hat the other had a shaved head." Phil replied.

"That's not a lot to go on is it, hardly narrows it down much."

"No, unfortunately not. The car salesman was only working at Millside temporarily, to cover the regular chap's holidays. He's from Harrogate and there aren't many ethnic minorities there. He says apart from the fact that one was bald and one had a hat they both looked pretty much the same. He was probably shitting himself to be fair. The only thing he can remember is that the one in the hat was very tall at least 6 feet 6."

"Well, we'd better talk to him ourselves see if we can jog his memory a bit, hadn't we? He may have remembered something since" said Kate. "Anything else there?"

"They've run Johnson through the computer. No previous. So that's another one we can cross off the list"

"DC Chatten, you can arrange an interview with this… What did you say his name was Phil?"

"Palmer, Ian Palmer, works at the Subaru main dealers on Wetherby Road, Harrogate. It's on the edge of the town just as you are driving in, near the cemetery" Phil replied.

Chatten wrote this down carefully. It wasn't a task he was particularly looking forward to. He felt it was getting away from the excitement a bit. But you could never tell and it was a nice day for a ride out. At least Rayner could start the door to door on his own this afternoon. That was always a bore.

"Phil, I want to go out and take a look at where they lived. Try and get some idea about what they did when they weren't working. There must be something that we're missing. Can you make yourself available to do that this afternoon? If DC's Rayner and Chatten could visit the car salesman and start the house to house that would be another angle covered. There'll be a team of uniformed officers made available to assist you. Here's a copy of the street plan with the areas we need covering highlighted. The different colours are for allocation to the various groups of officers. Make sure you don't miss anyone out and make arrangements to revisit the houses where the occupants are unavailable. And George perhaps you could find the manager of the nightclub and see how well he knew them, what's happening in club land at moment?"

"Will do" George replied. He thought he'd probably got off lightly in the job allocation.

She looked at Chatten and Rayner "Tomorrow I'll need you two to check through and follow up any paperwork we bring back from the house this afternoon."

Chatten tried to look enthusiastic and made a note on the piece of paper in front of him.

Kate began to gather her papers into a pile and slipped them into a wallet envelope, as a sign that the meeting was over. She looked down the length of the table at them all. "Thank you everyone, let's get cracking then." She stood and pushed her chair carefully underneath the table. Tucking the files under her arm she left the room.

Seven

Rayner felt a little put out that he'd been given the house to house enquiries to do. Like a lot of detectives he thought it was boring, routine work. He'd rather be out meeting and interviewing the real suspects, interesting criminal types in sleazy bars, not listening to bored housewives and elderly couples. Never mind, it wouldn't be forever he consoled himself. He was planning to go places in his career.

He turned up the garden path of No. 2 Old Park Road which was opposite the Rose and Crown. Nearing the white PVC door he noticed the net curtain twitch. Oh no, not another nosey old biddy he thought. Still they were often the ones who really knew what was going on in the street. As he raised his hand to knock at the door it began to open, stopping abruptly with a clank as the safety chain held.

On the threshold, looking through the narrow gap stood an elderly woman who could have been anywhere between sixty and eighty. Her sagging face under a cheap perm, peered up at Paul through national health glasses.

"Yes, dear?" she enquired.

Paul held his ID card to the gap in the door. "Police, we're calling at all the houses in the street in connection with the shooting on Saturday night. Can I ask your name and if you saw anything unusual during the evening, or on Saturday afternoon itself?"

"Elsie Smith, Mrs. No love, I can't say that I did." She sounded quite excited by the idea that she might have.

Paul made a note of her name and address. "So there was no one hanging about. No strange cars parked up in the road that you noticed?" He looked up and down the street as if to prompt her.

"No, I didn't see anything"

"Didn't hear anything, or see any strangers walking about"

"No, but I wouldn't have seen anything anyway" She continued to stand with one eye to the crack and made no offer to open the door.

No hope of tea and cake with this one then, thought Paul. "Why are you so sure that you wouldn't have seen anything, is your eyesight not too good?"

"Oh, no love I can see as well as you when I've my specs on. But I was at my daughter's in Morecambe all weekend. She picked me up on Friday in her car, drives you know, and has her own car too" she added proudly "and brought me back Sunday tea time. So I missed it all" now sounding disappointed.

Paul closed his notebook with a feeling of defeat and placed it back in his pocket. "Thank you Mrs. Smith. Sorry to have troubled you"

"No trouble dear"

He strode back down the path pulling the small single black wrought iron gate closed behind him.

He by passed the next house which was unoccupied and had huge solid metal sheets over the doors and windows to keep out the squatters and drug users. At No. 6 he tried his luck again. He rapped on the door and waited. There was no answer. He knocked again a little harder. The door swung open to reveal a large young man in his mid twenties, wearing a worn tea shirt and a pair of knee length union jack shorts. His head was shaved and he had three gold rings at the outer aspect of his left eyebrow and a bright red spiders web tattoo which radiated from the middle of his cheek and down across his thick bull neck.

"Police" said Paul by way of introduction.

"Yeah, didn't fink you was the bleedin' vicar did I? Could 'ave been one of them other Bible bashers though wot wears the suits 'cept they always travel in twos. 'Ere, do you reckon they're woofters then?"

"Can I take your name?" he suppressed a sigh. This one was going to be another complete waste of time.

"Dwayne Webster"

Paul jotted it down. "I'm making enquiries about the shooting over the road on Saturday night Mr. Webster. Did you see any thing unusual or anyone hanging about that you didn't recognise?"

"Nah mate, didn't see nothing, me. Watched 'Match of the Day' and had an early night. Sleep like the dead me. You know how it is" Webster smirked at Paul.

He was right. Hear no evil, see no evil, this one. A complete waste of space thought Paul "Well if you think of anything get in touch will you?" He knew that even if Webster had seen it all he wouldn't be forthcoming. Paul was the enemy, the filth. No point in leaving him a card. Paul was sure Webster knew his way to the local police station without directions.

"Yeah….."

Again Paul tucked the notebook away. Now he knew he'd drawn the short straw.

He trudged to the next house. Third time lucky maybe. Or maybe not. He knocked at the peeling green paint work of the front door. Yellowing net curtains on a stretched wire drooped sadly at the window and a plastic pot plant lay on its side amidst the bodies of last years blue bottles. If it was any other area he would think the house was uninhabited but the absence of metal sheeting at the windows told him otherwise. He hoped no one offered him a cup of tea here. At last the door creaked open and tall thin man in a dirty vest and brown checked trousers held up by a pair of navy blue braces stood before him.

"Aye, lad?" said the man at the same time as he tried to remove something from between his teeth with the orange fingernail of one who smokes untipped cigarettes.

"DC Paul Rayner. I'm calling at all the houses in the street to see if anyone saw anything unusual on Saturday?"

"You'd best come in then lad" said the man standing back for Paul to pass. "The lounge is on your right. Go in and have a pew. I'll go and put the kettle on"

Paul looked about him. It was like being in a time warp. A tabby cat wandered into the room and wound itself sinuously around his legs.

"Come on, Tiddles" the voice drifted through from the kitchen where Paul could hear the sound of a kettle being filled and switched on, followed by the sound of a tin of cat food being opened, and then the sound of a knife against a saucer. The cat dashed from the room, his legs scuttling like clock work.

At one end of the room stood a radiogram with a selection of LP records next to it in a wire rack. Against the opposite wall stood a sideboard bearing a collection of framed and ancient black and white photographs.

The man returned in a couple of minutes. "I've given him a tin of sardines" the man told Paul.

"Lucky cat" he replied not sure what comment was expected.

"Well they're cheaper than cat food you know"

He set down the tray he was carrying. It held two cups of tea and a metal biscuit barrel covered with a monochrome print of the river Thames. Paul was sure his granny had a one similar twenty- odd years ago which came free with six tops from OMO washing powder. It was either just before or just after the promotion for red plastic roses which could be collected one at a time until you had a bunch. He had a fleeting memory of soggy Digestive biscuits. The biscuit barrels hadn't worked when they were new and he was sure that it wouldn't now. He quickly refused the offer of a biscuit and looked warily at the stained, once white pyrex cup and saucer with the remains of hunting scene on it. Rington's tea, he thought. He put the cup and saucer down near his feet and got out his notebook. "Now as I was saying, Mr. Er…"

"Jackson, Bert Jackson"

"I'm here to ask about the shooting on Saturday night. Did you see anything or any one unusual in the day or evening?"

The cat came back into the room, and after a look at his owner jumped onto Paul's knee with the unerring certainty of an animal that could pick out someone who disliked cats. The cat proceeded to make its self comfortable and yawned at him with fishy breath. Paul tried to ignore the cat and concentrate on the man's reply. Realising that it was not going to cause offence, the cat in its contrary manner jumped down and rolled over in front of the hissing gas fire.

"Not during the day. No. I was in the bookies all Saturday afternoon, it's warmer in there. I always have an accumulator on a Saturday afternoon.10p a race and if they all win….." he tailed off leaving the resulting riches to Paul's imagination.

"What about later?"

"No I didn't see any one walking about with a gun if that's what you mean. He laughed to himself. Now there was them two lads in a fancy blue car. They were parked just up the side in the access road that goes round the back of the houses to the allotments. I only saw them when I went for a look out of the spare bedroom window. I got up to the toilet about one o'clock. There's no bulb in there so they couldn't see me looking out but I could see them alright. They had the little light on inside the car and they were just sat talking to each other. I wondered if they were planning to break in or something but they must have been waiting for somebody because in the end they just drove off"

They were waiting for someone alright. Leon Edwards and Eliot Nelson thought Paul. A breakthrough at last. "Did you see what they looked like?"

"One was black, had one of those big woolly hats they wear. And he was big"

"I thought you said they were sitting in the car? How do you know he was big?"

"I could tell…. His head was touching the top of the car. And then he got out and stretched. Like he was stiff you know. Only for a minute and then did something or looked at something under the front seat and got straight back in. He was big and tall."

"What about the other one?"

"He didn't get out, the driver. Looked normal sized and he was white"

"What sort of car was it Bert?"

"Ooh, now I'm not right good on cars, not nowadays. It was biggish, shiny, had a thing across the back of the boot. You know, makes 'em go faster or some such"

"If you saw that sort of car again would you know it?"

"Oh, I should say so. I seen 'em before. Fancy looking, not many about. Aye, I'd know it if I saw it again. I just don't know what they're called"

Paul looked at his watch. "Do you think if I sent a car round in the morning to pick you up, you could come down to the station and have a look at some photos of cars with me Bert?"

Bert sniffed loudly. "Is it like 'helping the police with their enquiries'"

"Yes, I think you could say that"

"What time have I to be ready then?" He could wear one of those shirts his daughter was always buying him for Christmas. He had three still in the cellophane wrappers.

"There'll be someone here at ten, and I'll meet you down at the station"

The straw suddenly looked longer. He wondered how Chatten was fairing in Harrogate.

*   *   *

They arrived at 41, Madeley Terrace. It was a large red-brick back to back Victorian terraced house, arranged over three floors and judging by the small cobwebby window just below pavement level probably had extensive cellars. It was in one of the streets of many similar houses in Chapel Allerton which used to be called bed-sit land, but because more and more young people were unable to get a foot on the property ladder, they increasingly had to rent property and so the type of tenant changed from students and ne'er do wells to young people who worked in the shops, offices, banks, and call centres of Leeds. The rooms were no longer referred to as bed sits but as house shares. And the condition of the houses improved accordingly.

Kate drew the bunch of keys from her bag and inserted the small Yale key into the lock of the wooden door. She pushed her weight against the door. Nothing happened. Trying a larger key in the mortise lock below she had more luck. It turned smoothly and the door swung gently open.

The house had a cold unoccupied feeling. The central heating had been switched off. Kate walked slowly into the hallway and into the first room on the right. It was a pleasant light and airy sitting room painted in magnolia with white cornicing and ceiling rose. A large bay window with the original sashes, draped with floor length cream curtains overlooked the street. There was a black leather reclining three piece suite and an oblong glass topped coffee table with chrome legs. A large screen television with satellite digibox, games console and DVD player underneath stood in the far corner between the fireplace and the window. Next to the television was a storage tower stacked with films and games. Kate walked across and studied them. They were just the usual mix of blockbuster movies, horror films and games. Looking into several of the cases it seemed that what it said on the outside tallied with what was inside. So, no porn film empire here. The magazines on the table were recent a mix of computer magazines and What Car. For two young men the place seemed remarkably clean and tidy. No unwashed coffee cups. No balled socks in sight.

The ground floor was well furnished. The kitchen/diner had a large rectangular table in the middle of the floor and six chairs were arranged round it. In the centre of the table was a glass vase holding a bunch of browning, wilted lilies. A residue of stagnant green water could clearly be seen. Again, the black granite work surfaces were clean and clear, everything had been washed and put away into the beech fronted units. Kate turned and walked out of the kitchen and climbed the staircase to the first floor.

There were three bedrooms and a bathroom. She walked into the first bedroom. On the bedside table was a framed photo of Leon Edwards, his arm slung around the shoulder of another young man. Both were casually dressed in T-shirts and track-suits. He smiled out of the frame, not a care in the world. From the dark background it looked as if they were in a night club. Leon held aloft what appeared to be a glass of lager. His friend punched the air and smiled for the photographer. Kate placed the photo back on the table and crossed to a chest of drawers. She slid open the top one. It contained underwear and socks. The next drawer down contained a selection of neatly folded t-shirts and a lower one a couple of long sleeved sweatshirts. The wardrobe held a variety of tracksuits, hooded tops and a couple of more formal cotton shirts and several pairs of jeans. Nothing untoward here.

Across the landing, the bathroom had a modern white suite with a separate shower cubicle containing a Jacuzzi shower. And the chrome rack to one side of the hand basin held a bewildering array of what Kate could only think of as men's beauty products.

Phil inspected some of the bottles, unscrewing the lid on a bottle of aftershave and sniffing at it cautiously. "Very nice, and I should say it's the real thing"

"And how would you know on your pay?" she joked.

"Because I always try a few when I'm in the duty free shop" he quipped.

The second bedroom was much like the first, and the third bedroom held an ironing board and a hanging rail.

Kate pushed the door to. She didn't feel that she was learning much. She decided to press on up to the attics.

The stairs were covered with a much cheaper brown carpeting, it was worn and the outline of the boards could be seen through it. The door to the attics creaked open at her push. As she walked in Kate flicked on the light switch. Natural light came only from two small square skylight windows. Again the rooms were clean and tidy. In the two attic rooms there were in total a dozen mattresses arranged side by side on the floor, each with a pillow and a couple of sheets and a blanket neatly folded at its foot. It reminded Kate of the films she'd seen of National Service establishments in the 1950's or the servants quarters in the old Victorian houses. Perhaps it was overnight accommodation for friends after late night parties. The rooms felt quite austere after the rest of the house.

Turning away and feeling a little puzzled by what they'd just seen Kate suggested that they look at the cellars. The door to the cellar was in the kitchen. Kate approached it cautiously, pulling it towards her. A flight of solid looking wooden stairs stretched away from her. She'd hoped that Phil would go first but he was hanging back, giving way to her seniority.

The reason for Kate's apprehension was that apart from the fact that she didn't like the dust and spiders, cellars always made her feel uneasy giving her flashbacks from the time when as a young PC she had been called out to attend a 'domestic dispute' and had been cornered in a cellar by a heroin filled idiot who mistook her for his wife. Kate remembered the feel of his hands around her throat. And the unexpected feeling of disbelief, that she was about to die, rather than fear. Fortunately back up had arrived just in the nick of time.

She remembered just how young and green she'd been. She'd thought that both mentally and physically she could take whatever the job might throw at her. She hadn't considered the realities of the job, her own mortality, or that her life might be held in so little regard by someone else. But after this incident she'd realised that she was expendable, that she might go in to work one morning and not go home at tea time. That was the nature of the job. It might seem exciting and glamorous, but it was also dangerous, and her confidence had taken a severe knock. Kate had been mentally shaken by the episode rather than physically harmed, and once she'd come to terms with it she was able to move on. Her confidence returned and from that time, it was onwards and upwards for the rising star Kate Peace. She'd shrugged it off as being part and parcel of the job but occasionally, as now, a part of her brain which she could not control clicked into overdrive. She took a deep breath, straightened her shoulders and descended the cellar steps. Again there were half a dozen mattresses side by side. The walls were whitewashed and it would probably have been reasonably warm when the house was occupied and the central heating system was on, as the boiler stood in the far corner and heating pipes ran round the walls before disappearing through the ceiling to heat the upstairs.

"There's something strange about this said Kate but I can't decide what."

"Do you think they were running a B&B on the side?" Phil joked.

"God Knows," replied Kate, "Let's go back upstairs and have another poke around in the kitchen and bedrooms. See if we can find anything to give us a clue about what they were up to" They climbed back up the wooden staircase and back out into the kitchen.

"I'll take the kitchen, you try Eliot's room see what we come up with." said Kate. She was ploughing through copies of old utility bills when Phil came back in and sat down at the kitchen table.

"What do you think about this then? It looks like Eliot's diary and the final entry in is for the Tuesday of last week."

Phil opened the diary, turned it, and slid it across the table to Kate. It read: *Collect Chris at 05.30, Hartshead Moor Service Station.*

Kate looked at her watch. "Could be something, could be nothing, we'll have to look in to it, but we'd better call it quits for now, I've got to meet Josie Arthur from Yorkshire Television shortly down at the Rose and Crown to do the appeal for information that's going out on tonight's news" She fastened her jacket and made for the front door.

"I'll leave you to lock up Phil if that's Ok and I'll see you tomorrow."

She drove down to Seacroft through the gathering afternoon traffic and met with the news team outside the Rose & Crown. They told her what form the bulletin would take and Kate in turn told them what information she would be giving.

The filming started and showed Josie Arthur standing by the front door of the Rose and Crown, she looked into the camera and said. "Here we are live from Seacroft this afternoon. This is the spot where two young men were shot, in what Police describe as a callous murder" The bearded camera man panned across the front of the pub. "And here we have Detective Chief Inspector Kate Peace, who is senior officer in charge of the investigation, to give us the details."

The camera cut to Kate, who was attempting to stop her dark hair blowing in her eyes as a strong breeze got up. "I can confirm that police officers were called to the scene here at the Rose and Crown Public House in Seacroft in the early hours of Sunday morning. They found two young men in the car park at the rear, who had been the victims of a shooting. One had received bullet wounds to the chest and was pronounced dead at the scene, the other man died later that day in the Infirmary as a result of his injuries. We are appealing for anyone with information about who is responsible for this callous act to come forward. Someone out there knows who is responsible. Do you know anyone who has been acting out of character. He's someone's husband, brother, son. Someone knows who this person is. They may have changed their usual routine or have become unusually quiet and withdrawn. All replies will of course be treated in the strictest confidence. You can call us on either of the numbers which will appear on your screens after this bulletin, or you can call in to your local police station. Thank you"

The camera cut back to Josie Arthur. "Thank you Inspector Peace. And now back to the studio."

*   *   *

Kate lowered herself slowly into the old roll top bath. She slid down and the Radox bubbles came up to her neck. Marvellous. The scent of the bubbles reminded her of the little muslin bags filled with dried lavender flowers which her granny had kept in the wardrobe. Her mind wandered sleepily and the water grew cooler. Was it worth letting some water out and refilling the bath? She lifted her hands from the water and studied them. No, her fingers already looked as wrinkled as prunes. She stepped from the bath and pulled the fluffy white Egyptian cotton towel from the cast iron radiator and wrapped it around herself tucking one corner in securely above her left breast. She combed some conditioner through her damp hair and applied some heavy- duty moisturiser which according to the television advert would make a noticeable difference after 14 days. Somehow she doubted it, but a girl has to try. Kate smiled at herself in the mirror. She was beginning to feel better already. She slipped into a cream silk nightie and a towelling robe. She wandered down to the kitchen, quickly crossing the flagged floor in her bare feet and pulled a tall green bottle from the fridge, where it had been cooling. She poured herself a large glass of the white wine. The surface of the glass misted over as Kate took a long drink.

She walked through to the snug and looked through her DVD collection. She selected 'Pride and Prejudice' slipping it into the machine, a dose of the dripping Mr. Darcy was just what she needed, and settled herself on the remaining bit of sofa next to Jasper who was sprawled full length. He opened one eye and tilted his ear trying to look alert. Kate took a sip from her wine and placed it carefully on the walnut occasional table beside her and with her other hand rubbed Jasper's ears. Before the film was 5 minutes in both Kate and Jasper were snoring quietly in stereo.

Eight

George had drawn a blank when he tried to get an appointment with the manager of the Glasshouse the previous evening. Shaun Moodie, he had been told, was out of town. George had passed between the two stone lions on either side of the top step, walking heavily down the flight of stairs, and under the ornate brass and Perspex canopy which gave the Glasshouse its name. House was actually a misnomer as the club was situated in a basement but that was ideal. It provided the dark airless conditions in which a lot of young people seemed to want to spend their time. He'd approached the ticket desk and asked the young girl seated behind it to take him to the manager's office. She looked up from painting her nails a violent green colour and tipped her head to one side, regarding him silently but making no effort to break off from painting her index finger.

"Police!" he yelled slamming his card on the desk as she lowered her head to carry on the task.

She jumped, upsetting the little glass bottle. It began to roll towards the edge of the desk, a thick trickle of pearlescent green, which reminded George of snot, ran across the surface. "Oh shit!" She quickly straightened the bottle, screwed the lid back on and jumped to her feet. She came out from behind the desk. "This way" she said and set off at as brisk a pace as her high heeled pink mules would allow.

George followed Karolina, the girl's name written across her chest in red on the pale pink t-shirt, or perhaps it was where she'd been on her holidays, through a dark passageway and into the dance area.

He knew Shaun Moodie of old and had a grudging admiration for the way he managed to move with the fashion in pop music. But then again he supposed it was more about business than music, about supply and demand. Moodie was nothing if not a shrewd business man

The heat and cigarette smoke hit him like a wall. Pulsating beams of different coloured lights almost illuminated the area. It put George in mind of what it would be like walking through a fairground ghost train. The pulsating drumbeat in counterpoint with the lights assaulted the senses of vision and hearing. Boom! Boom! B- b- Boom! Boom! Boom! b- b- Boom! Beat the drums. *Give it to me now; Give it to me rite now. Give it to me girl; Give it to me rite now.* The vocals competed. "What the bloody hell sort of music do they call this?" he called to the girl's swinging blonde ponytail as the distance between them increased. George puffed as he struggled to keep up with her. The view from behind was actually quite pleasing. The phrase "a couple of ferrets in a poacher's bag" sprang to mind. Pity her brains didn't match her bottom.

She must have caught something of what he said, as she turned to face him, her hand cupped behind her ear. "What?" she frowned prettily as she strained to hear him.

George saw rather than heard what she said. "Nothing, nothing, it's OK!" he waved her on. At least it had given him opportunity to catch up. They circled the edge of the dance floor, dodging the drinkers who were swigging from bottles with a variety of brightly coloured labels. It was something that really irritated him. He was convinced that it was an affectation encouraged by the bars to try and save washing up. He pondered the likelihood of the drinks being stored outside in the yard and how many dogs might have pissed up against the crates before they were brought inside. Give him a pint of draught beer in a dimpled pint glass with a handle any day. George was mesmerised by the bouncing mass of young bodies. It wasn't what he'd have called dancing. Scantily dressed young women, with huge bosoms which were almost contained in skimpy tops and short skirts gyrated in front of him. Exposed cleavages and navels seemed to be the order of the day. One generously built young women bent over, bottom in the air and laughed. Was she wearing any knickers? It was impossible to tell. If she was they were damn small ones, he couldn't see them. Quickly he looked away. Was it what they called a throng? Her friends thought it hilarious and clapped in encouragement. Another pulled down her lycra top and pushed her ample breasts together and pouted. A cheer rose from the edge of the dance floor. "Get yer kit off for the lads love!" someone shouted. A storm of laughter erupted.

George suddenly felt old he was glad he didn't have any daughters; he'd be worried sick if he thought they were in a place like this. Was there any hope for humanity or was he just tired. He pulled a crumpled and stained white cotton handkerchief from his trouser pocket and wiped his perspiring brow. They'd arrived eventually at the manager's office to find not Shaun behind the desk but his stand-in, a somber looking individual who introduced himself as Rick Gray. He wore a grey open necked shirt and a pair of denims so old that they were wearing into holes. His mousy hair was brushed to one side Gray by name and probably by nature. George had explained that he really needed to see Shaun, made his excuses, and said with a feeling of relief that he'd return in the morning. Escaping into the cold night air, he caught the smell of frying onions on the breeze, as he climbed the stairs to the street. He lifted his head and smelt the air trying to decide which direction it was coming from. Across the road and a hundred yards to his right, a group of young men were waiting at the window of a burger van. George headed across the road and arrived at the van just as the last of the group was liberally covering his hot dog in a squirting of mustard from the selection of plastic bottles on the counter. George looked on approvingly and his mouth started to water. "That'll make a hot meal of it lad" He rubbed his hands in anticipation and as the group moved away up the road he studied the menu, hand- scrawled on the inside of an empty burger box, and sellotaped to the interior of the window.

"How's business then mate?" he made a habit of engaging anyone he met in small talk. You never knew what you might learn.

"Quiet, always quiet on a Tuesday night. There's not so many about you know" replied the vendor who had a brush over hair style and the sagging face of a bloodhound.

"Better at weekends I suppose?"

"A bit better but sometimes they prefer a curry… or a Chinese. I think the days of burgers are done. I struggle to make a living mate on the prices I charge, but what can you do? Got to be competitive"

George tried to think of a sympathetic response and failed. "I know. Life's a bitch sometimes. Give us a quarter pounder cheese burger, mate and plenty of fried onions on it please"

"Yeah mate," the vendor replied morosely "Life's a bitch and then you die"

"I've got a mate who says 'Life's a bitch and then you marry one' " George responded in attempt to lighten the man's mood.

"Yeah well, I've got that to contend with as well"

Bloody Job's comforter this one, thought George. His food must be good. You sure as hell wouldn't come for the conversation. He looked up and down the street as the vendor turned the burger over on the hot plate. Two young women skittered, giggling along the pavement in the direction of the Glasshouse.

"There you are mate. That'll be £2.50" he said passing the burger across wrapped in a white paper serviette "Condiments at the end of the counter"

"Cheers" replied George moving to the end of the counter, and covering his burger in sauce.

The vendor looked over George's head to the next customer. "Yeah mate, what can I get you?"

George bit into the burger satisfyingly, the tomato ketchup running down his chin as he made his way beneath the orange street lights, back to the Omega.

*   *   *

Here he was again. The night club in the cold light of day seemed even seedier than it had done by night. The floor around the bar was sticky, and his shoes made a cracking noise as he pulled them free of the surface. The table tops were covered in sticky rings and overflowing ashtrays. The smell of stale beer and cigarette smoke lingered in the furnishings. A cleaning woman moved cursorily around the place wielding a stained dishcloth and a can of lemon air freshener. Only the sound of her plastic flip-flops as she moved about broke the silence. The cigarette hanging from the corner of her mouth added to the mess as ash dropped from it on to the floor. She ground it out in an ashtray she had just wiped with the dirty cloth and moved on to wipe the surface of the next table. She turned as she heard

George behind her. He stared hard. Yes it was Karolina. He recognised the green nails. Not so appealing without the war paint.

"Mr. Offord, to what do we owe this unexpected pleasure?" Shaun approached him, his right hand extended in welcome.

George swung round. "I think we've known each other long enough for you to call me George" They had an uneasy relationship. George was almost certain Shaun was straight and above board and would help him by answering his questions truthfully, but that depended on George getting the questions right. He was never sure if it was a bit of a game or a sort of psychological one-upmanship. Looking at Shaun, George couldn't help but smile to himself, he wasn't wearing well. Like a poor man's Pete Stringfellow, his greying hair pulled back in to a scrawny ponytail was becoming decidedly thin on top and the gold jewellery really needed a suntan to set it off. The tight black t-shirt emphasized Shaun's skinny arms and the gold metal watchstrap rotated on his bony wrist. When seen close to, the crows feet at the corners of his eyes were deep, as were the bags beneath them. At least George knew he was knocking on a bit and didn't try to fool himself. When would Shaun start to make concessions? There couldn't be much difference in their ages.

"I suppose you've heard about Leon Edwards" George said.

"Yes, a bad business"

"I understand he played here for you"

"That's right. He was getting quite a name for himself. A very talented lad, mixed his own music. People travelled from all over the North to come and listen to him. He was building up a good following. He'd just had an offer from Plan8 Records to release an album of his music. 'Fight or Flight' it was going to be called. Some good tracks on it too, 'Adrenaline', that was my favourite and 'Eternity' was really good as well. By the way George, what do you think will happen to his music now?"

"I haven't a clue Shaun, I suppose it'll probably be up to his family"

"Do you think they might still release it? He was very talented it would a shame for it to go to waste. I could help them you know. Point them in the right direction; give them a bit of advice and so forth, if they wanted"

Yes, thought George, for a fee, or a cut of any profits. He'd probably rob them blind. Same old Shaun, never miss out on an opportunity to make a bit of money. "By the way, where were you last night when I called Shaun, just out of curiosity?"

"Went up to Newcastle - listening to a lad who might just do as a replacement for him. Not as good as Leon, yet, but he's only young and still developing a style of his own. Very influenced by the jungle scene but this music has a lighter quality. Not so heavy on the drum'n'bass as Leon's music. Anyway, we'll have to wait and see how it pans out. I've got one or two others I want to go and see as well over the next week or two. Thought I'd nip up there mid week while it's quiet. Rick's capable of holding the fort if there's not too much going on."

"Bloody hell, what a racket it was, if last night was quiet I hope I never have occasion to call over the weekend!"

Shaun let out a hoarse laugh. "You know what George, you're getting to be a boring old man. Can't stay the pace any more!"

"But seriously, have you any idea what might have been behind this shooting? Did Leon Edwards have any enemies that you know of? Did he move in any dicey circles?"

"No, to all three. I can't believe what's happened. He was a quiet lad, just interested in his music. In fact at one point I wondered if he might be a bit......you know...gay. I mean a good looking lad like that, but he didn't bother with women that I could see, and believe me there's plenty here for the taking"

George thought he could well believe that based on some of the young women he'd seen.

"He just lived for his music. It's not the sort of business where you make enemies. Musicians, they're more like artists. They have a creative temperament, not destructive. I think he worked at a gym as well part time to make a bit of extra cash. That was probably why he looked so good. Plenty of muscle but not too big and he always had a very pleasant way with him. A bit of a charmer. It could have been put on, but I don't think so. He always seemed so genuine to me. The young girls couldn't leave him alone, loved him...but he wouldn't have any of it. And that only made him more of a challenge to them"

"Now don't jump down my throat Shaun. I'm not implying anything about what goes on here, and think carefully before you answer. Do you think he could have been involved in drug dealing, I don't mean here, but maybe through the gym?"

Shaun rubbed his chin thoughtfully. "I don't think so. I know you can never tell. Not 100%, but I just can't see it. You get a feeling for these things. The middle dealers usually get involved in the selling to make enough money to feed their own habit, and I'd be very surprised if Leon was a user. You just get a feeling and I didn't get it round him"

"What about the other lad who was shot, Eliot Nelson. Did you know him?"

"Not as well as Leon. He came in now and again, had the odd drink. Usually he dropped Leon off in his motor. A Jeep I think and sometimes he came in to help Leon set up his equipment and then went off again. But again he was a straight up guy, a pleasant lad. You know what I mean? No, I can't see it. Sorry, I can't help you

"It's Ok Shaun. You know how it is. Leave no stone unturned. If you do hear anything will you let me know?"

"Sure I will. A lot of people will miss the kid."

George handed him a card which he tucked into the pocket of his jeans and turned to leave.

"See you Shaun"

"Yeah see you later, and good luck"

George looked at his watch and made his way back to the office. He hated the paperwork but found the best way of dealing with it was to keep on top of it.

* * *

"Hi George" said Kate, as she arrived silently behind his chair.

George jumped, a long line of letter *aaaaaaa* s appeared on the screen of the computer in front of him. He swivelled on the round on his seat to face Kate. "Bloody hell, I didn't hear you come in. You scared me half to death!"

Kate was familiar with the amount of concentration George needed to come to grips with writing his reports in the word processed form. Despite attending several courses aimed at absolute beginners, George had still not progressed from a slow painstaking input of one fingered typing.

He turned his back on Kate and carefully looked for *save* on the drop down menu. To his cost he had been distracted before and lost all the work he'd taken two hours to input. He'd had to do it all again. It had cost him a lunch time pint in the Nags Head, much to his annoyance. He'd learnt that lesson quickly enough and always saved his work at 5 minute intervals. He carefully clicked the box and breathed a sigh of relief, the absorbed scowl disappearing from his face. He turned round again to face Kate relaxing back in the seat, hands clasped beneath the vast expanse of stomach which threatened to win the battle with the straining buttons down the front of his pale blue striped shirt. He realised just in time and sat himself upright on the seat waiting for her to speak.

"So what have you managed to come up with George, 'owt or nowt?'" she mimicked his broad Yorkshire accent.

George smiled back at her. He took her ribbing in good part. "Well, I called in at the Glasshouse and had a chat with our old friend Shaun Moodie. He wasn't able to tell me anything new but the picture I got of the two lads doesn't fit in with the drug dealing idea. Shaun was quite adamant that there was nothing to connect them with dealing that he'd ever seen. In fact by the time he'd done he made them sound like a couple choirboys. But they upset someone enough to go to the bother of having them killed."

"Mmm, we're missing something here. And we need to get on to it soon. Anything else to tell me?"

"Yes, and we've run a person check on Leon's brothers. There's nothing showing for either Wayne or Darren Edwards. I must say I was surprised. I'd have bet a pound to a penny that Darren Edwards at least, would have had previous form, but appearances can be deceptive. Or maybe he's brighter than he looks and just hasn't been caught"

"Anything showing for the gym owner, Johnson?"

"Ah, Devon Johnson. I think we're dealing with another breed altogether with this one. He's a much more interesting character. Never actually been convicted but his name has come up in connection with various activities. He is the registered owner of the gym where both the lads worked as well as a similar set up in Manchester, and also of the "Cut 'n' Tan" salons. There are four in all. I don't know if you remember but Operation Oracle was set up a couple of years ago by our counterparts in Greater Manchester?"

"Yes, I remember hearing about that. A lot of painstaking work went into setting it up. A series of dawn raids across the city. Pretty successful wasn't it as I remember?"

"It was, as far as it got several dealers off the streets in Manchester. But the upshot of it was as far as we are interested is that one of the dealers, a little jail bird called Mickey Philips was picked up in a raid on one of the houses, he was a small time player, about as small as you can get. The one that always carries the can for the others. Anyway Mickey thought he could save his skin by singing his heart out to try and save his miserable scrawny neck. He said the gym in Manchester owned by Johnson was being used to distribute from. He named several names, some of them went down with him, and some didn't. One of those who didn't was Johnson."

"So why did Johnson walk?"

"The word was he was a lot further up the pile and clever with it. Johnson always maintained that he had no knowledge that the gym was being used as a base by the dealers. He was also questioned in connection with making arrangements for Jamaican women to smuggle drugs into the country. As a result of information received several women were picked up as they came off the plane at Manchester. The sniffer dogs would have missed them, the drugs they were carrying as well as being in, let's say a very personal place, were industrially vacuum packed so that no scent could escape. The women all maintained that they had no idea who set it up. They were to do one run and then they would be given false papers and found work so that they could send money back home to their families. So same old story, no evidence to back the accusation up. If he was involved he made sure there was no trail leading back to him. I think Johnson's a wily bird who could do to be watched. The drug squad says that there's been no knowledge about Johnson being involved in drugs since Operation Oracle. Perhaps his near miss put the frighteners on him. I think he's mixed up in this somewhere. Shall I arrange to have him brought in for questioning?"

"No George, if he is involved in this, we need to keep one jump ahead of him. I don't want him to get wind that we're watching him or he might do a runner. But I think you're right. Johnson must be mixed up in this somewhere it's too big a coincidence if he's not."

"So what's our next move?"

"We found a diary at Madeley Avenue yesterday. There was an entry in it for Eliot to meet someone called Chris at Hartshead Moor service station. Might not be anything but it needs following up. I want to go Leon Edwards' funeral tomorrow morning. I don't expect it will be very productive but it's always good PR. So if I can leave it with you to have a ride down the motorway tomorrow and see what you can dig up?"

George wasn't sure if this was a good one or not. Pretty boring routine stuff but at least he shouldn't get cold or wet and there should chance of the odd bacon butty and pot of tea. "Ok leave it with me and I'll get back to you tomorrow afternoon?"

Kate smiled and picked up her jacket from the back of the chair. She knew exactly what he was thinking. She could read George like a book. He was a bit of a plodder sometimes but give him a job where he could eat and drink along the way and he'd put his heart and soul into it.

Nine

Carefully Kate reversed the Audi into a tight parking space at the edge of the main road outside the church. She won the space from a dark coloured BMW with blacked out windows, only because it was coming from the opposite direction and couldn't get across the traffic. The car radiated annoyance as its driver slammed it into gear and screeched off down the road. "Tough luck, loser" she said as she collected her shoulder bag from beneath the passenger seat and swung her shapely black Pretty-Pollyed legs from the car, a view greatly appreciated by a passing white van driver who tooted his horn and slowed for a better look. Kate gritted her teeth. If she hadn't been outside the church and surrounded by mourners, she'd have retaliated with a rude gesture.

The church was an imposing grey stone building erected during in the period of religious fervour of Victoria's reign, which swept across the country taking the city of Leeds in its wake. The local industrialists who made their fortunes firstly from flax and wool spinning and then later from the manufacture of machine tools, expected to see their employees attending the same church they themselves attended. It could be a route to gaining or losing promotion in the factory. Attendance increased and the churches, for a while had thrived. Kate doubted that many, if any of today's attendees regularly visited the church. Unless, perhaps it was to take the lead from the roof, or pinch the collection box. The grey finger of the spire pointed accusingly at the leaden sky. A row of bedraggled looking pigeons lined up along the ridge of the chancel roof, like a group of waiting Victorian mutes. Kate's black court shoes tapped smartly up the path to the church door like a blind man's cane. On either side of the path were headstones which had been laid flat to fulfill the new Health and Safety instructions after a child playing in a graveyard in a nearby town had been killed after a tombstone fell on top of him. Here, just last week, the verger had fractured his wrist after slipping on one of the self same damp mossy stones. So much for his health and safety. Kate eyed them warily.

The wails of the wheezing organ drifted out from the arched doorway to welcome her. She stepped into the shelter of the porch and folded the telescopic umbrella she'd been carrying. Collecting a hymn book and a prayer book from the wooden bookcase just inside the door, she took a seat in a pew towards the rear of the church, four rows down the aisle, and sat at its exit end. She bowed her head briefly in silent prayer and waited. Out of habit she ran a swift but practiced eye over the congregation. A few latecomers drifted damply in, pausing at the end of Kate's pew unsure if there was any system to the seating arrangements. She deliberately refused to catch their eye and they shuffled into a pew across the aisle. The coffin was brought in through the main double doors and wheeled in the modern way, on a chrome metal trolley to the front of the church. A single arrangement of white roses and lilies graced its lid. A figure stepped out from the shadows of the vestry, mounted the steps of the pulpit and began the service. He did a good enough job she supposed bearing in mind he'd never met his customer.

At his instruction they all moved outside. A straggling line of mourners trailed behind the vicar down the churchyard. The morning smelt sickly. A putrid combination of damp earth and lilies made her feel nauseaous. Kate stood near the open grave. There was a heap of soil next to it, shored up with a large section of plywood and improbably covered by a sheet of bright green artificial grass. In the far corner of the churchyard the gravedigger paused in his work and slammed his spade into the damp earth. He stood one foot resting on the blade of the shovel, and his elbow leaning on the handle, holding a roll up cigarette between his thumb and index finger, he took a couple of quick drags as he watched the funeral party through narrowed eyes, and then threw the fag end into the hole he was digging, before continuing with his task.

The vicar stood at the head of the grave, gazed into the distance, and made the sign of the cross in the air with his right hand. His cassock and surplice blew tightly around his legs as the wind gained strength. He drew himself to his full height, wispy red hair blowing, holding up the Bible in his left hand. The pages fluttered angrily, but it didn't matter that he was unable to read the words from the page. He knew the passage by heart and his voice boomed above the competition from the howling wind. His icy blue gimlet eyes pierced those gathered as he recited, as if daring anyone to disagree. "Fret not thyself because of evildoers, neither be thou envious against the workers of iniquity. For soon they *shall* be cut down like the grass, and *wither* as the green herb. The wicked *have* drawn out the sword and have bent *their* law to cast down the poor and needy" his voice rose higher and the congregation were transfixed, if not comprehending. "But the wicked *shall* perish and the enemies of the Lord *shall* be as the fat of Lambs, they shall consume *into* the same, they shall consume *away*. Remember not the sins of my youth nor my transgressions, according to thy mercy. *Consider mine enemies*, for they are many and hate *me* with cruel hatred!"

Wow! thought Kate, daughter of the vicarage, that was completely amazing. She had no idea that people still preached in this fire and brimstone style. Did he think it would have some sort of appeal for today's violent society, something they could identify with, that might even tempt them back to church? What happened to forgiveness? He wasn't far off going on to 'An eye for an eye, a tooth for a tooth' She risked a look at the Edwards family. Fortunately the speech seemed to have gone over their heads and as she looked around, the rest of the group also seemed unmoved by the content of the eulogy. Perhaps as non-attendees at church they just tuned out any religious talk as being above them. What a waste of a young life, Kate thought as looked at Leon Edward's parents, the mother being held up by a son at either side of her. Mr. Edwards stood to one side looking more hang dog than ever. Kate looked across first at Phil, who stood some 50 yards away under a damply dripping yew. Between them they scanned the crowd around the grave. Not really having any definite idea of who or what they might be looking for. There were no furtive figures skulking between the grave stones, or driving slowly by the cemetery gates.

The idea of the killer attending the funeral was a bit of a myth. At least she'd never witnessed it. All of the mourners looked perfectly legitimate if not slightly undesirable, and were behaving in an acceptable manner. The undertaker's men stood two at each side of the burial place and began to slowly let the coffin down into the black void. The webbing straps rasped, sliding through the brass handles of the oak coffin as it disappeared from view. Mrs. Edwards let out a muffled sob, holding a soggy paper tissue to her nose, and dropped a single white rose into the grave. The two brothers each threw in the customary handful of earth. Leon's father shook his head in disbelief, as tears streamed down his cheeks, and looked up at the grey sky as if expecting to find the answer there. The family turned at the signal from the vicar and began to walk away from the graveside towards the waiting black limousine. The rest of the group who had attended the committal retraced their steps.

As they passed Kate, Mrs. Edwards paused and said "Thank you for coming. We know you didn't have to. It's much appreciated love. If you want to come back to the Community Centre there's sandwiches and drinks put on. They've applied for a licence. Oh, that's if you're allowed, being on duty and all"

The two sons closed in protectively about their mother.

"That's very kind but I'm sorry I can't" Kate made a pretence of looking at her watch "I'm due in a meeting soon. But don't worry Mrs. Edwards, we *will* catch them you know"

Standing slightly behind his mother and so out of her line of vision, Daz looked down at Kate menacingly, and said "I 'ope you do!"

"'Cos if we catch them first…" continued Wayne.

Mrs. Edwards turned to them in distress. "Come on lads, don't talk like that. Not today."

"Okay mum, don't take on so, eh? Let's get out of here shall we, it gives me the creeps. And you could do with a stiff Brandy" said Wayne.

Daz maintained a thin lipped silence.

Kate felt the waves of hostility exuding from the two men but held her ground and raised her chin, resisting the temptation to take a step back.

The three continued along the narrow path to the waiting car. Mr. Edwards, hands in his trouser pockets, trailing unhappily in their wake.

Kate waited until they were in the car and made her way across the graveyard towards Phil who waited beneath the branches of the Yew, threading between the tombstones.

Phil couldn't believe how attractive she looked in black and tried to push the thought away. "Well how did it go?"

"About how you'd expect. I didn't see anything or anyone suspicious if that's what you mean. Did you?"

"Not in the way you mean, but there were a few unsavoury types about"

"I don't know why I came really. I suppose it's good for PR that's about all. I know the public like to think that the killer might have come to pay his last respects but both you and I know it's not likely"

"No, I've never known it yet"

"Let's get back to the then station then shall we? See what sort of a morning George has had"

*   *   *

George decided he would call into the station first before he set off down the motorway and check there hadn't been any further developments on the case. As he walked into the station the clock above the door told him it was 8.20am. He smiled to himself. That was about right it didn't do to risk losing his reputation and his nickname. "He'll be last one up on Judgement Day, that one" his mother had always said. His colleagues thought he was unaware that they called him "Minty" Offord. But as one young DC had explained when under put under pressure, "It's because you're always 'After Eight' sir" George had pretended outrage but was secretly amused. It was amazing what you could get away with if you pretended to be a bit slow. Passing the Desk Sergeant he asked "Anything come in overnight?"

"No very quiet. Just a couple of break ins over at Roundhay. One bloke had his Merc. taken. Apparently the burglar alarm on the house wasn't set. The chap said they never bothered with it or it meant that the cat couldn't have the run of the house overnight. All they had to do was put a brick through a pane of glass in the back door, the key was in the lock. They just reached through and let themselves in and what do you know? A bunch of keys on the kitchen work top, all ready and waiting, a gift from heaven. Garage key, car key the lot. Can you believe it? Don't they just bloody ask for it? And all *she's* worried about is that the back door was left open and the cat's wandered off!"

George shook his head. Not in disbelief, he'd heard it all before and far worse. Would people ever learn he wondered? He set off slowly up the stairs and pushed the opaque glass door of the office open. He looked at his desk, a small yellow post-it was secured under his unwashed coffee mug. "See you this afternoon - Phil" Bloody Hell, he'd been and gone early. Or perhaps he'd put it there last night. George looked at the mug for a second. Should he have a coffee first? No he'd best get off. There'd be plenty of time for a drink on the way. "See you later" he'd called to the sergeant on his way out.

"Aye, not if I see you first" was the reply.

He settled himself in the Omega and pulled out into the city centre traffic as a Pink Line double decker bus paused to let him out. He flicked through the radio channels finally settling on the local radio station where there was discussion of the day's horse racing meeting. It was at Wetherby this afternoon, over the sticks. A nice little course. Would he have time to call in at the bookies on the way back? Perhaps he should have set up one of those new fangled telephone accounts but there again that might be a bit too handy. He drove onto the M62 where a large B&Q lorry flashed him out. George took his cue and rapidly accelerated into the middle and then the outside lane. The overhead gantry warned of an accident ahead. George cursed and hoped it was further down than his destination. The traffic was becoming heavier. The accident had been cleared but had caused heavy tailbacks. He pulled into the car park of the service station at Hartshead Moor and parked near a National Express bus which was disgorging its hotchpotch of passengers. He walked through the foyer, the bored bus travellers aimlessly studied the rack of daily newspapers or the screens of traffic news. George passed on through and made his way to the restaurant. No harm in a plate of bacon and eggs washed down with a pot of tea first. He took his tray to an empty table with an ashtray. They were getting fewer and fewer. He spoke to the woman on the till and asked what the shift pattern was. 6-2, 2-10 and 10-6 she'd told him.

"So you wouldn't have been work at 5 in the morning a couple of weeks ago?"

"That depends, we all work an assortment of shifts. Depending on family committments. What day did you say?"

"Tuesday morning. Two weeks ago"

"Now let me think a minute. No. I was on the afternoon turn that day" Typical thought George.

"But Anne over on the breakfast counter was on nights. 'You were on nights weren't you Anne a couple of Sundays ago?'" She shouted across the room.

Ann broke off from her desultory stirring of the baked beans into a mush and came across. "Yes that's right why?"

"Don't suppose you get many customers at that time of day do you?" asked George.

"No not many, one or two on their way for an early flight at the airport. That's about it really"

"So, a lovely lady like you, you'd have remembered a good looking young man on his own?" George said in his best attempt at flattery.

"I'll say!" she joked.

George fished in his pocket for the photo of Leon Edwards and Eliot Nelson holding it out towards her "Either of these look familiar?" he said hoping she would pick out Nelson.

She took it from him and studied it closely. "Mm, Nice young men aren't they.... both of 'em" she passed the picture to her friend to admire.

"Ooh yes" she agreed

"Yes, very...and now they're both dead"

"Oooh!" shrieked the women in stereo, dropping the photo to the floor. "No they weren't in here. I'd have remembered them" said Anne clutching together the collar of her nylon blouse. "Perhaps they bought petrol?"

"Perhaps they did, I'll try there next" said George as bent to pick the photo from the floor.

He walked away from the women who couldn't decide whether to be shocked or excited. All he heard were snatches of "OOh" and "Well I never!"

He crossed the tarmac towards the filling station and gave the details to the middle aged man behind the desk. Ron, as his badge proclaimed him, promptly called through to the manager. George passed him the photo. He looked at it cursorily "Sorry, I wouldn't have a clue, we get hundreds of people through in a day, but I think we can do better than that. If he was in here it'll be on camera and if he paid with plastic we'll have the card details. Do you want to go and have some breakfast while I look?"

George declined explaining that the café had been his first stop.

"I'll just go to my car. I've a couple of phone calls to make. I'll be back in a bit" In the car he shook open his copy of the *Racing Post*. He flicked through the pages until he came to the one which listed the runners at Wetherby. The first horse listed in the 2.30 at Wetherby was "Leon's Luck" George thought it might be a sign but couldn't decide whether it was a sign to back it or give it a wide berth. He studied the rest and underlined a couple of likely candidates in black biro before making his way back to the manager's office.

"Here we are" said the manager "He's on the film. This is him isn't it?" he asked George pointing at the figure on the screen as it crossed the forecourt. "Bought some petrol, look, here he comes into the shop" The manager pointed at the image of Eliot Nelson as he looked directly at the camera when he approached the counter. "Paid by plastic too, E. Nelson was the name on the card" He held out the printout for George to examine. "Didn't cover his tracks too well did he?"

"Perhaps he wasn't trying to. Let's just watch the next sequence shall we?

"Yes, of course, that's fine by me. What are we looking for?"

"I don't know" George admitted.

The manager switched the tape on again. Eliot Nelson crossed the forecourt and got into the white van. It pulled out of the garage and towards the motorway. Behind it was a large white articulated lorry. George couldn't quite see the name on the side. '*Transport*' was the only word he could read. "I'll have to take these with me, but I'll give you a receipt for them" George added. He slid them carefully into the large brown envelope. A good mornings work all in all. Now would he have time to call in at the bookies he wondered as he sped back towards Leeds?

*   *   *   *   *

They all three sat round the table in Kate's office. George passed her the envelope containing the cassette and the copy of the entry of Eliot Nelson's credit card.

"Well done George a good result. I'll make arrangements to have the film looked at and enlarged. We need to see if there was anyone in the van with him or if he was just meeting this Chris at the at the service station for a chat"

"If he was, they didn't go into the café to talk. The woman in there was adamant she would have remembered him if he had. I think it's more likely that he picked someone up in the van"

"Yes I think you're right" said Phil. "It's a strange place to meet just for a talk at that time of the morning. I favour he brought the person he met back with him"

"Ok" said Kate "If we're going to follow that assumption for now I need to get a better look at the film and we need to see if there are any other cameras we could pick him up on. What about any overhead cameras on the motorway?"

"Or what about nearer home? What about the close circuit cameras on the roads coming into Leeds?" suggested Phil.

"Great idea" said Kate "I'll get on to that straight away" She looked up at the wall clock "Probably a bit late for today though. I'll give them a ring and see if I can set it up for tomorrow" She looked at the clock again. She felt they'd reached one of those sticky points in the investigation. There was a lot of work that had been done, but as yet not a lot to show for it. It was easy for the team to become demoralized, to feel they were losing their way in the maze of minutiae. She needed to show her appreciation. "Okay. I suggest you both take the rest of the afternoon off. You must have something you could do for a couple of hours?" she looked from one to the other questioningly.

George was already out of his seat and halfway to the door. "Well I've got a suit I need to pick from the dry cleaners before they close" he made a play of looking at his watch.

That would be great if it were true thought Kate. "Bye then, George. I look forward to seeing it tomorrow."

George faltered for a second and turned back to Kate.

"Only joking!" she laughed. "See you George"

She's not a bad boss, he thought, for a woman.

Phil was standing, ready to leave, but looking a little more thoughtful.

"Well Phil, what are you going to do for the rest of the afternoon? Round of golf….watch a film?"

Phil looked down at the carpet for a second too long and cleared his throat.

"Don't suppose you fancy a coffee do you, in town, er just go over one or two details?" he shocked himself by the suggestion. He'd been planning to suggest a meeting out of work. But this seemed to present a good opportunity, not too personal.

Kate looked at him but didn't quite meet his eye. "I don't think so Phil… .erm I've still quite a lot I need to do today"

"That's fine…..I just thought perhaps,… em. Well yes. I'll get off then" he turned and walked towards the door.

"Phil…" she called, thinking frantically. That couldn't have been easy for him. He probably wouldn't ask again If she turned him down now. "Really, I do have a lot I still need to do …….What about tomorrow?"

He looked at her in surprise which he hoped wasn't too obvious. "Tomorrow……yes tomorrow would be great. Perhaps a quick meal after work, pizza or something. Just to run over a few points?" Keep it casual Phil, he thought. Don't try too hard. Reel her in slowly like a trout. He'd never been fishing so where did that idea come from?

"Yes that sounds good. See you tomorrow then" She'd already turned back to her paperwork and didn't even lookup.

"Bye" he pulled the door to behind him. Was it a date? Should he have been a bit more daring? He took the stairs down two at a time, swinging off the newel post at the bottom. He loosened his tie and ran his hand through his hair. Roll on tomorrow. Things were looking up.

Kate looked up as the door closed. She lifted her cool palms to her warm cheeks. Fancy, blushing at her age!

Ten

She walked up the cascade of steps to the large white stone building which was Leeds University, through the automatic doors and crossed the foyer to the information desk. "Good morning, Detective Chief Inspector Peace. I've got an appointment with Professor Kenworthy at 10.30" she propped an elbow on the counter as she leaned across and towards the prim-looking woman sitting behind the desk. The woman looked over the top of her rimless spectacles, pushed them hurriedly back up into position and reached out to pick up the phone. She briefly studied both sides of a laminated A4 sized sheet of telephone numbers, and deftly pressed a sequence into the keypad.

After the others had gone the previous day Kate began to feel a little at a loss for where to go next with the investigation and had decided to take her problems higher in her search for help. Her call had not gone unheard, as Chief Superintendent Michael Southern had himself answered the phone, and after listening to the latest developments had invited Kate up to his fourth floor office to discuss the situation. Southern had rubbed his chin in thought and then gone on to point her in the direction of a Professor Kenworthy, who, he said, led the field in interpretation of video surveillance technology, and as luck would have it, was presently based at the University of Leeds. Hence Kate's appointment this morning, in academia.

"Good morning Professor, I have a visitor for you down in reception, An Inspector Pace. Yes, Yes, that's correct." She replaced the handset of the phone gently in its cradle and looked up at Kate, who did not correct her. "Professor Kenworthy will be right with you. Would you like to take a seat for a moment? I'm sure you won't be waiting long" The woman pointed at the seating area near the door.

"Thank you" Kate smiled at her, picked up her bag from the counter and walked across to the seats which had been arranged by the large plate glass windows where she could watch the traffic passing. She had just picked up that mornings copy of the *Yorkshire Post* when she heard the doors of the lift swoosh open and turned to look.

A tall redhead with twinkling green eyes emerged from the lift. Kate was about to return to her perusal of the local news, but the woman continued towards her, her right hand held out towards Kate in welcome. "Good Morning. Fenella Kenworthy" she introduced herself "Great to meet you. I understand that you need some help with some camera footage that you have?"

"Yes, that's right" Kate got to her feet and held out the large brown manila envelope that she'd taken from her shoulder bag.

"OK, lets go up to my room and have a look shall we?"

Kate followed her into the lift. Professor Kenworthy pressed the button for the third floor. They got out and walked along a carpeted corridor, lined with large leafy green pot plants and went through a door which had Professor Kenworthy's name on a brass plate.

She showed Kate to a seat, and said "I won't be a moment, I'll just give this to one of the technicians and they can get it set up for us" As she left the room Kate looked about her. There was paper work on the desk and Kate tried to read it upside down, but the top one was only a sheet of tabulated numbers. The one partially underneath it was a graph. There were no prints on the wall, not even a book case to study. It was difficult to get a handle on the vivacious woman.

Professor Kenworthy returned and reached in to the top drawer of the desk from which she pulled a pink cardboard folder. "Ok, follow me. We'll go and see what they've managed to come up with shall we?" They went back into the corridor and took the second door along going through a small anteroom and then through another door into an IT suite where banks of computer screens filled two of the walls. The third had huge plate glass windows which had a view over the Infirmary and across the rest of the city. Professor Kenworthy sat down in a small leather bucket chair and gestured for Kate to take a seat in the one beside her.

"Ok Kate, Can I call you Kate, or must I stick to Detective Chief Inspector?"

"No you can call me Kate, of course, as long as I can call you Fenella instead of Professor" she laughed "You don't look like a professor!" both women smiled. Kate was secretly ashamed to admit that she had been expecting a jowly, greying, middle aged man wearing horn-rimmed glasses and a bow tie.

"No and I have to admit that I thought that K. Peace would be Ken rather than Kate" This time they both laughed.

"Well, before we look at the footage Kate, I'd like to explain a little about the camera system around Leeds. When I was told that you were bringing some footage from a private close circuit camera, I have to say that I was a bit concerned about the quality. Anyway…, most of the cameras in the city centre are operated by the police. As I'm sure you are well aware. These are the ones which look like big black globes which you can see attached to the sides of buildings, and they are cameras which are capable of filming at any angle covered by the dome The only place it isn't able to film is directly above it. And that wouldn't be relevant for your purposes would it? I take it we're not looking for a plane or a helicopter?" she joked.

"No, what we're looking for is some information about the movement of a particular vehicle, where it was and who was travelling in it if that's possible?"

"Oh I should say that it's more than possible Kate. These cameras have remarkable focusing and zoom facilities and have a magnification rate of 15 times. That means you would be able to see details of a driver's face or number plates of the vehicle from at least half a mile away. Then there's the equipment we know as 3rd Generation Cameras and are also operated by the police, again as I'm sure you're aware. They are similar in appearance to the other cameras but are usually sited slightly differently. These cameras are actually open circuit television cameras as they can transmit to a monitoring station situated elsewhere in the city. As it happens I and my team are currently running a study on traffic congestion in the city and have use of some of the cameras. I thought that this might be helpful so if you can narrow down what part of the city it is that your vehicle was in I'm sure we can get hold of the relevant film from our archive."

Kate was astounded. It sounded like something out of big brother. "You mean that if we can get an idea of the vehicle from the footage from the service station, you should be able to find it on one of your cameras?"

"That's entirely right"

"Well, let's go shall we?" Kate leapt to her feet.

"Hey, not so fast" Fenella put a restraining hand on Kate's arm. "Let me grab a coffee to take through and then we'll make a start." She reached across and poured them both a mug of coffee, passing one to Kate as they walked across to one of the computer screens. They sat side by side at one of the terminals. "We'll look at your tape first. It may be reproduced more clearly on our equipment" They ran the video tape from the service station and could clearly see Eliot Nelson getting into the white transit van and driving away. A lorry could be clearly seen on the security cameras following the white transit van out onto the motorway. They ran the film a few times but the picture was still poor and grainy. It was hard to see any more detail. "You say this film was taken at a service station on the M62?"

"Yes, that's right."

"So we know which way he'll come into Leeds. That should save a bit of time" Fenella wrote a few lines on a sheet of paper and passed it to one of the passing technicians. He looked at it briefly and left the room.

"It won't take him long to find the discs" A few minutes later the bespectacled technician gestured through the glass and Fenella typed a few words into the keyboard. Kate was amazed. A white van was driving along the dual carriageway. Fenella paused the disc and zoomed in. The white transit could clearly be seen driving into Leeds with Eliot Nelson behind the wheel, but the passenger side was in shadow.

"I need to see who's with him. Can you get in closer?" Kate peered at the image on the screen.

"Hold on then, let's get in closer" Fenella froze the image on the screen and then magnified it until all that could be seen was the windscreen of the van.

"But, there's no-one with him!" Kate's disappointment was intense. She'd been pinning all her hopes on being able to identify Eliot's passenger and give herself another lead to follow.

Fenella panned out again. "Alright, let's just watch and see where he went shall we. That might give you some ideas?"

"Stop! Stop!" Kate put her hand over Fenella's in an attempt to stop the film running. "Can we look at the vehicle behind him?"

Again Fenella froze the frame and zoomed in. A large white articulated lorry came slowly into focus. The name of the company *Transportes Routiers* was now easy to read on its side.

"It's the same lorry which followed him out of the service station. He did meet someone there and bring them back to Leeds with him after all, just not in his van"

Every detail of the lorry could clearly be seen. Even the French registration of the vehicle could be picked up from the open circuit system above the road into Leeds.

"OK, can we see where they went now?"

They studied the disc as a series of images picked up across the city plotted the route of Eliot Nelson and the French lorry taking them across Leeds centre and out towards Chapeltown. Kate watched in delight as the van and the lorry drove past the forecourt of the gym, down the access road at the side of the building and into the warehouse area behind it. Kate was grateful that the cameras installed after the Chapeltown riots had been left in position. They watched as the driver jumped down from his cab, a small man in a fleece jacket and wearing a baseball cap, who started unloading the crates from the lorry with a fork lift truck which had been attached to it.

Four large crates were piled on pallets in the warehouse. The driver of the white transit van then got out, walked across to the warehouse and pulled down the huge metal roller door, closing himself inside. The lorry driver meanwhile crossed to a dimly lit Portakabin with some paper work to get it signed by some one inside. He could then be seen on the picture coming out again folding the papers lengthwise and putting them in his inside jacket pocket as he crossed the yard to his lorry. He then climbed back into the cab and carefully manoeuvred the lorry round to face the gate and drove back out onto the main road.

"Is that what you wanted to see?" asked Fenella sitting back in her chair

"That will do very nicely. I'm not sure if it's what I wanted or even expected. But, yes. I think you can call it a good result. At least I've got something more to work on now. I don't mind admitting I was getting a bit stuck for where to go next with this investigation. And thank you very much Fenella for sparing the time to do this. I'm sure you must be very busy"

"No thanks needed. I've enjoyed myself immensely. It beats sitting and counting how many lorries use a certain stretch of road in an hour. And then doing the same again for cars, and the same again the next hour. Then it gets really exciting....I get to put it all on a graph! Do you fancy a drink after work, celebrate your breakthrough?"

"That would be fun.... Oh sorry, I can't tonight, I've just remembered, I've already something pencilled in. Perhaps another time?" Kaye replied ruefully. She'd enjoyed Fenella's company, she didn't get to meet many fun, intelligent women.

"Fine, no problem. Hey, are you doing anything tomorrow?"

"No, nothing I can't put off" The ironing and cleaning could wait, especially if she wasn't there to look at it.

"Have a ride out, come to my place I live out at Thornton, it's really pretty and we can have a long walk in the fresh air. It's just what you need after being in Leeds all week"

"That sounds super. I'll do you a deal. I'll buy the coffees"

"I'll take you up on that. How about if we meet in the big public car park down by the river? It's well signposted as you drive into the town. You can't miss it"

"See you tomorrow then"

*   *   *

Kate had spent most of the rest of the afternoon at her desk writing up a report on the film evidence that she'd watched at the university. Luckily for her, DC Rayner had spent his previous summer break motoring round France and it just happened that he still had a copy of the French Michelin Road Atlas in his car boot. From this she'd found out that the number plate on the French lorry which ended in the two digits 34 meant it came from the Herault Department of France. A strange place to buy your weight lifting equipment from she'd thought, but conceded that she was no expert in this. She'd even asked Rayner where most gym equipment was manufactured.

He said he didn't have a clue but the stuff he'd seen in a catalogue had 'York' on it.

On the strength of her findings she'd had to arrange another visit to Chief Superintendent Southern's office and try to persuade him that because of what she'd discovered from the tape at Leeds University with Professor Kenworthy, a visit to France in order to follow up the company who owned the lorry and it's driver might throw some light on what was going on, although he'd grudgingly agreed, due to constraints of the budget she'd had to concede to making the trip on one of the low-cost air lines. Ryanair had a daily flight out of Stansted to Carcassonne and she could be down there in time if she got the early train out of Leeds just before 7o'clock. Southern gave her permission to travel on the following Monday morning. He would ask for someone to liaise with the local police force and arrange for some one to meet her at the airport.

She was just tidying away the items on her desk as the door of the office creaked open. "Hi, Phil. You ok?"

"Never better….Are you ready for that pizza?"

She looked up at the clock. It said five to five. "That time already! I hadn't realised" she stood and pushed back the chair with her knees, turning to lift her jacket from its back. She lifted her bag from the bottom drawer of the desk, slid it closed and locked it, replacing the small silver key into an empty coffee jar.

"I always wondered why you kept that instant coffee there when we always have filtered" Phil laughed.

"I'm just the same at home. I keep a set of spare keys in an old dog food tin" she admitted. "Actually Phil, I feel a bit frazzled. I think I'd rather just go home and freshen up a bit"

Phil did his best not to look disappointed. He'd looked forward to their meeting all day.

"I could have a quick shower, while you pour the drinks, and then I could rustle us up some supper. Nothing flash…I might even have a pizza in the deep freeze if you're really set on that, but there's been some big developments today and I really do need to bring you up to speed if you can spare the time to drive out. If not I could give you a ring later if you prefer?"

"No, that's fine by me. I've nothing else planned for tonight." Invited back to her place. It sounded promising. He'd better text his mate Gary and tell him to pass a message on to the others that he wouldn't be able meet them as planned. Anyway they were only going to drive out to the cinema at Junction 27 and watch …. He couldn't even remember what it was they'd been going to see. And suddenly it didn't seem at all important.

Kate knew the traffic on Friday teatime would be heavy leaving the city centre and she'd probably lose Phil at the first set of traffic lights. "Just follow me. If you lose me, driving out of town, I'll wait on the forecourt of the Texaco garage at Harewood. Then it's not far at all. Is that ok?"

"Yes, that sounds like a good idea" said Phil who wasn't sure where Kate lived. He knew it was somewhere between Leeds and Harrogate, out in the sticks by all accounts. The traffic was even heavier than usual and he soon lost sight of Kate but sure enough as he swung round the bend leaving Harewood he saw the silver Audi parked at the exit of the filling station. He flashed his headlights to let Kate know that he seen her and she pulled back on to the road in front of him. He followed her along a stretch of increasingly narrow country roads, passing between dry stone walls. At one point they'd had to pull into a gateway to let a car travelling in the opposite direction get past. At last to his relief he saw her left hand indicator flashing. She pulled in through an open five-barred gate and parked by the front door of the farmhouse. Phil's Astra crunched across the gravel and drew up next to her. He climbed out of the car slamming the door closed as he walked towards her. "Very nice" he said looking up at the front of the double fronted farmhouse, which was obviously old but had been well maintained.

She shrugged, "I like it" and selected the door key from the bunch in her hand and let them in. They went into a small entrance hall where an old dog struggled to his feet to meet them. He wagged hid his tail so hard he almost lost his balance. "Hello Jasper, had a hard day sleeping?"

"I didn't know you had a dog Kate. How do you manage when you're out all day?"

"I'm lucky, there's a girl comes up from the village to do a bit of housework for me three mornings a week, she lets him out for a while before she goes home and my next door neighbour pops in at lunchtime on the other days. Anyway let me show you through. They went into the old stone flagged kitchen and Jasper trailed behind. "What can I get you to drink Phil?"

"A coffee will be fine" he didn't like to ask for anything stronger in case she thought he might be expecting to stay.

Kate moved across to the work surface and switched the kettle on. She opened a wall cupboard which held a box of pyramid tea bags, a jar of freeze-dried instant coffee and a selection of mugs. "Can I leave you to make the coffee, I won't be a minute?"

She left the room and he heard her feet on the stairs.

"Oh can you give Jasper a scoop of dog food…it's in the paper sack under the sink" her voice trailed away.

He fed Jasper first and then assembled everything next to the kettle whilst he waited for it to boil and opened a line of matching wooden unit doors until he found the one which concealed the refrigerator and a carton of milk. Phil heard the shower stop running upstairs. Jasper sat to attention near the kettle. Phil listened, he could hear the floor boards creaking as Kate moved about. Quickly he took a chocolate digestive from the packet and passed it to the dog.

"Phil!" she stood in the doorway, her hair damp from the shower, and wearing a pair of pale blue jeans and a cream roll neck sweater. "He's not supposed to have those!"

"But he looked so hungry, and desperate and he was slavering on my foot"

"Yes, well he's good at that" she laughed as she walked across and took the coffee he held out. She took a sip and set it down. "Actually, I've got a nice white wine in the fridge. I think I'll have a glass of that. Do you fancy the same?"

"No, it's Ok. I'll stick with the coffee for now"

Deftly she pulled out a chopping board and a selection of knives and then put an onion, a red pepper and a courgette on to the wooden board in front of Phil. "OK, start chopping"

"How?"

"Just chop them small into little squares. Look, first this way, then that" she demonstrated. Whilst Phil concentrated on the vegetables Kate started to dissolve a vegetable stock cube in a jug of boiling water, and poured some olive oil into a large frying pan. She stirred some rice in the oil. It hissed as she added the stock. They prepared the vegetable risotto in an easy companionship and carried it into the living room and sat side by side on the sofa. "Right I'd better bring you up to speed on what I've been doing today"

Phil nodded and continued eating the risotto. It really was very tasty and the grains of rice were different sizes and colours.

"I went to Leeds University and spent a very productive morning with a lady called Professor Kenworthy. She's some sort of IT wizard. Anyway she was able to improve that footage that George brought back from the service station. It showed Nelson there as we already knew, but better than that they have access to all this film taken of the roads into and out of Leeds, and around the city centre. And it picked Nelson up driving in Leeds. I was hoping we'd be able to see who was in the van with him" she paused.

"And did you?"

"No, he was in the van on his own"

"But I thought the diary said he was meeting someone called Chris?"

"Yes he did"

"But you just said he was in the van on his own"

"He was but he was being followed from the service station and into Leeds by a bloody great articulated lorry from France. I can only assume it was being driven by 'Chris'"

"So what happens next?"

"Well I've spoken to Southern and he's given me the go ahead to make a flying visit to France to track down this lorry and the driver"

"Some people have all the luck."

"Well it's the only good lead we've got at the moment so, I think that brings you up to speed"

"Yes, I see what you mean. By the way that was great" he said, turning to her and forking the last spoonful of rice into his mouth. He leaned forward to put his plate on the coffee table and managed to move closer to Kate as he sat down again. Their legs touched and Kate tensed. The atmosphere was charged with expectation. She suddenly felt awkward and wondered what interpretation Phil had put on her inviting him back. Probably the right one. But now she wasn't so sure if it had been sensible.

"Look Phil, I'm sorry. I don't want you to get the wrong idea. I'm not sure this is such a good move. I'm going away on Monday as you know.

So let's just leave it for now, hey. A cooling off period, isn't that what they call it and we'll see how it is when I get back? I don't want us to get into anything we'll regret later. I depend on you heavily at work Phil, we work well together and I don't want to spoil that. Sorry if I'm sending out mixed messages. If I'm confusing you" Kate gabbled as she smiled ruefully and ran her fingers through her hair. "Actually, I'm confusing myself too" She picked up the glass and took a sip of the cool white wine, setting it back carefully on the table so Phil couldn't see the tremor of her hand.

Phil stood up. "Yes, you're right of course. There's a lot at stake, its pretty complicated isn't it and now probably isn't a good time"

Kate smiled slowly, feeling both grateful and relieved that what could have been a difficult situation seemed to have been resolved amicably. "Anyway Phil, can I ask you to hold the fort until I get back? I'll probably be away three or four days at the most I expect, depending how things turn out"

"Kate, you can leave everything in my very capable hands anytime you like!" he leered at her comically and laughed to show it was a joke. He looked at his watch. "Good grief, is that the time! I'd better push off. I arranged to meet some friends. I didn't realise what the time was" He grabbed his jacket, and got to his feet. If he put his foot down he could still meet the lads for a quick kebab when the film finished.

As she watched him walk away from her and out into the hallway with his head down she had a sudden flashback of the night that Keith had walked away from her. How he'd stood for a second, half turned towards her with one hand on the door frame. She'd just let him go. For a moment she'd wanted to stop Phil, to call him back, but the moment in time when she could have done that had passed. Had she done the right thing in letting Phil walk away? She wasn't sure. He was through the front door, and in three crunching strides he was across the gravel and into his car. She stood and watched as the red taillights of his Astra disappeared down the track, out onto the road and into the night. Half of her felt regret for an opportunity missed. The other half felt relief.

Eleven

Kate had carefully studied the directions written on the piece of paper that Fenella had given her, and calmly swung the Audi round the tight bends on the back roads which led towards the small market town of Thornton where Fenella lived. It was still early and as yet there was little traffic about on the country roads although the weather looked promising, still cool but with a bright watery sun peering intermittently between the clouds. Kate had dressed in brown corduroy jeans and a cream wool sweater over a brown checked blouse. She'd topped off the outfit with a waxed jacket and a cream cashmere scarf to keep out the chill. If Fenella was going to drag her on some wild hike over the Yorkshire Dales she might as well dress the part.

The Greatest Hits of Robbie Williams was on the CD player. She'd bought it last week in shop in Leeds and hadn't until now had chance to listen to it. Easy listening, for driving. The occasional buildings grew closer together, changing from agricultural to residential and Kate knew she must be getting close to the edge of the small country market town. She drove down a steep hill, past a church and a scattering of large detached houses with well kept gardens heading towards the River Thorne and just before crossing the ancient stone bridge, turned right into the large public car park on the edge of the river where they'd arranged to meet. Kate looked at her watch, climbed out of the car and walked across to the ticket machine. She wasn't sure how long they'd be staying so bought a ticket for the day. As she carefully peeled the backing off the ticket and turned it over to attach the other half to the inside of the windscreen she studied the advertisement printed on it promoting two meals for the price of one at the local drive-through. Hearing the purr of a powerful car approaching she turned just as a bright yellow Honda sports car pulled up alongside her.

Fenella opened the door and holding onto the edge of the windscreen pulled herself out.

"Wow! Some car, girl" said Kate enviously "I didn't have you down as the sports car type, it looks fun though"

Fenella tossed her long red hair back and tied it securely with an emerald green silk scarf she'd pulled from her pocket. "Yes, I like it and I haven't had it all that long but I think its days are numbered. It's a bit low to get in and out of gracefully"

Kate looked closely at Fenella. There were a few lines at the corners of her eyes, otherwise her skin looked good, but perhaps she was older than Kate had first thought.

"I know what you're thinking"

"What?"

"You're wondering how old I am, aren't you?" asked Fenella.

"I was not!" objected Kate trying not to blush.

"Well, I still think you were and what's more, I'm not telling" laughed Fenella raising her chin "The only thing I will say is that I'm probably about the same age as you. But I do have a chronic medical condition which means that my joints play up a bit. It's not an age related thing. Unfortunately I've had it for years so I'm used to it and I won't let it get the upper hand"

"Good for you" said Kate thoughtfully "Are you sure you're Ok to go for this walk though, because if you're not feeling up to it we could just go and get a bite to eat instead. My treat remember. Look there's an offer at the drive-through, 2 burgers for the price of one!"

"I do hope you're joking. I haven't got you to come all the way out here to eat a burger. No really, I'll be fine. I've been looking forward to it - and I'm actually better if I keep moving. A bit of gentle exercise is best. The less I do, the more I tend to seize up. So shake a leg and get your walking boots on, you're not getting out of it that easily"

"Yes, don't worry, I was only having you on. Actually I don't eat meat, and I shudder to think what gets minced and put into burgers" said Kate as she walked behind her car pressing the button on her key to open the boot. She took off the leather loafers which she kept for driving in, threw them into the boot and changed into her walking boots whilst Fenella wandered across to the machine and bought a ticket. They set off out of the car park, walking side by side, Kate zipping up her jacket and adjusting her scarf.

"Ok which way?" asked Kate.

"We'll go over the pedestrian crossing here and walk along the edge of the river, shall we?"

They waited for the traffic lights to change in their favour and walked down the single width road which ran parallel to the river and aptly called Riverside.

"It's a nice walk and there's lots to look at. If we carry on along here we'll pass the old dye house in a minute. It's used for storing and maintaining the rowing boats over winter now. You can see one or two on the river. There are a lot more in the summer of course, but it's a pretty old building which dates back to the time when there was a textile industry here. They grew flax in the fields around the town. It was then bleached or dyed and made into linen. We'll go past the old linen mill, along to the next river bridge and walk back up into the town. It'll probably take us the best part of an hour I should think and that's without eating. Does that sound ok or are you pushed for time?"

"That sounds just perfect. I've got all day. You just lead the way and I'll follow"

They paused to look at the old dye house, a single storey stone building. The door was open and in the shadows they could see a young boy painting one of the rowing boats which had been upturned and secured on a frame to allow him to inspect and paint the underneath of it. Fenella pointed out a steep stone stairway which disappeared round the back of the building. The steps were narrow and worn down in the centre.

"That's a short cut up into the town but the steps are a bit steep and there are 99 of them so I think we'll take the easy option and keep going along here"

Shortly they arrived at the old linen mill. A three storey building constructed of locally handmade red bricks, with the huge, small paned

Georgian windows which were needed to let in the maximum amount of light for the weavers to work. Kate could see from the board attached to the gate way, which read *Flat 3, For Sale* that it had been converted into residential accommodation. "Oh this is pretty, look Fenella, right next to the river!" Kate stood on tip-toe to look over the high fence. "It's even got its own landing stage with a little boat tied up! Oh and ducks in the garden. I bet it's expensive though, such a lovely area"

"£395, 000 for that one….. It's called Flax Flatts. I live round the back. Mill Master's Cottage" Fenella gestured somewhere over the fence in the direction of the river. Kate could just see the rooftop of what appeared to be a very substantial detached house, which stood slightly apart from the main building "And you're right it's lovely down here in the summer. The developer did a really good job of converting it. You can still see the mill race and where the water wheel was, although it fell into disrepair a few years ago and had to be removed. There was a bit of opposition initially to it being converted into housing, but people just don't like change. It looked as if the building was going to become derelict, and I know the use has changed but at least by doing this the structure of the building has been preserved hasn't it? People think conservation is about the past, about keeping things as they were. But it's not. It's about the future, about enabling a building to continue to be useful, even if its use has to change. Anyway don't let me get on my soap-box or we'll be here all day. Let's press on then shall we?"

The narrow road meandered past a row of old stone cottages on their left and on their right a little tea room with a walled garden which went down to the river. The sign in the bow window read *Closed*. Inside Kate could see one woman dressed in black wearing a white pinafore polishing the tables. Another sat at a table wrapping serviettes round knives and forks and placing them in a small wicker basket. At the end of the road they turned left and were confronted by a very steep hill. Kate listened to the cars changing down through the gears as crawled up the hill.

"Are you sure you'll be ok walking up here Fenella, it looks awfully steep?"

'I'll be fine, the trick is to take it slowly. I often walk this way into the town. I prefer it to the 99 steps"

They plodded slowly up the steep hill pausing to turn and look back down at the view of the river before they turned around a curve in the road and it was lost to their view. Kate noticed a shop across the road called *Thorne Gallery* with an eye catching abstract painting displayed in the window.

"Oh, can we just call in here Fenella and look at some of these paintings? Do we have time? I quite like the look of that one. I wonder what else they've got"

"Of course, actually I've never been in here before. It's funny isn't it, but when you live somewhere and go past places every day you don't always make time to look at them properly. Let's go in and have a look"

They pushed open the door and a small bell tinkled above their heads. A sign propped on a small table next to a little hand bell read:

You are welcome to browse.

Please ring the bell if you would like any help.

The ground floor of the building which had originally been a two up two down cottage had had the central wall knocked down and was now one long light room which allowed natural light to flood in from three sides. At the rear of the shop, a small, middle aged woman with cropped grey hair and bright blue eyes, wiped a paint brush on the hem of the man's shirt she was wearing over denim jeans. She turned back to her canvas and studied it, clicking the handle of the paintbrush against her teeth. Kate couldn't see the painting she was working on as the easel was turned away from her to catch the light coming in from the side window. The two of them strolled slowly round the shop looking at the many different works displayed on its walls.

"Anything you fancy?" asked Fenella.

"I'm undecided. There are one or two nice paintings I quite fancy but I never like to buy a painting in a hurry. It can be a big mistake you have to live with if you make the wrong decision. I can always come back" They left the shop, the woman so engrossed in her work she seemed not to notice them leaving.

The pause in the shop had given them both a chance to catch their breath and they managed to climb the rest of the hill without too much difficulty. At the top Kate had to stop to remove her scarf and unzip her jacket. The walk up the steep hill had made her quite warm. Turning left at the next corner they passed an old chapel which, from the three doorbells, Kate could see had also been converted into housing. Next door to it was a traditional sweet shop with shelves of glass jars on view. Turning left again into a narrow road which ran down the side of a pub called 'The Castle' they arrived at a public car park. Walking through this brought them out at the edge of the putting green. Following the footpath around it, they arrived at an expanse of flower beds which had been newly dug in preparation for planting with spring flowers. Finally they arrived in front of the castle ruins. Kate studied the sandstone remains briefly before passing in front of it where she was able to look down over the gorge and see the road along the edge of the river where they had just walked a little while earlier. The people looked tiny. And the train which trundled across the viaduct which spanned the river looked like a toy. She hadn't realised how high they'd been climbing. No wonder she'd felt so warm, it was quite a climb.

"What an amazing view!" she turned to Fenella "If I'd known we were coming here, I'd have brought my camera"

"It is a super view isn't it, a bit of a surprise really. Don't worry. If you want a picture of it there are plenty of shops where we can get a post card of the view. In fact I'm fairly sure they'll have one at the café I was going to suggest we had lunch at."

"Actually, now you come to mention it I am beginning to get a bit peckish" Kate admitted. "It must be all this fresh air and exercise. I've worked up quite an appetite"

Turning away from the castle they walked past Thornton police station, a small but relatively modern building, which, as it was a weekend was unmanned. A sign blu-tacked to the inside of the glass door gave those searching for assistance a number to ring. That was Ok Kate supposed as long as you were able to find your way here to read it in the first place. She shook her head in dismay. A sign of the times. Hopefully the lack of police presence meant there was very little crime, but she wasn't convinced.

They crossed the cobbled market square with its stone market cross and went into an old red brick building which had a sign above the lintel which read. 'The Apothecary's House, 1746'. Downstairs was a shop, the walls were whitewashed and the beams dark with age. There was a huge display of traditional and alternative medicines. Kate picked up a bar of Lavender scented soap, but put it down in favour of one containing oatmeal. "On second thoughts I'll take them both" she said joining the queue at the counter. She wasn't exceptionally tall but had to duck as they opened a small wooden door at the bottom of a staircase. Once through the door, the stairwell meant that she could stand up straight again and they walked up the short flight of wooden stairs to the tearoom upstairs. Oak boards creaked beneath her feet. As luck would have it a couple were just getting up from their seats at a table in the window. Kate and Fenella quickly took their seats and enjoyed an unobstructed view across the market square. Shoppers went about their tasks. Business was brisk at the greengrocers. A constant procession of buyers stocked up with vege for their Sunday lunch. Women studied the display in the window of the "Woolly Backs" knitting wool shop, whilst their husband's gaze drifted to the display of bottles in the window of "Beeritz" next door.

"Can I take your order?" the voice made Kate jump. A young girl dressed in a period costume of a muslin print frock with her hair twisted back into a bun at the nape of her neck stood expectantly with a pad and pen.

"I'm sorry, I haven't even looked at the menu yet, but you could bring me a black coffee while I decide, er decaff. If you've got it, please"

The waitress looked at Fenella. "Can I get you anything at the moment or shall I come back?"

"I'll have a pot of Chamomile tea please, and we'll order when you bring the drinks, if that's ok?"

The girl made a note of the two drinks and went through a door into the kitchen.

"Well, what would recommend?" Kate asked. "It all looks very nice" as she scanned the menu.

"I think I'm going to have a sandwich in the Swedish bread, it comes with a salad too and the portions are pretty generous, but there are cooked meals or jacket potatoes with a variety of different fillings if you prefer something a bit more substantial" replied Fenella.

"The sandwiches sound really nice. I think I'll have the same, but I can't decide between the brie and grape filling or the mature Wensleydale cheese with red onions"

"Tell you what, why don't we order one of each and share them. That way we both get to have some of each?"

The girl came back with the tray of drinks, placed it gently on the table and took their order for the sandwiches.

"So tell me, I know you can't discuss your work in detail, but what was the outcome of our work with the film the other day. Was it any help?"

"Oh, yes. Well actually I'm going to France on Monday" Kate took a sip of the coffee and nibbled the little almond biscuit from the saucer. It's the best lead we've got at the moment. I need to find out about the French lorry we saw on the film. We need to know what he delivered to the gym. The thought is that he was probably bringing, either knowingly or unknowingly..." Kate looked round but there was no one else within earshot. A couple stood at the till, some distance away waiting to pay and at the only other occupied table a young father struggled to persuade a toddler to eat his toast amid shrieks of protest. Kate continued, "...drugs into the country and that they were using the gym to distribute from. Obviously the two who were shot have either tried to muscle in on the act and were raking off more of their fair share or were just playing out of their depth, and for some reason not needed anymore. Anyway next stop France"

Kate sat back as the waitress put the plate of sandwiches down in front of them and tucked the bill under the sugar bowl.

Fenella distributed the sandwich so that they both had a selection and bit into hers. "France hey, whereabouts?"

"Down in the South. Somewhere near the Mediterranean coast. It should be an improvement on Leeds anyway"

"Well, lucky you. I'll think about you on Monday when I'm at work"

"Oh, I'll be working too, don't forget. It's not a holiday you know" Kate ate the last of her sandwich and dabbed the corners of her lips with the serviette. She picked up the bill from underneath the sugar bowl and unfolded it.

"Let's go halves?" suggested Fenella.

"No, my treat. I've really enjoyed it. The walk and the fresh air have done me good. Perhaps we can do it again sometime?" Kate rummaged in the pocket of her jacket and pulled out her purse.

"Yes, that would be great. And next time I'll pay"

"It's a deal" said Kate moving across to pay at the till. The girl gave her some change which Kate dropped into the saucer containing tips for the staff. On the way out Kate bought a postcard with the view of the river. "I think I might enlarge this and frame it. It would look good in my kitchen" she told Fenella as they walked back to the car park. "You could come out to my place and see it when I get back from France. There are some lovely walks nearby and perhaps we could have a pub lunch en route?"

"Give me a ring when you get back and we'll arrange to do that"

They paused to cross the road into the car park waiting for a gap in the traffic, having come full circle on their walk. Fenella slid back into the yellow Honda, moving much more easily than she had earlier in the day. "See, I told you the walk would do me good" she waved to Kate out of the window as she backed carefully out of the parking bay and then accelerated smoothly away into the afternoon traffic.

Kate took off her boots placing them next to the neatly folded waxed jacket and changed back into the black leather loafers. She settled herself behind the wheel of the car and switched on the ignition, swapping the Robbie Williams CD for one Charles had sent her in the post. *The Senior* by Ginuwine… what sort of name was that, she skipped forward to track 5 as he'd recommended as she drove out onto the main road and the strains of "In those Jeans" filled the car. Kate smiled to herself. Good taste Charles, she thought. Ginuwine certainly beats Robbie into a cocked hat.

Twelve

It was just another in a long string of cold mornings when Kate set off on her journey. France really seemed quite inviting. In fact she almost felt guilty when she thought about Phil and George questioning people in Leeds. But hey, this was one of the privileges of rank and God knows there sometimes didn't seem to be many. Ryanair had a daily flight out of Stansted to Carcassonne and she could be down there in time if she got the early train out of Leeds just before 7o'clock.

As usual Leeds station was freezing cold with a strong wind blowing the length of the platform. Kate pulled her coat round her and dashed into the deserted ticket sales area. She followed the instructions on the machine and managed to extract the ticket which she had paid for earlier by credit card over the phone without too much difficulty. She then went and joined the growing queue of travellers who were waiting to buy drinks and snacks in the café.

"Good morning Madam what can I get you?" asked the young man behind the counter.

Kate studied the vast selection of teas, coffees, and other hot drinks available. "I'll have a large Hot Chocolate, please" she replied.

"Will that be to take out or drink inside?" asked the young man.

Kate checked her watch, still almost 15 minutes until the train was due, if it was on time, and it was freezing cold out on the platform. "I'll drink it in here please"

The young man poured the drink into one of the largest cups Kate had seen and she wished she'd asked for a medium. "Anything else... a pastry, or a sandwich?"

Kate eyed the All Day Breakfast sandwich on the counter warily. "No I don't think so, thank you" Ugh cold bacon and eggs. You probably *would* know about it all day if you ate it she thought.

"That will be £3.50 then please" he said.

Kate raised her eyebrows, but said nothing. Better not put too many of those on expenses she thought. Old Southern would have a fit. She handed over a five pound note, zipped the change and receipt away in her purse and went and took a seat near the door where she could keep an eye on the platform and watch people coming and going. Not that there was any need as there was a screen detailing Arrivals and Departures on the wall in the café. It was just habit and part of the job to "people watch"

As the train came into view everyone took up positions at the edge of the platform trying to find the most advantageous spots from which to board the train. They couldn't get on to the train quickly enough to escape the cold and damp weather of Leeds. Kate had just made herself comfortable and was reading a copy of Labyrinth she had bought especially for the train when the guard appeared.

"Can I see your ticket Miss?" he asked.

Kate patted her pockets and then rooted through her bag. She had an embarrassingly large pile of used tissues, Sainsbury's till receipts and scraps of paper with cryptic remarks on them which must have meant something to her at the time she written them, on the table in front of her. Impatiently she swept the pile back into her bag and was starting to feel panicky when she realised that she'd been using the ticket as a book mark. She handed it over and the guard clipped it and handed it back. Kate sat back and looked out of the windows for a while. Rattling south through industrial Yorkshire the cooling towers of the power stations were only just visible through the dense fog. They had an eerie quality reminding Kate of the film setting for a science fiction film. Kate tried to doze but without success. A little while later the landscape changed to agricultural land and a flock of seagulls swirled in the air behind a tractor like snow flakes, and in the next frame the brick boxes of suburbia flicked by. Soon they were at Peterborough, with a 45 minute wait between connections and the weather although brighter with a weak sun which was beginning to disperse the mist, was not any warmer. Kate picked up her small case and made her way over the footbridge to the buffet on the opposite platform. She took comfort in another cup of Hot Chocolate, this time accompanied by a rather sickly mass produced caramel slice. At this point she wished she'd been organised enough to make some sandwiches. After this all there was to look forward to, was airport food. She wandered aimlessly up and down the platform for a while and looked at the Departures screen from time to time. There were one or two delays, and the affected passengers headed for the waiting room, or a connecting coach service, but thankfully her train was not one of them. Eventually the connecting train arrived and the journey to Stansted continued. The train rolled onward across England, small farms dotted the vast openness of the fens, which were broken only by the ditches which criss-crossed the view. Kate felt her head starting to droop. It had been an early start. Suddenly the carriage rocked, jolting Kate awake as another train blasted by travelling in the opposite direction. She dozed briefly again and awoke after some time just as the train swayed slowly into the picturesque city of Ely, it's massive medieval cathedral brooding over the pretty pastel coloured cottages which faced the riverfront.

A further change of passengers took place, a number carrying briefcases left the train and were replaced by others carrying suitcases. Thankfully the train arrived at the airport on time, as there was not a lot of time to spare before check-in. Kate dashed up the escalator from the station and into the airport. After two large cups of Hot Chocolate and a cup of coffee she was now torn between the need to quickly locate both the Ladies loo and the Ryanair check-in desk. Fortunately in the distance, a long queue had formed at check –in, so Kate decided it was safe to make a rush to the loo first. Check-in went smoothly though slowly, with the typical hold ups caused by women pleading for small suitcases to be classed as hand luggage, people with faulty passports and the usual number of travellers who were either in the wrong place, or at the wrong time, or both, and wanted the airline to accept responsibility for it. Finally after the numerous checks, scans, x-rays and baggage searches Kate found herself in the departure lounge. She walked across to the window and watched as a constant stream of planes took off and landed. Becoming bored she wandered into the newsagents and picked up a copy of the *Independent*. Perhaps a crossword would help fill the time.

The plane had just landed, slightly late, and Kate watched as it was swiftly "turned-round" within twenty minutes. They were called forward to board.

"Boarding passes 1-90 only please" announced the boarding staff. Kate produced her boarding pass and passport for inspection and walked with the other passengers across to the plane. Passengers and suitcases were being put on at the same time. At this time of year the plane was only three quarters full and she had no difficulty getting a seat near the window. At last she was on her way to France.

*   *   *

Carcassonne was only a small airport and the suitcases arrived in the terminal almost as quickly as the passengers. Kate was able to pass quickly through the arrivals area and outside to the row of prefabricated huts under a row of pine trees, which accommodated the car hire companies. Southern had offered to arrange for someone to meet her but Kate had assured him that she didn't mind driving down. It was only an hours drive down the motorway.

"Good morning Madame, do you have a reservation?" asked the elegant woman behind the desk.

Kate pulled out the voucher she had printed on the internet and passed it over the desk to the woman.

"Thank you" replied the woman, peering at it over the top of her black rimmed spectacles. She compared it to the details on the computer screen in front of her. "And may I see your passport and driving licence?"

Kate slid them across the shiny surface of the desk.

"Do you have your credit card in the same name as the booking too?"

Kate pulled it from her purse and passed it over.

"That all appears to be in order, here are your keys. In this wallet are the documents for the car, the carte gris. They must be kept in the car at all times. Not to do so is an offence. You will see also telephone numbers in case of a problem. She underlined them firmly in black biro. These are the numbers if you have an accident or a break down. You must ring them, not me. If you go out of those doors, straight ahead, then turn left and you will see your car parked in the first row on your right. A black Renault Megane. The registration number is written on the key. Please return the car full of fuel. All the bays are numbered. Yours is number 5" added the woman.

"Thank you" said Kate picking up her keys and insurance documents. She breathed a sigh of relief. She had been dreading having to resort to her school girl French. The old remembered phrases she had learnt parrot fashion at the Church school she had attended of "Madame Marsaud is in the kitchen" " Jean-Paul is at school" " The sun is bright" were of no help whatsoever in adult life. They hadn't studied useful topics such as "What to do when your car breaks down" "Buying a railway ticket" or "I would like to order a meal"

Kate looked around as she got into the car to make sure no one had seen her shame- faced first attempt at getting in the wrong side. She executed a cautious couple of circuits of the airport car park before pulling out onto the main road and heading for the motorway. It was all well signposted. She took the exit from the roundabout which read A61 Narbonne. She had been told to take the road to Narbonne and then the A9 towards Montpellier. She looked at a map, Narbonne then keep to the left when the road divided. If she got in the wrong lane she'd end up in Spain. Not so bad she thought to herself as she settled back in her seat and put her foot down, heading off towards the south coast at a steady 110 kilometres an hour.

It was the first week in March and the weather was being kind. The bluest of skies provided an exquisite backdrop to the almond trees that were covered in a smattering of white blossom. There was a quality of light peculiar to this part of the world. Kate could understand what had attracted Van Gogh and his colleagues to Arles. The sky was bluer and the grass greener than any she'd seen before. Everything was more vivid and sharply defined, like the stained glass in the bottom of a kaleidoscope as it falls into focus.

She pulled off the motorway and studying the display, paid the toll of 5 euros at the booth. As promised the road to Sauvignan was clearly posted although, in the usual French habit, not the distance. She had been told to follow the signs for the town centre and just after the ancient stone bridge crossed the river there was a large public car park where her French counterpart Monsieur LeClerc would meet her and show her to the small house where she would be staying for the duration of her visit. It belonged to a relative of his and was used in summer as the family's holiday home.

She got out of the car and looked about. Directly across the road a man in a pale suit sat at a table outside the *Pont du Relais* drinking coffee from a tiny cup so favoured by the French. He waved, and she waited for a gap in the post lunch traffic, hoisting her hold-all over her shoulder. Almost 2 o'clock and the French were returning to work after their two hour lunch break. As she approached the table he stood up.

"It must be Inspector Peace, enchante" he took her hand and sketched a bow over it. "Capitaine LeClerc" he introduced himself. "You have had a long journey, no? Perhaps you would like something to eat?"

"Please, call me Kate." She shook his hand in a more businesslike fashion and then released it. "Actually I'm fine at the moment. I had a meal on the way. But don't let me interrupt your lunch"

He drained the last drop of black coffee from the little cup and replied "No that is fine, we will take a walk through the *Place* and I will show you the shops and then I will show you to where you will be staying. Let me take your bag" without waiting for Kate's comment, he picked up the bag and set off down the street. At the bottom of the road they turned right and found themselves in a pretty square. LeClerc pointed out two *Boulangerie*, the *Tabac* and the *Pharmacie* "Although, I don't think they will have the English newspaper at this time of year. In the summer, yes. We have many English visitors. At the moment no" They crossed the square and walked up the side of the *Boulangerie*. Kate looked longingly at the pastries. They turned another corner into a narrow street. The jumble of houses were arranged not only in long rows and back to back, but also with back to side, and because the streets had evolved over several hundred years some of the houses had noticeable changes to their structure. Some had blocking or creating of doors and windows, but the original ancient decorative stonework could still be plainly seen. Kate was quite entranced. In the exterior walls of a couple of the houses Kate could see where a beautiful carved but weathered stone archway had been completely filled in, captured like a fossil, no longer able to fulfil its previous purpose but still preserved for display. Looking at the changes, Kate could only begin to try to guess why they have been carried out, perhaps two houses had been converted into one, or a passage way between the little buildings incorporated into the house.

The house was approached from the street through a large solid wooden gate set into a surrounding stone wall approximately ten feet high. The gateway was tucked away in a quiet, shady corner of the narrow, twisty medieval streets. It was between two other houses at right angles to one and parallel to the other at a dog-leg in the narrow road. There were two steps down into the yard, where directly to the left stood an ancient stone well in one corner, with a wall of about thirty inches high, and for safety, a wooden lid covering it. The front exterior wall of the house had been painted a warm creamy-yellow colour, the doors, windows and shutters stained in dark wood varnish, and against this backdrop were displayed, terracotta pots, with young hydrangeas, impatiens and geraniums, which in the summer would blossom into a riot of colour, in various shades of pink, ranging from the delicate pastel of the hydrangea, to the hot pink of the impatiens.

"We are arrived" said LeClerc. And indeed they were. It was like arriving at the centre of a maze.

"I'll never find my way up and down all these little streets"

"It's ok, there's a street map here" said LeClerc, picking it up from the kitchen table and handing it to Kate. "See, I have marked with a cross where we are to save you time, or you would be going round in circles to begin with, because to you, one narrow street looks very much like another, and the ten minute walk to the square would take you half an hour, or even more" he smiled. "Well, I will leave you now. There's food and milk in the fridge but the shop is open until 7.30 if you want anything else. He handed her the keys and disappeared up the steps and through the gateway.

*   *   *

The next morning Kate woke suddenly, feeling disorientated. Was it night or morning? It was still dark. What day was it and where was she? She rolled onto her side and picked up her watch from the bedside table. The luminous display read 08.05. She fell back on the pillows for a second. It came back to her. She was in France. She put on the bedside lamp and walked across the tiled floor to the window. It was still dark because the shutters were closed, completely blocking out all the light. Lifting the latch she pushed them back, folding them in half at the hinge and securing them to the wall with the metal clasp. She could hear the sounds of voices and car engines passing outside in the street. Turning back she went into the bathroom, flicking the switch on the kettle as she passed. A quick shower and a cup of coffee and she'd be right as nine pence. Not due to meet LeClerc until 10.30 she decided to have a walk down to the square after her coffee.

Her senses were assailed by the colours and scents of the produce which were on display, and the contrast between the supermarket shopping which she was used to. There was no pre-packaging and no feeling of having to choose quickly as six people waited behind with their trolleys, clutching a plastic bag torn from the roll. Kate always felt under pressure to choose her goods quickly and then ended up coming home without something vital such as potatoes or onions. And why she wondered, do all the English supermarkets have their fruit and vegetables just inside the door where it creates an immediate jam of trolleys as we all inspect the box of half ripe identical watery red blobs which tried to pass themselves off as tomatoes. She had been reliably informed by someone in the trade that it's a marketing ploy, to make our first sight of the interior of the shop seem inviting, but was nowhere near as inviting as Kate's arrival at the French open air market. The quality, quantity and variety of produce available on this market was excellent. She wished she could take some home with her, perhaps she would. The very irregularity of shape and varying degrees of ripeness of some of the food seemed proof that conformity is not always best and in France is cause for celebration rather than rejection.

The market was held in a pretty square, flanked by two rows of ancient plane trees which offered shade to the goods and vendors as well as the shoppers in the summer. The stalls were set up under huge canvas parasols. The pride taken by the stallholders in the presentation of their goods reminded Kate of an English village agricultural show, everything arranged to its best advantage. The huge spring onions lay proudly in serried ranks, their massive white globes secured in bunches. The potatoes though quite clean gave the impression of just having left the ground. They begged to be bought. The scent of the delicately shaded apricots drew her towards a stall where a plate of freshly sliced fruit was being offered for tasting prior to purchase. This did not seem to be unusual at the market, the stallholder only had to see someone pause for a second and they immediately offered a sample of what is being considered.

The cheese seller was equally keen for his wares to be sampled and handed out cubes of cheese to a constant stream of passers by. He was handily found in the narrow street between the boulangerie and the wine seller where the two tradesmen could be seen in the street in earnest conversation discussing the merits of their various wares and jointly able to chat to their clients. Kate tried some of the locally produced Fromage du Chevre it certainly left the one that she'd had at the Caraway standing. That was something else she'd have to take back with her. Kate came away from the market feeling as if she had had a small meal. Several bars and cafés were set around the square with tables and chairs outside in the area between the front of the café and the market stalls. Kate had agreed to meet LeClerc at the PMU café. But her eye was caught by the lingerie stall which was incongruously sited outside the butchers. The underwear was in vivid shades of cerise and lilac, the silks and lace concoctions were cheekily displayed by the young Frenchman with curly black hair and merry dancing eyes. But perhaps he felt the anatomy displayed close by had something in common with his wares. Kate went across and looked at some of the underwear it was out of this world and not expensive. She needed to take some of this back too. Perhaps she should look for somewhere which sold suitcases.

There was a stall which sold olives outside the Office du Tourisme with herbs, oils and different varieties of olives displayed below olive branches which the stallholder had tacked onto the parasol. Next to this was a small stall selling hand painted ceramics. Serving dishes, and bottles for serving olive oil.

She'd pop in to the information office later and see if there were any sites of interest close by that she could see whilst she was here. Looking at her watch Kate decided that she'd better set off for her meeting. If he was prompt he'd be on his way now.

Thirteen

Walking uncertainly into the PMU, Kate thought that it seemed strange to suggest meeting in a bookmakers shop, but as she walked in she was surprised to see that although there was a television by the bar with the odds for the afternoons racing and another with the Rapido game ongoing, there were also several other women in there, some with bags of shopping and one armed with her knitting, who seemed to have no interest in the gambling but were just enjoying a cup of coffee. She looked around the room but LeClerc hadn't yet arrived. She approached the bar and haltingly ordered a coffee and a pastry from the man serving drinks.

"I'm sorry Madame, but we do not serve the food in winter" he must have noticed her crestfallen look as he went to say "If you would like I will make the coffee and you can buy a pastry from the Boulangerie and fetch it in here. I will bring the coffee to where you are sitting. Kate picked up her bag and walked to the boulangerie which LeClerc had pointed out the previous day, whilst the barman prepared the coffee. Pushing open the glass door of the shop she was met by a wall of heat and the beautiful smell of freshly baked bread. There was a glass topped counter and incorporated below it on the glass display shelves all manner of freshly baked goodies. Strawberry tartes jostled for position alongside cream buns and sacristan, long sticky, flaky pastry sticks covered with flaked almonds. Friande saucisse, veau, and Roquefort, best compared to sausage rolls with a frankfurter, veal or Roquefort cheese filling. Whilst in the queue Kate was able to watch as the baker shaped the next batch of baguettes and placed them between the folds of fabric, to keep them in shape, on a large tray. He then took a long iron rod to open the door of the wood burning stove, where they would be baked. As the door opened the intense heat from the oven could be felt in the shop. He pulled out a tray of baguettes which had just finished cooking and deftly turned them out of the tray into tall lined wicker baskets on wheels, which he pushed across to the counter, where the girl who was serving used them straightaway. She 'wrapped' them skillfully by placing a small piece of paper, three inches wide, bearing the bakeries name 'Freres Anton', around the middle of the baguette, giving it a quick twist to secure it, before passing it to the customer. The bread was then carried home through the streets exposed to the elements. Suddenly Kate was at the head of the queue. Unsure of the pronunciation, she pointed at the sausage roll. The woman behind the counter said something which Kate did not understand. She raised her shoulders in puzzlement and said "Sorry" The woman pointed at the microwave oven in the corner. Kate shook her head in reply and took the small paper bag she was handed.

Back at the café she took out the sausage roll and placed it on top of the empty paper bag to serve as a plate. As the bar tender approached the table Kate recognized her mistake. The tiny cup he was carrying contained coffee of the super strength French variety. She could smell it before he got anywhere near her. He placed it in front of her and she promptly passed him a ten euro note. Taking a small sip she shuddered and placed the tiny cup back on the saucer. Never mind the sausage roll would soak it up. She dabbed her lips with a napkin and looked up just as LeClerc walked in.

"Bonjournee Kate, Ah, enjoying a cup of coffee I see, to help you wakeup, did you sleep well?"

"Like a top!" If she carried on drinking coffee like this she felt sure that she'd never sleep again.

LeClerc tilting his head to one side, looked puzzled.

"Sorry, it's a figure of speech. It means I slept exceptionally well. Thank you"

"Like a top…. I'll remember that. It's the little house. It's a very restful place. I don't know why but all our visitors always say how well they sleep there. Have you had breakfast?"

"Yes, thank you. I always have a good breakfast"

"Excellent. When you have finished your coffee, we'll get going. I've arranged a meeting with Commissaire Cassin of the Police Judicaire at the Hotel de Police in Beziers. It is purely a courtesy visit but I think that we will discuss with him the case, yes?"

"Yes, of course that's fine" Kate had expected something of the kind.

They walked round to the car park where Kate had left her hire car the previous day and got into LeClerc's large, dark blue Peugeot saloon. They drove sedately into Beziers, the road passing between the railway line that runs along the south coast between Montpellier and Perpignan, for a while journeying alongside the TGV. and the beautiful Canal du Midi.

"I have made us an appointment to visit Monsieur Bels, who is the manager of Transportes Routiers, this afternoon. After we have spoken to Commissaire Cassin" LeClerc informed her.

The Hotel de Police was a light coloured squat rectangular building. Symmetrically designed with four rectangular windows, filled with opaque glass and covered with metal bars on each side of the door, it was in appearance an unattractive unforgiving building. LeClerc expertly swung the large Peugeot into a space which Kate wouldn't have attempted. The left front wing was across the footpath, and the angle it was parked at prevented the Renault Twingo parked in front of it from getting out.

"Are we Ok parked here?" asked Kate not liking to make an obvious criticism of LeClerc's parking.

LeClerc took a step back and looked at the car and then up and down the street. "Yes, there are no parking restrictions here"

She followed him round the corner to the front door of the Police Station. "Abandon hope all ye who enter here" thought Kate, passing through the door. The inside of the building did little to alter her opinion. The heels of LeClerc's highly polished leather shoes clicked as he strode ahead of her along the corridor. Kate's soft soles squeaked in his stead.

LeClerc paused in front of a door with an opaque glass panel in the top half, and knocked. Without waiting for a reply he pushed it open and waved Kate through to proceed him into the room. A man with a grey crew cut looked up from what he was writing, pen held in mid air. At first it was difficult to distinguish any other of his features for the swirling cloud of dense blue cigar smoke which surrounded him.

"Let me introduce you to Commissaire Cassin" said LeClerc.

Cassin stood up, a slight and not very tall figure, she could now see as the smoke swirled away, but exuding authority. He held out his hand towards Kate, who reached out into the fog to shake it.

"Capitaine LeClerc has told me something of your case, and of course we wish to assist you in anyway we can. He paused to rub the outside of his nose with his index finger as if giving himself time to think. However I'm sure you will understand that also we are busy with our own work so it would be difficult for me to spare any more staff to help you in your investigation...."

"Of course I understand. At the moment all I would like to do, with your permission of course is interview the manager of the transport company and the driver involved" replied Kate "And I would like to take this opportunity to thank you for the assistance you have given us so far. Capitaine LeClerc has been invaluable in helping me find my way around"

Cassin nodded, picked up his cigar and looked at Kate down the length of it through narrowed eyes. As if waiting for her to make further comment.

She felt that she was missing some subtle point here but couldn't work out what it was.

Cassin leaned back in his leather chair, and although he was not a big man it squeaked in protestation. He leaned forward again and placed his elbows on the desk, making a steeple with his fingers. "At this point we are willing to leave the investigation to you. It would appear at this moment in time that the offence has occurred in England. However, I must ask that you liaise closely with Capitaine LeClerc, as any issues which arise and are a crime in this country will have to be pursued separately, and when you bring your case to a successful conclusion in England, as I have no doubt that you will" He looked at Kate meaningfully over the top of his metal rimmed spectacles "I will of course expect to be informed of any irregularities which you may find have occurred in France?"

The crafty sod, thought Kate. So that was it. She would do all the donkey work and afterwards he would use it to serve his own purposes. Well, at least they weren't going to try and step in beforehand. She'd be allowed to play it her way and as long as she got the glory for the big drugs bust at her end, they could do what they liked about investigating the doings of Transportes Routiers at their end afterwards.

"Of course" replied Kate, giving one of her most winning smiles.

Cassin stood up to indicate the interview was over, and reached out to shake Kate's hand again. "Bon chance, Madame, et a bientot"

Kate shook his hand in return. "Thank you for your help Commissaire, you have been most kind"

"The pleasure has been all mine" he replied.

Yeah, I bet it has, thought Kate as she followed LeClerc from the room.

Walking out, down the steps of the building into the sunshine, LeClerc extended his arm in order to examine his wristwatch. "Ah Kate, it is midday, I think it is time we had something to eat, don't you?"

Kate nodded her assent. To her surprise she was starving.

LeClerc gently took her elbow and led her to the edge of the footpath where they waited for a gap in the stream of lunchtime traffic. The French workers were possessed of an urgency to get home and relax during their two hour break. Noticing a space between a large blue Citroen and a bus which were slowing down as the traffic lights changed to red, he took her hand and expertly steered her between the traffic and onto the safety of the opposite footpath.

They walked into a small restaurant called "La Fontaine" where they were swiftly shown to a table for two in the window. Kate thought that the speed with which they had been seated, and the desirable position of the table probably indicated that LeClerc ate there regularly. The waiter pulled out Kate's chair and then carefully pushed it into position beneath her as she sat down. Carefully tucking a strand of straying hair behind her ear she took the menu which the waiter was holding out towards her.

"Un aperitif?" the waiter asked her.

"Not for me thank you" Kate addressed LeClerc, hoping that she wasn't committing some awful social gaffe.

LeClerc shook his head at the waiter. "Nor for me" He looked unperturbed and Kate began to relax.

"What would you like to eat?" LeClerc asked her.

Kate's eyes skimmed haphazardly across the range of dishes on the menu, most of which she could not identify. She looked to LeClerc for guidance. "What are you having?" she asked.

"I'm going to have Le Menu, the set meal," he explained, pointing to the section of the sheet which detailed the three courses, all of which had three choices.

As he was reading the menu Kate studied him surreptitiously from beneath her lowered lashes. His face was lined, though not by age she thought, but rather the product of too many hot summers. That being said she found it hard to put an age on him. Perhaps mid to late forties, or even fifty. He was certainly quite attractive in an understated, elegant way, where less is more. He carried the light coloured linen suit off very well.

Kate brought her attention back to the menu and studied it closely. There seemed to be options which would suit her. Salade Composee, and Salade Hareng would be OK and a selection of cheeses for desert would be pleasant.

LeClerc chose a selection of Charcuterie to start followed by the Daube de Toro. "And we'll share a bottle of the local red wine please" LeClerc said to the waiter "If that's alright with you Kate?"

"Red is fine by me" She wasn't accustomed to drinking at lunchtime but LeClerc was driving, so when in Rome and all that, she thought.

The waiter returned with the dark green bottle and held it out for LeClerc to inspect. "Reserve Vermeil, Coteaux du Languedoc" LeClerc read from the label. "Yes, that's fine" he nodded to the waiter, who opened the bottle carefully with a satisfying pop of the cork and poured them each a glassful before wiping the neck of the bottle with a dark red napkin and setting the bottle down on a small rush mat.

Kate watched LeClerc take a sip of the wine as she bit into a piece of the crisp baguette. A flurry of crumbs landed on the red checked tablecloth.

Are you enjoying your visit so far Kate? It's a pity we don't have time to take in a few of the sights" said LeClerc as he speared a piece of cold meat from the charcuterie selection.

"I've enjoyed what I've seen very much, but as you say. I haven't really got time to visit the sights"

"Perhaps having seen a little of what we have to offer you might want to return?"

"Yes, I think perhaps I might"

The waiter came and took the plates away giving Kate back her knife and fork. He quickly reappeared with LeClerc's beef and Kate's Herring salad. Even Kate had to admit the wine the beef was cooked in smelt divine.

"What will you have for desert Kate?" LeClerc asked her "I can recommend the Mousse au chocolat. Madame makes it herself"

"I'm sure it's lovely but I really don't think that I could eat another thing"

"That's fine. What about coffee?"

Kate remembered her earlier experience and quickly nodded towards her glass of wine. "No, really. I'll just finish this. But don't let me stop you"

The waiter hovered just behind LeClerc's shoulder.

"Just one coffee for me then please" he said to the waiter. "Well, Kate has this visit been useful?"

"Yes, it's been everything we wanted, and more. I'm sure that once we've got to the bottom of what's going on with the lorry driver and where in the journey the drugs are being put on board I'll be able to bring the case to a successful conclusion. I can't thank you enough for all your help"

LeClerc gave a Gallic shrug. "Do you mind if I smoke?"

Usually Kate would have objected but there was something fascinating about watching a Frenchman with a cigarette. Kate tried to settle on what it was that appealed to her but was unable to decide. As she looked out of the window, a small terrier dog wearing a blue and white bandana round its neck sailed by in the wicker basket of a bicycle. The female cyclist's smooth brown legs twirling as they both disappeared from view round the next corner. Across the road, a heavily made up woman leaned into the driver's window of a parked car. The car drove on and the woman, seeing herself to be observed, winked at Kate and walked slowly towards the corner. She leaned down to another car. Was she asking for directions Kate wondered?

LeClerc insisted on paying the bill, handing over his credit card to the waiter and Kate, relaxed by her half of the bottle of wine couldn't be bothered to argue. In fact she had a feeling that she had probably had quite a lot more than LeClerc. They drove through several streets of shops and then along an open stretch of road a short distance from the town to an industrial park where several large lorries emblazoned with the logo that

Kate recognised were parked up in a compound. LeClerc showed his card at the gatehouse and the barrier was raised to let them through.

"Right Kate, let's go and see what Monsieur Bels has to say for himself shall we?" said LeClerc as they crossed towards single storey brick building which housed the office for the business. Bels greeted them effusively, showing them to a chair and offering them coffee, obviously puzzled and concerned about what could have brought them to his door.

"Do you have the information that I asked you to supply?" asked LeClerc.

Monsieur Bels pulled a thin cardboard wallet across the desk towards him and pulled out a sheaf of papers. "Here are the records for last month. I understand that is what you wish to see?"

"We are only concerned with any of your lorries which have made a delivery to England" said LeClerc.

At this Bels looked a little less worried. He rifled through the pile of papers until he found the one that he wanted "Here it is. We made only one journey to England last month" He held out two sheets of paper which were stapled in the top left hand corner and handed them to LeClerc. "This is the record of the journey which was made by our driver to Leeds. You will see that he was to deliver four pieces of machinery. Is there a problem, did they arrive safely? We've had no complaint from the customer" Bels looked wary.

"And who was the customer?" asked LeClerc.

"Johnson it says here" replied Bels.

Well they were certainly talking about the right lorry thought Kate.

"We need to interview the driver of the lorry. How can we get hold of him?" she asked.

"Monsieur Dubois is away on holiday this week. I believe he is visiting his parents in Alsace. They are very elderly. His mother has not been well. But he returns tomorrow I think. Next week he will drive to England again"

"Has he driven to England many times?" Kate queried.

"No, that was his first time but he is to go again next week. We deliver to Leeds roughly once a month or thereabouts. The driver who always did that run has left recently. Dubois was the only person I had available. I don't think he really wanted to do it. He doesn't enjoy the long journeys now. He's not a young man"

How many rowing machines and pieces of weight lifting equipment could one gym accommodate Kate wondered?

"I would be grateful if you don't tell Monsieur Dubois about this interview. I think it would be more helpful if we spoke to him in England."

Bels looked puzzled "You can't think Dubois is involved in anything......" he struggled to find a word and was forced eventually to settle for "...illegal. He wouldn't. He's worked for me for the last 15 years. I couldn't show you anyone more reliable"

"We have reason to believe that someone is using your vehicles to take drugs into England!" said Kate "It may be that Dubois is not aware of what he is carrying among the cargo."

"Oh, Mon Dieu! You don't think?" his face was ashen; he slumped in the seat and rested his head on one hand despairingly.

"At this time I've no reason to think that either you or Monsieur Dubois knew anything about the drugs which are at some point in the journey, being hidden in your lorry. But two men in England have been killed....murdered for their involvement in this. Do you understand?"

Bels sat there his mouth agape.

"Do you understand how serious this is?" Kate repeated. She turned to LeClerc "Does he understand?"

LeClerc spoke staccato to Bels.

Bels gave a short reply.

LeClerc turned back to Kate "Yes, he understands"

"Good, because I intend to get to the bottom of this mess and he will assist in any way he can"

LeClerc again spoke to Bels.

Monsieur Bels gulped and nodded.

"Good, I think that will do for now, but I will be in touch with you in a few days to verify the exact route and journey times that will be made by the lorry"

LeClerc drove her back to Sauvignan and dropped her off in the car park.

"Thank you again" said Kate "Perhaps I'll see you again before I go back?"

"Perhaps" replied LeClerc driving away, his hand raised in a wave through the open window.

*　　　　　*　　　　　*

Overnight the weather had changed again. When Kate opened the shutters grey clouds scudded across the sky, accompanied by a cool breeze. Out in the street small children with large bags were gathering to make their way to school. How would she spend her last day? The thing she had come to do had been accomplished; her time to all intents and purposes was her own. She'd have to write a report on her interview with Cassin and with Monsieur Bels but she had made rough notes that she could work from. She could write up her report on the plane or even on the train at the other end. It would be a shame to waste the day.

She went to the fridge and poured herself a glass of fresh orange juice and prepared a bowl of muesli. Then she slipped into the shower and dried herself on one of the fluffy white towels. Pulling on a white T-shirt, her jogging bottoms and trainers, she picked up the car keys tossed them into the air and then pocketed them. She walked round to the car park, half expecting to bump into LeClerc on the way and was, she had to acknowledge a little disappointed when she saw nothing of him. Now that he didn't need her to be watched Cassin must have called him off. She followed the road signs which directed her towards the beach, driving carefully along the country lane, still not completely confident at driving on the other side of the road. A quarter sized tractor, small enough to fit between the rows of vines puttered along in front of her giving her an excuse to drive slowly and study the countryside. She drove between field after field of vines, with the occasional one which would be planted with sunflowers. In a gateway a group of men gathered waiting to start their days work trimming the vines. At last she reached the car park and left the car beneath a Fig tree. The beach was in a conservation area and at this time of year frequented only by the locals, and precious few of them.

The rasp and swish of the sea was becoming a crash and wash, and a strong wind carried droplets of foam, like a damp mist onto the beach. The marbled grey clouded sky was reflected in the heaving sea. There were only a few other people on the beach, one woman sat in the shelter of the dunes and appeared to be absorbed in a paper back book. A couple well wrapped were walking a small wire-haired dog, which, excited by the buffeting wind dashed frantically back and forth along the beach. The calm open expanse of the beach contrasted with the heaving unrest of the sea. A young angler wearing combat trousers, a baseball hat and sunglasses had grown dispirited with his meagre catch and was busy packing up his equipment. He bore away the few fish he'd managed to catch, triumphantly in their Tupperware coffins.

Kate looked at the sky and studied a couple of indignantly shrieking seagulls which were only with great effort able to maintain their flight path in the wind. She tightened the laces of her trainers and began a series of stretching exercises. First she bent her right knee and extended her left leg behind her for ten seconds, feeling her calf muscles stretch. She then alternated, performing the same movement with the other leg. She then reached behind her and with her right hand caught hold of her left ankle and pulled her foot up towards her buttock, feeling the stretch in her quadriceps muscle on the front of her thigh. She alternated the movement again and then jogged gently on the spot for a couple of minutes. She then turned towards the west and set off at a smart jog in the opposite direction to the yapping dog.

She jogged at first slowly along the water line. Pausing only to pick up a couple of delicate shells, which had been tossed onto the beach by the waves. She zipped them into her pocket. She felt good. For the first time in two weeks or more Kate was relaxed and at ease as she got into her stride, working up to a swift sprint, her feet drumming on the firm sand. Her dark hair was whipped by the breeze which brought a pink glow to her cheeks. Looking briefly behind her Kate was satisfied to see the long line of footprints left in the compact sand stretching away as far as the eye could see.

As she slowed down from her run, wanting to walk for a while in order to cool down slowly, she removed her trainers and pulled the bottom of her elasticised joggers up over her knees and paddled out into the chilly water. She could feel the firm sandy ridges of the sea bed under foot. Finally she turned and slowly she made her way back to the car. It was time to pack and head for home.

Fourteen

Leaning with her elbows on the top of the wooden five barred gate, she watched the small the yellow sports car becoming larger as it zipped round the bends of the narrow lane up to the farmhouse. At last, when she judged the driver was near enough to see her, she stood on her tip toes and waved her hand vigorously in the air. The driver of the sports car flashed its headlights in response, roared on towards her and turned in through the gate. It parked on the gravel, next to a bed of daffodils which were presently in full bloom below the living room window.

"Hi, how are you?" said Fenella as she lowered the car's window, and leaned out to speak to Kate "Did you have a good week?" she peered up at Kate, "I say you've caught the sun a bit haven't you"

"It was a very productive working visit" Kate replied "And as a bonus the weather was lovely!"

"Huh, some people have all the luck. I don't know how you managed to swing it. Couldn't you have just made a few phone calls?" She climbed out from the car and swung the door to. It closed with a quiet click.

"Probably, but I enjoyed the change of scene" Kate joked " Anyway, did you manage to find your way here without too many problems?"

"Well I set up the sat.nav. But there was a point about halfway up this lane when I began to wonder if I was going to end up as the subject of one of those newspaper articles where they delight in talking about satellite navigation systems not being able to tell the difference between a road and a bridleway. I could just see the headline 'Nutty Professor takes four faults at the wall' and a picture of the car nose first in the dry stone wall"

Kate laughed, and as she turned towards the house, waved briefly to her neighbour Betty, who she could see in the distance struggling to anchor her sheets to the washing line in the playful spring breeze. They'd be dry in no time thought Kate "Well come on in then, I expect you could do with a drink after your journey up here into the back of beyond" she walked ahead of Fenella towards the house "I've got a pot of coffee percing and a few sticky buns"

"Excellent, I'm starving"

As they walked in Fenella studied the exterior of the old building. The farmhouse had obviously been extensively renovated, but very carefully so. The old chimneys had been fairly recently re-pointed and the front elevation appeared to have been sandblasted, but that must not be as recent as it appeared, unless they'd found some way of protecting the wisteria which grew above the door. "You've had quite a lot of work done on the house, haven't you?"

"Yes, and it hasn't come cheap, I can tell you. It's lovely living in a conservation area but there are a lot of restrictions to comply with, so the work you can have done is very tightly controlled. The window frames are suffering from the effects of the weather, we catch quite a bit of wind here on the tops, it's very exposed as you can see, too much rain in the winter and too much sun in the summer. It plays havoc with the woodwork. It always seems to need repainting"

"You sound jut like a farmer Kate. It's never the right sort of weather!"

"Well look at this" she led Fenella across to the dining room window "I think this one probably needs replacing altogether" she poked an index finger into the rotting wooden sill and fragments of wood dropped the ground "I'd wondered about having PVC put in. I know they're not as nice but they're much more practical, so I wrote and asked the planners at the town hall. It was a complete no, no. I have to stick to the original materials. So if you know of a good joiner, send him along"

"Oh, but that window is beautiful. You couldn't have had that done in PVC" Fenella pointed to a tall arched window, set halfway up the wall, which had a three inch band of royal blue stained glass around the top of the pane. It looks almost like the sort of window you'd see in a chapel"

"It's interesting that you should notice that. There's an old chap down in the village, Mr. Tebay. Well I say old, he's probably about seventy. He's a retired teacher and local historian, and he was telling me that the house was once used as a chapel. So that would explain the style of window. Apparently in April of 1759 John Wesley visited the village and according to the records 'preached to a small but well-behaved congregation in an orchard' It may even have been the orchard here, but there's no way of knowing that for certain. I thought this was a bit odd, having a church service in an orchard but Mr. Tebay said that initially a lot of Methodist meetings were held in the open air and it wasn't until around the turn of the nineteenth century that they started to build their own chapels or convert existing buildings for use as preaching houses. So that's probably around the time when the upstairs of this house was converted into a preaching room for the local Methodist congregation. This area is quite isolated, so they'd either have to have travelled on foot or come by pony and cart if they were lucky. It was too far for them to walk into town. The downstairs of the house was kept as living accommodation for the farmer and there was probably an external stair case built onto the side of the house to give them access to the preaching room. The staircase is no longer there, perhaps when it was dismantled the stone was used for building the pig sties or something but if you look carefully there is an area at the top of the wall which looks as if it is where the door way has been filled in. Anyway, here endeth the first lesson, as the preacher would have said. Let's go and get that coffee shall we?"

Fenella smiled "I was quite enjoying the history lesson Kate, I think you've missed your way. You could have been a History teacher, but for now coffee would be marvellous"

"Well, Mr. Tebay is gathering some more material about the history of the house so when he let's me have it, I'll give you a call shall I?"

They walked through to the kitchen where the view from the rear window gave an open vista across a scrubby looking field and then on to open moor land with areas of gorse and heather. The land rolled away into the distance and was dotted only by the occasional stone field-barn and outcroppings of Millstone grit.

"Here you are" Kate poured out the drinks and passed Fenella the mug of coffee "Let's go through to the sitting room" Kate picked up the plate of cakes, pushed open the door and let Fenella follow her into the room. "Oh! I've forgotten something. Have a seat Fenella, I won't be a minute" Kate placed her mug on the coffee table and went out of the room.

Instead of sitting in the chair Kate had indicated Fenella wandered across to the window and studied the view from the front of the house, of the narrow lane winding down between the dry stone walls to the village. It really was very well situated. Then she took the opportunity to study the shelving in the alcoves on either side of the stone fireplace. One side contained a selection of DVDs and CDs, the other side was filled from floor to ceiling with books. Large coffee table books were on the bottom shelf, the higher shelves were filled with an assortment of classics, with what appeared to be the entire works of George Elliot, Jane Austen and Elizabeth Gaskell and an assorted jumble of this years best sellers, probably not due to be kept with the same care as the classics which had been carefully arranged in alphabetical order. She then turned to study the walls. You could tell a lot about a person from the contents of their walls and bookcase.

"Ah, here we are. Just a little something I brought back from my 'holiday' for you" she handed Fenella a lumpy paper bag.

"What is it?" she looked puzzled.

"Open it and see. It won't bite"

Fenella squeezed the bag and then satisfied that it contained nothing unpleasant she opened the bag slowly, reached in and pulled out a beautifully soft, tan leather shoulder bag "Oh that's really nice, but you shouldn't have" she protested half heartedly.

"It's Ok, it wasn't expensive, the leather goods were really cheap and I got one for myself too"

"So how did the trip go from a work point of view, was it useful and did you find anything out?" said Fenella, replacing the bag on the table.

"Yes, I managed to get an interview with the manager of the company whose lorry we saw on the film. I felt a bit sorry for him actually. I don't think he knew anything about the way the lorry was being used and there's another shipment due soon. So if our assumptions are correct...." she tailed off unwilling to tell Fenella exactly when the lorry was due to arrive.

"Well, good luck with that but be careful. My granny always said 'to assume makes an ass out of 'u' and 'me'"

"I hope not" replied Kate "You know, this thing is nagging me like a toothache. I go over and over it in my head. I feel we're so close, but something's missing. I get this awful feeling that it's staring me in the face but I can't recognise it for what it is"

Fenella leaned over and picked up a copy of the previous day's *Yorkshire Post* from the lower shelf of the coffee table beside her. Idly opening the first page she was met by the headline **Double shooting; Police Close In.** She read on. "It says here 'The Police say they are hopeful of making an arrest soon' and are you Kate?"

"Well you can always hope can't you?"

Fenella let the newspaper fall to her lap. She looked at Kate from beneath her lashes and studied her for a second. Kate looked distracted. She decided not to ask any more questions. Kate was clearly under quite a bit of strain. Closing the paper and folding it into four she replaced it on the coffee table again. She looked out of the window. The landscape, though brooding in appearance was washed by subtle spring sunlight.

She leaned back in the armchair stretched and yawned. "I don't know about you but I could do with the cobwebs blowing off me. What about a short walk?"

Kate started, and came back from wherever her thoughts had taken her. "Fenella, I'm sorry, you must think me really rude. I haven't been sleeping well. Yes, I think a bit of fresh air will do me good. I'll go and fetch our coats"

They walked through the kitchen, left by the back door and crossed the yard. Passing through the small gate into the orchard, Jasper struggled along after them on stiff old legs. As they passed beneath an apple tree a blackbird shrieked his alarm. Jasper plodded on, tongue lolling, oblivious to the perceived threat he posed. At the bottom of the orchard they climbed over a small wooden stile into the field. Jasper stood with his head poking between the rails of the fence, and whined wistfully as he watched them walk away from him.

"Oh listen to him!" Fenella turned to Kate, plucking at the sleeve of her jacket "Can't he come too?"

"He'll be fine there Fenella. He knows he really can't do it anymore. He'll still be there when we come back. Just ignore him he's just trying to make us feel guilty for leaving him behind"

"Well, he's succeeding. I feel awful"

"I can tell you haven't got a dog. You'd be hopeless"

They walked along a narrow beaten foot path between clumps of tussocky grass and through another field towards the open moorland, but when they reached the dry stone wall at the end of the field, Kate turned abruptly left and walked alongside it. It was much pleasanter here, they walked in the sunshine and the wall protected them from the light breeze which blew down from the moor.

Fenella looked back along the footpath at Kate's house. "Who does this land belong to?"

"The two fields actually belong to me, but as you can imagine I don't have a lot of time to plough the fields and scatter the good seed, only joking. The land is poor quality, only any good for grazing a few sheep on. So I rent to Bill and Betty next door cheaply, on condition that they maintain it. That way I get the unspoilt view without any of the hard work"

At the bottom of the field the dry stone wall had been constructed to incorporate a set of stone steps and they scrambled over it into the lane on the other side.

"Do fancy walking down to the village while it's so nice?"

Fenella judged that it was probably another half mile walk down hill to the village, then turned and looked doubtfully at the steep lane back up to the farmhouse.

Kate read Fenella's mind and looked at her watch. "It's OK, if we wander slowly down and have a Shandy at the Drovers Arms, we'll just be in time to hitch a lift back with Bill. He's always in there at this time of day"

The two women wandered along the lane. On the banking was a sprinkling of bright blue periwinkle and beneath the hedges several clumps of primroses. They walked past the pretty lytch gate of St Michael the Archangel, with its graveyard of ancient leaning headstones. They had become tipped and tilted by time. Grown mossy, or worn smooth by age, their inscriptions were weathered and difficult to read. At the edge of the path were the more imposing tombstones of the few moneyed families, the further from the path the cheaper plots accommodated the smaller plainer memorials. Fenella peeped over the wall to get a better look, and was shocked to come face to face with a black, horned head and a pair of malevolent yellow eyes "Oh my God, what is it?" she cannoned backwards into Kate who lost her footing on the grass verge, and fell into the road.

"Bloody Hell, Fenella. They're only a few Jacob's sheep" Kate laughed "What did you think it was?"

"I wasn't sure. You hear all sorts of things about strange goings on in these isolated rural communities. Have they escaped from somewhere?" she asked Kate as the sheep eyed her balefully before taking off to join its friends in the shadow of the small grey stone church.

"No the vicar keeps them in there to maintain the churchyard. The old tombstones are too close together to get a lawnmower in between them even if he could find someone willing to do it. At least he hasn't gone the way of a lot of churchyards and had the headstones laid flat or even worse, removed altogether"

They passed a row of cottages and the village's General Store, before arriving outside the Drovers Arms. "Shall we sit outside?" Kate asked.

"Yes, let's. It's a shame to be inside on such a nice day. This good weather won't last, I'm sure"

"I'll go in and get the drinks"

"Are you sure it's not my turn to pay?" said Fenella pulling out her purse.

"No I don't think so. You have a seat. I'll get the drinks in and tell Bill that we're here. What would you like?"

"A Shandy sounds good. I feel I've worked up a bit of a thirst" replied Fenella, making herself comfortable at one of the wooden table and benches, and replacing her purse in her bag.

Kate returned with the two glasses of Shandy and two packets of salted peanuts on a round metal tray. "They're just bringing us a plate of sandwiches out, and Bill says he'll be ready to go back in about half an hour, if that's ok?"

"It sounds absolutely perfect" replied Fenella. She pulled a pair of sunglasses from her bag, shook her hair away from her face and turned to catch the meagre warmth of the sun's rays.

*   *   *

Kate waved as Fenella drove away down the hill and then turned back to the house. Jasper was waiting patiently in the back porch. She bent to stroke his head, it felt bony through the silky golden hair. Opening the back door she watched as he shambled across to his basket. "Oh for goodness sake, come on Jasper. You can stop sulking now. You know the walk would have been too much for you" she crossed to the glass cookie jar, where Jasper's treats were kept and extracted a couple of marrow bone biscuits. His claws scrabbled on the stone flags of the floor in his haste to get to the biscuits. Taking them gently he slobbered on Kate's hand. She rinsed her hands at the sink and then made a coffee which she carried through to the living room and looked at the page of the newspaper which had earlier caught Fenella's attention. Unbidden a picture of Leon Edwards lying in the car park of the Rose and Crown flashed before her. She hoped that they were at last closing in. Tomorrow would tell. Quite what it held she wasn't sure but they should be further forward and with a bit of luck they'd have a good haul to their names and be able to close the case. For now she should try to relax. Tomorrow could well be a long and hectic day.

Fifteen

The weather was kind on the drive south. It was a pleasant morning, dry and bright which seemed to have improved the mood and driving of the other road users. Kate enjoyed the drive, relaxing back in the leather seat as the silver Audi cruised happily in the outside lane, leaving the HGVs to jockey for position in the other two. Flicking the U2 CD into the player Kate stole a glance at Phil. He sat quietly in the passenger seat, she thought at first that he was looking out of the passenger window at the traffic, but as she leaned forward she could see that his eyes were closed and his head had lolled slightly away from her with a lock of sandy hair flopping across his eyes. She couldn't tell if he was dozing or merely sitting with his eyes closed.

Christian Dubois was probably approaching Calais at this moment. Bels had told them that he would usually overnight at Rheims to break the journey and be on one of the lunchtime ferries. Did Dubois really have no idea that his lorry contained a shipment of drugs? Of course when it came to court he'd plead that he knew nothing about it. And, she supposed, it was possible that he could be telling the truth. How many lorry drivers really knew what was in the containers they were carrying? She looked at the digital time display on the car's console as Bono sang that he still hadn't found what he was looking for. She sighed "Yeah mate, I know just how you feel, and I'll tell you what. Sometimes I'm not even sure I know what it is anymore" Phil stirred, opened his eyes and yawned hugely. "Are you talking to yourself now?"

"No, I was talking to you" she lied "I was just testing to see if you were asleep"

"Was it anything important?"

"No, you know the price of eggs, the meaning of life and all that. Nothing important"

"Oh, sorry. I must have nodded off for a minute. I don't suppose there's any chance of something to eat is there?"

Kate reached into the door compartment and tossed him the remains of an ancient packet of Polo's. "Well the menu's a bit limited. Will these do you?"

Phil inspected the packet doubtfully and blew on it to dislodge the grey fluff protruding from the centre of the top mint and then thought better of it and put them in his own door. "Best keep them for an emergency. We might need them later."

Kate pushed her foot to the floor and smiled at the car's smooth and immediate response. "We'll get a bit nearer and then stop for something to eat if we've got time" The miles slipped past, and the mileage on the signs for Dover grew less and less. Eventually she pulled over into the forecourt of a large filling station on the approach road to the ferry terminal. She handed Phil a £20 note "See if you can find me a salad sandwich and a bottle of water, and whatever you fancy"

"I could kill for a portion of fish and chips actually but I don't suppose they'll have any"

"You know, you get more like George every day" she called to his departing back.

He came out with the food and drink in a small paper carrier. "There wasn't a lot to pick from, is egg mayo Ok? It was either that or roast beef and horseradish."

Kate envisaged the limp white sliced bread and anaemic egg. The beef was probably rubbery too. She regretted too late that she hadn't bothered to make a sandwich and bring it with her. Why did it always seem such a chore first thing in the morning to accomplish the simple task of putting something between two slices of bread. She knew full well at the time that she'd regret not doing it. Oh well, now she'd have to pay the price, and serve her right.

They left the filling station and drove a little further along the road where they were able to park up and wait in a lay by. She turned off the engine and lowered the car window, tilting her seat back slightly as they settled to wait. Watching the empty crisp packets tumble around in the breeze, Kate peeled the plastic seal from the egg mayonnaise sandwich, regarded it balefully and ate it more for something to do than because she was hungry. Her appetite had gone. Whether it was the soggy sandwich or the feeling that they were getting near to closing the case which made her feel slightly queasy, she couldn't tell. Phil tackled the beef sandwich enthusiastically and delved back into the carrier, producing a couple of Mars Bars. "Fancy a pudding?"

"Wow, Mars Bars, you really know how to treat a girl. But no, not for me thanks"

"Suit yourself" Phil shrugged and ate them both in quick succession.

Kate reached into the door pocket and produced a small canister of wet-wipes. Wiping her fingers on one of the perforated cloths, she pushed it into the empty sandwich container and then passed them to Phil. "Wipe your hands, I don't want greasy marks on the upholstery" He raised his eyebrows but did as she asked, and then put the empty sandwich containers and sweet wrappers into the paper carrier and took them across to the concrete litter bin. Turning quickly, he dashed back to the car and climbed in, slamming the door in his haste. "He's here. I'm sure I saw the top of the wagon above that hedge. You'll see it in a second as it comes round the next bend. Yes, there look"

Sure enough the large white lorry from *Transportes Routiers* laboured up the slight gradient towards them.

Kate started the engine and drove slowly to the exit of the lay by, ready to pull out behind the lorry. She let a couple of cars pass, in the hope that Dubois wouldn't notice that they were trailing him, and then pulled out into the stream of traffic. They followed the truck slowly back northwards weaving in and out of the traffic. Kate maintained a safe distance and was sure Dubois had no idea they were behind him. She sped past him as the lorry took the turn off to Manchester. He had some equipment to drop off there first and then he'd cross the Pennines to Yorkshire. They'd meet up again later. She wanted to make sure that the lorry was safely on her own patch when it was stopped. There was probably time for a few hours break before they were due to meet it outside the gym. "Phil, do you want me to drop you off at home, you can grab something to eat, have a shower or what ever, and be back at the station about 3 o'clock?"

"No, it's hardly worth it. I'll get something to eat in town and then come back to the station and get on top of some paperwork" The truth was now they were getting near the arrival of the lorry, it suddenly felt real and Phil too was excited. Being in on a big drugs haul would be a boost to his chances of promotion. Kate dropped him outside the station and he didn't ask where she was going. He made his way up to Pizza Palace and joined the queue in the takeaway. "A deep pan meat feast pizza and cheesy garlic bread to go please" He told the guy behind the counter. That should keep him going for a while. It was going to be long night and if he didn't eat it all now he could always wrap it up and take it with him.

"Is that it?"

"Oh, and a can of coke please"

"£5.95 please"

Phil handed over the money and sat on the window sill to wait. He picked up the Evening Post and idly flicked through it, sipping from the can of coke. There was another article about the possibility of amalgamating the county's police forces to create a new Yorkshire Super Force. He wasn't sure if it was a good idea or not. He didn't suppose it was going to create any new jobs and more than likely was a cost cutting exercise, although it might mean they would cover a larger geographical area and see a greater variety of cases. Or it might never happen.

"Meat Feast and Garlic bread"

Phil folded the newspaper and dropped it back on top of the pile of well thumbed magazines. He collected the two boxes of food and wandered back down the hill to the station. The street was pretty quiet. Half a dozen people straggled off the National Express coach from London and wandered off into the night.

*   *   *

They'd been told to expect the lorry to arrive around 5.30 and had been sitting in the car since 4 o'clock. They'd had to keep both the headlights and interior light off and although it was cold Kate didn't dare risk running the engine. She'd thought briefly about bringing a flask of coffee, but decided against for fear it might mist the windows of the car and give away the fact that it was occupied. They had to look just like any other resident's vehicle which was parked up in the street overnight. Just up the road a white Luton box van, bearing the slightly altered logo of a nationwide rental company, with blacked out windows was parked. It held several armed officers. This was going to be the biggest drugs bust they'd had. Kate could feel it. She was so sure she'd really prove herself on this one. Just for a second she had a fleeting doubt. If she was wrong someone would have her head on a plate. There'd been a lot of extra manpower and money put into this case. She was jolted back to the present as the headlights of a white transit van sliced through the night. It drove slowly up the road towards them, followed by the white lorry, and turned down the side of the gym and in through the gateway of warehouse.

"I wonder who's driving the van tonight?" asked Kate, not expecting an answer.

Phil chomped quietly on the remains of his pizza and shrugged.

As the lorry manoeuvred slowly and reversed towards the metal roller doors of the warehouse, the transit van came back out of the yard its job as escort done and started to drive back down the street and way from them.

"Should we stop him?" asked Phil

"No, it's Ok; DS Rayner is just round the corner. They've formed a road block with a couple of patrol cars. Don't worry they can't get far"

Kate was about to turn her attention back to the yard where the lorry had reversed up to the open door of the warehouse, when the silhouette of a portly figure stepped out of the shadows into the path of the departing transit van. The driver put the headlights on full beam in warning, and the figure in the road faltered, raising an arm in front of his face as the lights momentarily dazzled him. The transit instead of braking began to pick up speed.

Caught in the glare of the van's lights they realised who the figure was.

"It's George, what the f...." yelled Phil.

"George, no!"

The muzzle of a gun protruded from the passenger window of the van and three loud bangs rent the air. George hit the deck like a felled oak.

"Officer down, Officer down!" Kate shouted into the radio. She leapt from the car and started running across the slick tarmac. She couldn't see properly for the drizzle but as she dashed the tears away, she could see that George wasn't moving. At the same time the rear doors of the Luton van burst open and four armed officers leapt out taking up positions to shoot. The white transit van had stopped at the top of road when the driver realised its exit had been barred by the Volvo estate patrol cars. The reverse warning lights came on momentarily but went off again as the driver realised that for him there was no going back and no place to run.

"Oh my God! Oh Christ! George what were you thinking!" Kate shouted into the darkness as she ran towards him, instinct over ruling training.

"Get back ma'am" Kate was spun round as an officer from the armed response unit grabbed a handful of material at the elbow of her jacket and thrust her roughly behind the Luton van and out of the firing line. "Sergeant Smith Ma'am at your service"

She looked up not sure if was attempting to lighten a grim situation or had a weird sense of humour. He was she guessed, a little over six foot tall and almost the same wide. Built like a brick shit house, as George would have said. She didn't know they made uniforms that big. "Er, Good morning Sergeant" She leaned against the side of the van breathing heavily and feeling helpless.

The armed officers surrounded the transit van and the one with Kate picked up a loudhailer. "You are surrounded by armed Police. Put your weapons down and get out of the van slowly, with your hands on your heads"

Two figures emerged one from either door of the van.

Lights began to come on in some of the surrounding houses but the occupants had the sense to stay indoors.

"Move away from the vehicle slowly. Any residents stay indoors and keep away from your windows"

The two men took a few cautious steps away from their vehicle.

"Keep your hands on your heads and turn round. Keep your backs to the officers"

The figures turned away simultaneously in some awful synchronized parody of a dance.

"Slowly lie down on the floor on your stomach and place your hands behind your back"

The men did as they were instructed.

"Don't move. I remind you that you are covered by armed officers"

As he was speaking the last words of the sentence four uniformed officers slipped out of the shadows. Putting a knee in the small of the gunman's back they slid on the handcuffs before doing the same to the driver.

Meanwhile George lay motionless on the wet tarmac, as the siren of an approaching ambulance grew louder.

Phil and two uniformed officers ran into the yard. Dubois sat in the portakabin his delivery note on the desk was being signed by Alf White both looked stunned. "You two sit there and don't move"

Kate ran into the yard and across to Phil. She'd recovered some of her composure.

"How is he?" Phil asked quietly.

"I don't know… the paramedics were with him and they were just getting him into the ambulance. He hadn't come round. They had an oxygen mask on and connected him up to some machinery. They said he was still alive"

"What was he doing here?"

"It was my fault…"

They both turned at the sound of Alf White's voice.

"It was my fault" he repeated "I know George. I rang him and said I'd overheard a conversation. They said that there was something being delivered here this morning. I didn't know what it was, but I could tell it wasn't above board from the way they were talking. I heard them say something about needing a driver now they didn't have Eliot Nelson. The name rang a bell. George said that if ever I heard anything to ring him so I did."

"Who was having this conversation?" Kate asked.

"It was the boss here, Mr. Johnson. He was asking that young lad from the gym, Liam I think he's called to drive the van for him but I don't think he trusted him to do it on his own so he said he'd have to go with him"

"Johnson" said Kate "I wondered when he'd come to light"

"OK Mr.….?"

"White, Alf White. Is George alright?"

"Ok Mr. White, stay here for now. And you Mr. Dubois"

Dubois seemed surprised that she knew his name.

"An Officer will be along in a moment to take some details and then we'll need you both to come down to the station and make a statement" They left the portakabin and she called across for DS Rayner to take the details of the two men.

A Mondeo estate car with two sniffer dogs peering eagerly from their cages at the rear was being driven in through the gate.

"They're here Ma'am if you're ready" it was the uniformed officer who'd pulled Kate out of the way while the occupants of the van were being arrested.

"OK let's go then" she looked at Phil and they walked across to the car and introduced herself and Phil to the dog handlers. They got the dogs out of the rear of the car, slipped on their leashes, and the small group crossed to the warehouse. At the front walked the two officers, wearing the navy blue fleece tops and baseball caps of the dog handling section. Four large wooden crates had been fork lifted down from the back of the lorry and stood in the middle of the warehouse floor.

"This is a passive dog" the handler explained as he patted the head of the black Labrador which sat at his feet. "He's been trained to locate opiates and cocaine, as well as one or two other illegal substances. The other dog" he pointed at a liver and white Springer spaniel "has been brought along purely as a precaution" He paused for dramatic effect. "He's trained to sniff out explosives. We'll let them work together and if either of them identify a substance which they have been trained to locate, they will sit down where they find it and remain perfectly still. Most people think they are trained to bark but that's not the case. Right are we ready?"

"Ready when you are" said Kate trying not to look fazed at the idea of explosives.

"Ok lads off you go and play" said the handler as he slipped the dogs lead off. The Springer spaniel lived up to his name covering the distance between his handler and the crates in a series of excited leaps, his stubby tail twirling before getting down to the game of finding a hidden object. The black Labrador was altogether more businesslike and plodded from one crate to the next huffing and snuffling his way round, his tail giving a constant slow wag. Kate held her breath waiting for the Labrador to sit. He circled the crates several times nose to the ground. The Springer spaniel leapt on and off the four crates but did not sit, much to Kate's relief. At length both dogs returned to their handlers. Neither had "sat" both looked as if they had enjoyed the game but were ready to go and do something more interesting.

"Think you're going to be out of luck on this one Ma'am. I don't know what's in there but it isn't drugs and it isn't going to explode. Can we get off then?"

"Yes of course. Thank you for your help"

The handlers reached into their pockets, rewarded their dogs with a biscuit each, praised them, put the leashes back on and returned them to their cages in the rear of the estate car.

Kate turned to Phil "Shit, shit, shit" she said under her breath. She turned to brawny Sergeant. "Sergeant Smith can you get a crow bar and get these crates open. I need to know what's inside"

"Never mind Kate, I could do with a new exercise bike!" said Phil.

"Phil don't even joke about it. I don't think I can bear it"

"Yeah well we might both be on our bikes after this farce" he said gloomily.

Sergeant Smith returned with a crow bar and set to work. As the wood of the first crate creaked, Kate closed her eyes, unable to look. Finally with a scrape and a groan the crate splintered open and she opened her eyes to find her self looking into six pairs of terrified dark brown eyes.

Smith opened the crates one at a time and a similar sight met their eyes each time a crate delivered its contents. In each sat six young men, clearly of African origin, in two rows of three, facing each other, their backs against the sides of the crates. They had been given litre plastic bottles of water to sustain them during their journey, but the food if there had been any, was long since gone. The young men huddled in a dejected group, tired, hungry, and dirty. Kate stood dumbstruck and then suddenly things began to click into place like the coloured pieces of glass in a kaleidoscope shifting together to form a pattern. The receptionist at the gym. The assistant at Cut'n'tan. Devon Johnson had been smuggling people into the country, not drugs. She looked at the forlorn figures in front of her and began to wonder at the enormity of it. Which crime was the worst? Before today she'd have had no hesitation in saying the importation of drugs. The effects of illegal drugs reached out, damaging and taking young lives, tearing apart families, in turn, creating their own crime wave. But were the effects on these people and their families any less? People trafficking was like throwing a pebble into a pool and watching the ever widening ripples. In the yard right in front of her, lives from three countries were being shattered. She could almost hear it. Dragging herself back to the job in hand she turned to Phil. "Get on the phone and get some vans down here pdq, we're going to have to take them in" They'd got their result and it was going to be a big one, but somehow it left a bitter taste in her mouth.

"Please…" said one young man beseechingly, holding out his hands palms uppermost. "Please…" It was obviously the only word of English that he knew.

Kate turned and started walking across the yard and back to the car. She'd have liked to go home and get a nice cold bottle of wine out of the fridge. Instead she waited until Phil caught up and climbed into the car beside her and turned it towards the station.

Sixteen

Phil, can I leave you to co-ordinate things here? I'm going to give the hospital a ring to let them know I'm on my way, and then I'm going down there to see how George is"

"Of course, I'll take DS Rayner if that's ok and we'll start getting the paper work together to process them all"

"Just do the bare minimum with Johnson and Nevin for now, and then see to the others. There'll be White and Dubois to take statements from and I think it's probably going to take an hour or two before they can get hold of an interpreter for you to help with the immigrants"

"Look Kate, you get off, don't worry about us, we can get the ball rolling at this end"

"Yes, I know you can. I won't be long though. I'll be back as soon as I can. And Phil. Thanks, Ok"

"It'll be fine, try not to worry, see you soon" His words felt hollow even as he spoke but what else could he say? He felt sorry for her; she looked so tired and worried.

Kate parked outside the infirmary. She felt as if she'd spent too much time here lately. Just inside the door was a small shop selling newspapers, magazines and a selection of essentials for anyone who found themselves having an unexpected stay. What might George need? It was hard to say. It depended on how ill he was and how long he'd be staying. She didn't like to arrive empty handed so selected a couple of items from the counter, paid a lady wearing a green tabard with WRVS embroidered across the front, and went on her way.

The hospital was just beginning to awake to another day. The nurses for the morning shift were already hard at work. Some of the doctors were still arriving and the administrative staff would be following them very soon. Kate approached the front desk and waited for the receptionist to put the phone down. "DCI Peace I've come to see a Mr. George Offord. He was brought in by ambulance earlier this morning. Could you tell me where to find him?"

The blond receptionist crossed to the monitor and clicked on to the page which listed all the admissions and which wards they were on. She scrolled down the first page. "Ah yes. Here we are, it looks like he's on Ward 35, but just let me ring them and check for you. It's only early and sometimes the ward clerks haven't quite got the system updated" the woman sniffed.

"Thank you" Kate fiddled anxiously with the strap of her shoulder bag and distractedly rearranged her hair.

The receptionist picked up the phone and punched in a series of digits and waited. "Is that Ward 35?"

"I have a Detective Peace here who would like to see Mr. Offord. Is he with you?"

"Oh, is that right?"

"Well I would imagine so"

"No, I don't think so, not at present"

"Yes, I see. Yes I'll try and do that later"

"Well I think that would be the case, yes"

"So is it OK to send her along?"

There was nothing more irritating than listening to a one sided telephone conversation, concerning oneself, or perhaps they were discussing something else entirely. Kate resisted the desire to interrupt and ask "Excuse me, can I see him? Is he ok?" She made a conscious effort to calm herself.

"Yes I'll do that, see you later" she replaced the phone and said to Kate "Mr. Offord has just come back from the operating theatre and is still quite sleepy but Sister says that it will be Ok to pop in and see him for a few minutes as long as you don't disturb him. If you follow the red markings you can't go wrong" The woman was already answering another phone call.

"Thank you" she replied to the woman's back. She felt a little at sea, her rank and experience was of little help to her here and she resented the feeling of vulnerability and dependence on these strangers. Kate walked a little unwillingly down the hospital corridor; worried about what she'd find when she reached the ward. George had taken at least one bullet to the chest and she wasn't sure how extensive the damage had been or what state she would find him in. Following the red arrows which had been painted on the floor towards Ward 35, she eventually arrived at the nurse's station.

A plump, middle aged woman with an iron grey, pudding basin haircut and wearing a grey uniform, had just replaced the phone in its cradle and was trying unsuccessfully to sort a pile of unopened envelopes, several of which had just slipped to the floor. "Good morning, Can I help you?" she asked as she ducked under the desk to retrieve the dropped letters.

"Yes, I'm here to visit Mr. Offord. He came in earlier this morning"

"Are you a reporter?"

"No, I'm not!" Kate was surprised. Were the media coming out of the woodwork already?

"Can I ask if you are a relative?" she looked down her nose over the top of her heavy black oval framed glasses as she bounced back down into her seat.

"Erm, no. He has no close family. I'm DCI Peace, a colleague" Kate had been only a short time in the hospital and could see how easy it would be to feel intimidated by these officious women.

"Ah yes, Sister said to expect you" The guardian looked a little less severe, standing up and pulling her tight uniform dress down into position over her rounded hips.

Perhaps her rank did carry a little influence in here after all.

"Let me show you to his room"

"No it's Ok, I can see you're busy. Just point me in the right direction and I'll find it"

She leaned out over the top of the desk, preceded by a huge expanse of bosom, which tested the strength of the dress's poppers, and pointed "If you walk down to the end of the ward you'll see two doors next to each other on the right. Mr. Offord is in the furthest room"

"Thank you" 'and Carry on Matron!' she thought as she set off down the ward. That must be a good sign, surely. Didn't they keep the most poorly patients in view of the nurse's desk so that they could be more easily observed? - Or was it that the most gravely ill were kept furthest away so that they could be moved discreetly without distressing the other patients when they died! Her step quickened momentarily. Which of the two doors had the woman said? She bent to read the small hand written piece of blue card in the metal holder near the first door. *Joan Smith*. It must be the next one. She bent again. *George Offord*. Suddenly she felt apprehensive. She took a deep breath and pushed back her shoulders. Gently she pushed open the swing door to the side ward, and stepped through, the self closer let it swish closed quietly behind her. From just inside the door she studied George. He was propped up in bed, seemingly asleep. A plastic bag of clear fluid hung from a metal pole attached to the bed frame. It dripped slowly into the tubing which disappeared under a bandage secured around George's wrist. Thin wires were attached to stickers at the top of his chest and snaked out towards a monitor that had green line squirming across it. His jaw sagged and his head was turned slightly to one side, looking grey against the pile of starched white pillowcases. She was shocked how much older he suddenly looked and wondered, even if he were able, whether he would want to return to work after this. She wouldn't blame him if he didn't. He wasn't far off retiring anyway and he'd have no trouble getting signed off by the police doctor.

She paused, for a moment undecided what to do, not wanting to disturb George. Perhaps he was still under the effects of the anaesthetic. She tip-toed across to the bedside locker and had just put down the bottle of Lucozade and the bunch of grapes, and was about to creep out again when George's eyes opened. She took in the mass of bandaging to his left shoulder, where the back-fastening gown had slipped down at one side. "Oh, George, how are you?" Her voice quavered. What a bloody inept thing to say, she could feel a lump in her throat, and had to fight hard to keep at bay the tears which pricked her eyes.

"I feel like shit" he croaked, his gaze swivelled to the bottle of Lucozade which stood on the locker. "For Christ's sake, I hope that's not what it says on the bloody bottle. I hope you've chucked it out and filled it with a can of bitter. I could do with a drink. And you know where you can put the bloody grapes as well. For God's sake see if you can find me a bacon sandwich... .and not from one of them damned vegetarian pigs of yours either!"

"Oh, George. Thank God you're alright! I was so afraid" Kate took a final step towards him and put her wet cheek against his, unable to contain the tears of relief, which now ran unchecked, any longer .

"Come on now lass, don't take on so" he said enveloping her in a bear hug with his good arm "It'll all be alright, you'll see. He only winged me. I'll be right as nine pence" He coughed and tried to reach out for the Lucozade bottle "I'm dry as the bloody Gobi desert"

Kate unscrewed the lid and passed it to him.

He took a long slug and shuddered "It is Lucozade!"

Kate sat down on the grey moulded plastic chair and dashed away the tears with the back of her hand. She sniffed, leaned back in the chair and then laughed in relief. "You know George, I think you're right. I think it will be alright"

*   *   *

An hour later she breezed back into the office, a heavy weight had been lifted from her shoulders. "OK everyone how's it going?"

Phil gestured to the mountain of paperwork on his desk. "We're winning but only just" he took his cue from her cheery manner, and although anxious asked nonchalantly "Is the silly old sod going to be OK then?"

"Well, he's sat up complaining and wanting someone to fetch him a bacon sandwich. I think they'll want him out as soon as they can or he'll drive them mad. I'd better give the welfare officer a ring. He might need a bit of help when he goes home"

"I can't imagine George taking to that idea, and I can't imagine anyone doing the Florence Nightingale bit for long either"

"Point taken, We'll have to see. Right Phil, I've been thinking... I want those two girls in here. I want them grilled. Where are they from? If they are local girls that's fine but I have my doubts. That one on the desk at the gym that day when we went to interview Liam Nevin had very little English. And the girl who was helping Carla in 'Cut 'n' Tan', we need to speak to her too. I want to see their passports and their work permits and any other documents they have that might support their case. Do we have an interpreter here yet?"

"There are three on their way now"

"Let's grab a coffee and set up in interview room one. Send DS Rayner and WPC Capstick out to pick the girls up"

The first girl who had been picked up as she arrived for work at the gym had a forged passport. Kate, Mrs. Nyala, the interpreter, wearing a native African dress in floral yellow pattern, and the girl Sebina, wearing her blue track suit, sat round the table.

"Mrs. Nyala" said Kate "Can you ask Sebina to tell us how she came to England?"

"It had cost £2000 and another £1000 for the journey" she told them through the interpreter. "My family paid, my sister was forced to work as a prostitute, my brother is a 'bumster' at a hotel, my aunts and uncle all helped to save up the money to send me. There is no good work at home in Senegal. I was told that I would be able to get work here easily, that the wages were high and I would have enough to send home to support my family. I was one of the lucky ones. At least there was a job for me when I got here but the pay isn't as much as they promised. By the time I have made a payment towards the journey and paid for my accommodation and food there's hardly anything left." She gave a sob and a tear ran slowly down her cheek. She hung her head in abject misery.

"She says that she is very afraid about what will happen to her. She says that Mr. Johnson told her that if she ever told anyone about how she had got here her family would-be killed" said the interpreter.

"You can tell her that Johnson has been arrested. He cannot harm her or her family now"

"She says that she is afraid that she will be sent back home to Senegal"

"You can tell her that I'm afraid that, that is not our decision, and not within our power. Her case will referred to the Home Office. At the moment we need her help. She must tell us every thing she can about how she made the journey over here, so that we have as much evidence against Johnson as possible. Please explain that the more we know about what he has been doing. The less chance there is of him being released. We need to make sure that he is locked up and for a very long time"

Kate knew that there was no way Johnson was going anywhere but she needed to extract as much information as she possibly could from the frightened girl. The knowledge would passed to Interpol who needed all the evidence that they could gather in order to help the countries involved to combat the problem of people trafficking. Haltingly and with the help of the interpreter the girl began to explain.

"Her family had scraped together most of the money needed to send her. The rest could be paid off a bit at a time from the money she sent home when she got a job in England. It was seen as an investment in the family's future. She would come to England and get a good job, perhaps as a nurse or a hairdresser, or even a nanny. She had been told that rich people paid handsomely for someone to look after their children whilst they went to work. She remembers how she was so happy when the man had come to the house with the passport and visa for her. She knew of many cases where the man who had been paid to provide the documents had simply pocketed the money and disappeared. It was a big risk. Her family were simple people, naïve and trusting, not used to people who would deceive them but the man had provided the documents as he had promised" The woman paused whilst she waited for the girl to tell her more .

Kate rubbed her face and sighed. It was an awful story. There was going to be no happy ending for anyone involved.

The woman took a breath and continued. "They travelled overland for days and days. Sometimes they were on foot, and sometimes in vehicles. Sometimes they slept in the open air and sometimes they found shelter. They crossed the Sahara desert, a small band of them, young men and women, who carried the hopes of their families. Eventually they arrived in Morocco and were crowded into a small fishing boat to make the sea journey across to Spain. She says it was terrible, this is when she was most afraid. The sea made her sick and the boat was overcrowded, she was cold and wet, and sure that it would sink and she prayed to be saved. It was cold and it was dark and it seemed to take forever. They were landed near a beach and were pushed out into the water. She couldn't swim. She and Gina struggled onto the beach together where there were two trucks waiting. They were put into the back and covered with canvas and driven north all the next day. She says at one point she looked out from under the canvas and saw mountains covered in snow"

Kate imagined by this stage they had probably reached France.

The woman continued that they had been kept in a large metal, building for a short time where they given food and water. That night they had to sleep on the floor. There were no covers. She was afraid they'd be found.

The next day they were put into large wooden boxes, given some bread and plastic bottles of water, and were then put into a lorry to complete their journey.

Kate listened sympathetically but felt saddened. "Ok I think we'll take a break. Interview concluded" she said for the benefit of the tape, and stood up and left the room.

*   *   *

In the next room Gina was telling Phil a similar story. WPC Capstick sat by the door taking notes. Working in the hairdressing salon had given Gina chance to practice her English and she managed reasonably well with only minimal assistance from the interpreter.

"We travelled for two or three days in the lorry. I'm not sure. It was very cold and uncomfortable. We were hungry and soon all the water was gone. I was afraid. I started to think that we would never get to England, that we would die on the way. I know now that does happen"

"Can you tell me what happened when you arrived in England?"

"The wooden boxes were opened and we in a big cold building. The men pushed us into the back of a white van. They were rough, they shouted and pushed us. We were treated like animals. I wished I had never come"

A tear landed silently on the table and Phil passed her a tissue. "What happened to you next" he asked half afraid of the answer. He was glad of the presence of the WPC Capstick

"They took us in a van to a house and kept us there"

He wondered how to broach the question "I'm sorry that I have to ask you this, did anyone ever harm you physically, hurt you or touch your body in anyway?"

"No nothing like that" she looked surprised.

Phil thought they had been lucky. "Can you tell me the address of this house where you were taken?"

She shook her head.

"Can you describe the house?"

She looked at him blankly.

"OK, was it a big house?"

"Oh yes"

"Did it have a garden?"

"Oh no, no garden. Many houses in a line, joined together and some steps up to the door. The door is green and two numbers on it 4 and 1."

Thoughtfully Phil noted this down and circled it in black biro.

"Inside it was very beautiful, I look into the rooms as we walk past. Lovely carpets, and lovely curtains. I think if I have come to live here in this house then I am very happy, but we go through another door and down many steps into a dark room with only a little window up high. There is one light from the ceiling and we are told 'You sleep here' There is a mat and a blanket on the floor and some clean clothes in a black plastic bag"

Things started to click in Phil's head. "OK let's take a break shall we? I need to go and have a word with someone. Would you like me to get you some sandwiches and a drink sent up?"

Both women nodded gratefully.

"PC Capstick can I leave it with you to sort out some food and drinks for these ladies?"

Capstick rolled her eyes heavenward and pursed her lips "Of course, Detective Sergeant Simpson. I think I can manage that" as she stomped out of the room.

"I'll be back shortly" Phil told the two women.

Phil hovered outside the door of the adjacent interview room. He could see Kate in profile and tried to catch her eye as he peered through the small glass panel of the door. At last she seemed to sense his presence and looked in his direction. He gestured for her to come out. She excused herself to the other two women and went out into the corridor.

"What's the matter Phil? Is there a problem?"

"No, no problem. Just the reverse, in fact. You're going to love this. The house Gina says they were kept at when they arrived here….She described it as a big house. There were houses joined together and a 4 and a 1 on the door. It sounds like it could be Madeley Terrace!"

"Well that fits. They were receiving illegal immigrants and keeping them there until they were found other places to live"

"Yes that's how it looks. I bet that's where the latest lot were going as well"

"I wonder how long Johnson's been running this operation. Twenty four of them, and roughly once a month or so….that's almost three hundred people a year. I'm not sure what percentage of the fee he takes, but if he's then employing them, taking rent and an unspecified amount to pay off their loan. I can't begin to think… but it's big money by anybody's standards."

"Could he employ that many people Kate?"

"I don't know but I bet he knew people who would….for another fee. I understand employment agencies don't always ask too many questions. The more people they place in local factories or in agricultural work, the more they make. And I suppose the rest would just disappear and fend for themselves. Try and get a bit of work cash in hand somewhere. Maybe in a restaurant."

"So what will happen to this lot do you reckon?"

"Well our nearest Immigration centre is at Lindholme. It's an all male establishment, which is next to the prison, I understand. I suppose they'll go there first. I think it holds just over 100. If they're full I imagine they could be dispersed round the rest of the country. Where the girls will go, I've no idea"

"And eventually they'll all be sent back?"

Kate shrugged "I would think so, unless they can claim asylum. I'm not sure about the political situation where they've come from. Anyway that's out of our hands, thank goodness. It's not a decision I'd like to have to make"

"Do we need to ask the girls anything else now?"

"No, I think we've got as much as we need to know from them for the moment. Let's take a break for lunch and then we'll talk to Mr. Johnson and Mr. Nevin. I need to get out for a breath of fresh air. I'll see you back here in an hour"

Seventeen

Kate collected her jacket and bag from the coat rack in the corner of her office and left the police station. She crossed the road, dodging between the heavy traffic coming into the city centre, and walked towards the West Yorkshire Playhouse. For a little while she sat outside on the low wall, taking advantage of the improving weather, just watching Leeds go about its daily grind and enjoying being in the open air. Buses arrived and departed from the bus station with astonishing frequency. Where were all these people coming from and going to? Others scurried along the pavements, head down, engrossed in their own business, like purposeful ants. Life goes on complacently for most of the world, she pondered, whilst for a few, their lives were being shattered. But that in itself was all part of the greater pattern. She sighed, got to her feet, dusted off the seat of her dark brown trousers, and walked into the Playhouse.

She walked up the wide staircase to the pleasant, airy café. At the counter she studied the variety of light snacks on offer and then ordered a decaffeinated black coffee and a Danish pastry. She wasn't particularly hungry but just fancied cheering herself up with a treat. There'd been too many snatched and makeshift meals over the last couple of weeks and she was starting to feel sluggish and jaded. As soon as this case was concluded she'd take herself in hand, have a good shopping session in Sainsbury's and restock the cupboards and fridge with all the fresh healthy, foods she knew would make her feel better. Then she'd throw herself into a strict exercise programme, starting with a long early morning run, and some workouts in the gym.

Nibbling at the syrupy pastry, she remembered the last time she'd been here. It could only have been a couple of months ago, though it seemed longer. She and her sister had been to watch "Dead Funny" by Terry Johnson, although she had to admit, she hadn't found it very funny at all. It centred on sex therapy and adult relationships. She thought the humour rather overdone in parts and couldn't understand why it had won so many awards. Perhaps it was a case of the Emperor's New Clothes and people were saying they liked it because they felt they should. To give it the benefit of the doubt, perhaps the marital dysfunction theme had been a little close to home and she wasn't the best person to give an unbiased opinion. Happily, Clare had seemed to find it amusing. They'd both enjoyed the meal afterwards though and agreed to meet up in a few weeks time for a day going round the shops. Yes, once, this case was sorted she'd ring Clare and they'd make a day of it. Too many things had been getting neglected lately she decided. The weather was starting to get better for shopping too. There was nothing drearier than dashing from one shop to another, struggling with a flapping umbrella through the rain and ending up looking like a drowned rat. Though to be fair, there was quite a lot of shopping in the city centre now which was under cover. The Bond Street centre housed many of the chain stores and there were lots of smaller shops and boutiques in the Queens Arcade. The Light seemed to cater more towards the young and the fashion conscious, and abounded with designer retail shops and several bars and cafes, which all advertised themselves as '*The* place to eat' or suggested themselves to be the ideal place to meet for 'after work cocktails' They always seemed to full of people who were trying to be someone or something else, and were willing to pay handsomely through the nose to fail. She looked at her watch; it was time to be getting back. Draining the remains of the black coffee and licking the sticky syrup surreptitiously from her fingers before wiping them on the napkin, she picked up her bag and left. The end was in sight and suddenly she felt much more alert. 'Ok,' she said to herself, smiling and standing tall 'Seconds away, round two. Let me at 'em.' She turned a few heads as she left the café.

They met up again in the squad room. Phil was standing in front of the mirror, studying his reflection, and adjusting his garishly patterned purple and pink tie.

She chose to ignore his flamboyant dress code. His ties were as loud as his profession allowed, without her actually being forced to ask him to tone it down "Right Phil are you ready?"

"Yes" he showed her the small microphone hidden under the lapel of his jacket, which would relay his interview with Liam Nevin to her, as she sat in the adjoining room, on the other side of the one way glass. They would also both have a small earpiece, and if Kate wanted to intervene during the questioning she could speak to Phil undetected.

"Ok let's go for it then. Get in there and give him a hard time"

Phil walked into the small airless interview room, it smelt of sweat and dust and defeat. He took a seat at the opposite side of the table to Liam Nevin. DS Rayner sat on an upright hard-backed wooden chair just inside the door. Nevin's solicitor sat next to him. Phil knew the duty solicitor Jack Garland of old. A scruffy fifty year old has been, who managed to eke out a living from legal aid paid out to the desperate. Garland ground out his hand rolled cigarette in the foil ashtray, in response to Phil's disapproving glare.

"Ok, Liam let's just go through this in a little more detail shall we. Where were you on the night that Leon Edwards and Eliot Nelson were killed?"

Liam Nevin looked up and paused from the intense biting of his fingernails and pulled at his pierced ear.

"I called in at the Glasshouse. I was bored. I just called in to see who was about, if any of my mates were there"

"So there'll be someone we can ask to verify that you were there?"

"Yeah I should think so" he sounded uncertain.

"Ok Liam, so give me the name of someone I can talk to, who can confirm that they saw you there that night? Who were you with and who did you speak to?"

"I wasn't exactly with anyone. I was on my own. I just called in had two or three beers, hung around a bit, you know how it is, there wasn't a lot doing so I left"

"So, if you bought two or three drinks, the bar staff will remember serving you?"

"Dunno" he rubbed his spotty chin "It was busy. I bought a drink and wandered round a bit. You know how it is?"

"No, Liam, I don't know. So you're saying that you didn't stay because 'there wasn't a lot doing'"

"Yeah that's right, it was pretty boring and I didn't stay long"

"But then you said no-one would remember you because it was too busy. So was there nothing doing or was it busy Liam?"

"A bit of both…" he scratched his head in concentration "there were lots of people about but no one I knew"

"So let me get this right, what you're saying is, that you didn't actually speak to anyone there, there was no one you knew and no-one will remember seeing you?"

"Yeah, that's right. That's what happened" he shuffled in his seat and scowled, deep in thought, and then risked a sly smile at his cleverness.

Garland rolled his eyes and shook his head.

"Ok Liam, so when you left the Glasshouse, where did you go next?"

"I can't remember. Another bar I think. But before you ask me, I can't remember which one. I'd had a few drinks right. Then I went home and watched the tele." he now sat upright becoming more confident.

"You never went to the Glasshouse that Saturday, did you?" Phil asked.

"Of course I did. Why would I say I did, if I didn't?" Nevin sounded indignant.

Phil tapped his pencil on the desk, then turned and tapped it again." I should have thought that was obvious …"

Nevin gave a puzzled frown in response.

Garland folded his arms and studied the cracks on the ceiling. The number of times he'd had to sit through stories like this…

"I don't think you went to the Glasshouse at all, Liam. I think it's just a story you've made up. We can see straight through it" Phil laughed.

Nevin didn't know if they were having a joke at his expense. He looked from one to the other, searching their faces for a clue.

"No Liam, do you know what I think you did? I think you went for a drive to the Rose and Crown"

"No, I've never been in the Rose and Crown"

"Right, Phil, start putting the pressure on" Kate's voice came through the ear-piece.

Phil ignored Nevin's remark "So what did you do…. Wait for them outside the Rose and Crown. You were parked up round the back where it was dark. You waited for him to come out. And then you shot him didn't you? You were jealous of Eliot Nelson, you got angry and lost control. Why should he get everything? He's been shouting his head off about the holiday he was going to have in the South of France, he was the one who had the flash car, the flash clothes, plenty of money to throw about, and you had wanted in on it hadn't you? But Eliot Nelson and Leon Edwards were big buddies and they wanted to keep it to themselves, they didn't want you pushing your nose in and having to split the money three ways instead of two, did they? They gave you the cold-shoulder, and that made you angry, didn't it Liam?"

"I don't know what you're talking about"

"Oh you don't?…..Well I think you do! If they weren't going to let you in on the deal, then you were going to get your own back and they had to go didn't they? That way you could be top dog. You could muscle in on their deal and have it all to yourself"

"No, it wasn't like that!"

"O.K. but you shot them, there's no two ways about it"

"I didn't. It wasn't me. I wasn't there!" a film of sweat appeared on Nevin's forehead.

"Well it looks that way to us. And we *know* you were there" Phil bluffed, "The landlady of the Rose and Crown remembers seeing you. She says she saw you go in and talk them. Then she says you all three of you left together. We've got another witness who saw you parked round the back near the allotments and he's willing to stand up in court and identify you too. So if you're saying that it wasn't *Like that*, and it *wasn't* you who shot them….. You'd better tell me what was it like, and who the cold blooded killer was" said Simpson trying to wear him down "Because if you don't start talking soon and talking fast Liam, you're going to take the rap for this, all on your owney own lad and it'll be a hell of a stretch for double murder, and the attempted murder of a policeman….. If it wasn't you, like you keep telling me, I need a name, Liam. And I need it now!"

"O.K. O.K. So I was there but I didn't have the gun….." Liam stood and took three steps away from the table. Rayner reacted quickly and jumped to his feet. Nevin had nowhere to go, so came back. A short pause fell like a pebble into a pool and the silence rippled.

"Right, we're getting somewhere at last. Sit down again Liam" Phil could see Nevin was starting to crack.

Liam Nevin took his seat again, cowed and defeated, his eyes darted from side to side as he tried frantically to think of a way to limit the damage.

"The next question's an easy one Liam. Your starter for ten.... Who was it Liam. Who had the gun?"

"It was Devon Johnson" he whispered.

"A bit louder for the tape please, Liam"

"I said it was Johnson. Johnson had the gun and he shot them both. I swear to God and on my mother's life... I didn't know he had a gun. I didn't know that's what he was going to do"

"So what were you doing there?"

"He came into the Glasshouse. I'd just got there. He asked me to drive for him that night. Said he needed to meet Eliot Nelson. That he had some business that he needed to discuss urgently but he said he couldn't drive himself, he'd been drinking"

"And you fell for it Liam, big time. He set you up. You were the last person seen with them. Johnson set you up to carry the can"

Nevin dissolved into a snivelling wreck. He folded his arms and laid his head on the table.

"Interview concluded" said Phil for the benefit of the tape and stood up looking at Liam Nevin in disgust. "Rayner pass him a tissue, I'm out of here" he paused at the door and called to the custody Sergeant "Lock him up again"

Jack Garland, who had sat in silence throughout the interview reached into his pocket for his cigarettes as Liam Nevin was marched back to the cells.

Phil walked next door to the room where Kate had been watching the interview through the one way glass. "So Kate, you've got your man, Devon Johnson"

"It sure looks that way. We'd better have him up here next and see what he's got to say for himself then"

*   *   *

They took their seats at the small square table, with Kate facing the door and Phil sitting slightly behind and to the left of her. Johnson was ushered in. Phil had never seen anyone so big. He was well over 6 feet 6 inches tall and because of his size the two escorting police officers, Sergeant Smith and another uniformed Pc who Kate hadn't seen before, had to let Johnson walk in front of them in order for them all to pass through the door. Johnson had his waist length, shiny black dreadlocks loosely gathered into a ponytail. This was the first time they'd seen him up close. No wonder the super sized Sergeant Smith had been asked to attend. Grenville Harrington, Johnson's solicitor followed them in, and after carefully pulling up the knees of his immaculately pressed trousers, placed his briefcase on the floor and took a seat next to his client. Kate immediately took a dislike to him, he reminded her of a snake. Aged around thirty, with slicked back, black hair and prominent high cheekbones he had an Italian look about him, or that could have been the black and white pin-striped Armani suit and black Fozieri Oxford shoes he was wearing.

"Turn on the tape Phil please" She carefully recited the names of the occupants of the room, the date and time. "Is every one comfortable? Mr. Johnson would you like a glass of water before we begin?"

Johnson shook his head.

"Devon Johnson we have information that three weeks ago you received a number of crates containing equipment for your gym which were delivered from France by a company called Transportes Routiers to your warehouse in Chapeltown?"

"I can't remember man" Johnson shuffled his bulk in the chair trying to get comfortable. First he sat up straight and then slid down on the seat, settling for a slouch, legs apart and hands dangling loosely between his massive thighs, in an attempt to look contemptuous.

"Well I would like to inform you that we have someone who can"

"Oh yeah, and who might dat be Miss?" his chin jutted at her insolently. He would have been exceptionally good looking Kate thought, except his looks were marred by his narrowed eyes and sulky down turned mouth. He flared his nostrils and looked down at her as if she were a bad smell under his nose.

She ignored his question. "So you deny knowing anything about this shipment of cargo from France three weeks ago *or* the one which arrived last night?"

He didn't even deign to reply but instead made a detailed study of the backs of his large hands, and after a moments apparent thought adjusted a heavy gold ring on the third finger of his right hand to a position more to his liking. He held his hand out away from him and continued to study it.

He was infuriating; she wished she could think of a way to annoy him as much as his attitude annoyed her. "Mr. Johnson, what do you have to say?"

Johnson looked up from his contemplation of the ring, his cold, hard eyes, totally expressionless locked with Kate's and she felt a shiver run down her spine. She felt that she was in the presence of someone not only bad, which she was used to but of someone evil.

"I don't have anything to say to *you* Miss"

There was a pause in which you would have heard a pin drop. Into it Phil calmly announced. "Devon Johnson, you are being charged with people trafficking, that is illegally bring immigrants into this country"

Johnson folded his brawny arms across his chest and smirked. "You can't prove I knew anything about them people. Yeah, it was my premises that were being used. But I knew nothing about it. I'm being set up here. You're trying to frame me. Just like last time. Well it didn't work then and it won't work now."

"You were in the white transit van which escorted that lorry to the warehouse last night weren't you?" said Phil.

Johnson remained silent.

"Mr. Johnson declines to comment" said Kate for the benefit of the tape.

"And you are also charged with the murders of Leon Edwards and Eliot Nelson" added Phil.

"And I had nothing to do with that either. So don't try to pin it on me" he placed his right elbow on the table and gazed around the room as if completely bored and gave a sigh.

"Well, firstly we have a witness who says you paid him to be there to open the place early this morning. Alf White says you paid him £250 in cash to open up and receive the lorry"

"Well he's lying. I don't know who paid him. £250 to open the gates you say? Don't make me laugh" sneered Johnson. "He was just a casual worker, did a bit of sweeping up in the warehouse from time to time, and it wasn't me who paid him the money. Right!" Johnson started to breath heavily and gritted his teeth, the cool exterior slipping.

"…..And secondly, your accomplice, Liam Nevin, well he hasn't got a lot of nerve has he? You picked a bad one there. I don't know what you were paying him Johnson, but it sure as hell wasn't enough, because we've been playing Jackanory next door and he's been telling me a very interesting story. Now let me think, how did it go?…. 'Once upon a time, there was a wicked man, and he was called Devon Johnson and he had a gun which he used to shoot Eliot Nelson and Leon Edwards'. So it looks like you're in deep shit Johnson"

Johnson leapt to his feet, face contorted with rage. He placed one enormous hand squarely in the centre of Grenville Harrington's chest and sent him sprawling from the chair. "Can't you say anything? What, the fuck am I paying you for, you stuffed shirt" Kate looked on in amusement as she saw the pristinely clean soles of Grenville Harrington's expensive shoes as he shot backwards off the chair. Johnson swung back to the table as the two uniformed officers moved smartly forward and slipped on the handcuffs. Only their speed prevented Johnson from reaching Phil across the table.

"Oh and don't forget the attempted murder of a Police Officer" Phil continued taking a deep breath and a step back. "Take him back down to the cells please" he said to their already departing backs.

Grenville Harrington slowly picked himself up from his undignified position flat on his back, in the corner of the room and tried to rub the dust from his pinstriped trousers.

"I think this is yours?" Kate handed him a cream silk handkerchief which she'd picked up from under the table.

He took it, mopped his brow and chanced peering down the corridor, out of the door before he wordlessly left the room.

The sounds of a scuffle in the corridor could be heard and Johnson's voice raised in protest, fading into the distance.

"Jeez Louise" said Kate taking a deep breath "I wouldn't like to meet him down an alley on a dark night"

"No but the chances of that are pretty slim. He's going down for a long time. In fact when the shrinks get hold of him it might even be a stretch in Rampton. Did you see his face? He looked completely unhinged"

"Best place for him I'd say. Anyway how's the rest of it going? Has some one taken statements from Dubois and Alf White?"

"Yes, I've had Chatten on that side of things and think the paperwork is pretty well on schedule"

Kate looked at her watch "Have you seen the time Phil?"

"Yes time flies when you're having fun doesn't it?"

"Let's just call in and tell everyone to wind it up for today. That's if they haven't already gone home"

In the office the team were still there, but were making signs of packing up for the day. Computer screens were being switched off. Papers were being straightened into piles and filed away. And desks cleared of pens and other paraphernalia, ready for the arrival of the cleaning ladies.

Kate stood just inside the door and waited until she had everyone's attention, "I'd just like to take this opportunity to thank everyone for their hard work on this case. As you know of course we've had a very successful outcome, the only near tragedy was the injury sustained by one of our colleagues. However, it would appear that he's had a very lucky escape and should make full recovery in time" a polite ripple of applause greeted the last remark "That being said, I don't know about you lot but I'm off to the pub and if anyone else wants to come along, the first drink's on me"

The team cheered and trouped out of the office behind her, Chatten and Rayner providing a ragged chorus of 'For she's a jolly good fellow'

Kate turned holding up her hand "Ok, lads don't go overboard, that'll do. I'll make that the first two drinks".

Eighteen

The noisy group happily tumbled in through the doorway of the pub. They were welcomed by a wall of heat and music.

Outside the rain poured relentlessly. A double decker bus full of homeward bound workers who goggled from the windows, swished past the open door.

Appropriately "Riders of the Storm" was being piped over the music system, as the company shook the rain from their jackets. Strategically placed soft lighting flattered everyone and created a relaxed mood.

"You go and grab a seat, I'll go to the bar Kate. What do you want?" asked Phil.

"I think I'll just have a slim line tonic please" she smiled up at him, getting her purse out and hoisting her shoulder bag into a more comfortable position.

He wondered if it some sort of code that equated to his chances. "Just a tonic Kate, I thought we were celebrating?" he reproached her playfully.

"Oh, go on then put a gin in it" she laughed "And put this fifty quid behind the bar. I'm feeling generous"

He raised his eyebrows thoughtfully and walked across to the bar, looking briefly over his shoulder to check she wasn't watching him. Engrossed in conversation with Superintendent Southern, who'd followed them in she had her back to him. Phil caught Southern's eye and raised his arm in a drinking motion. Southern waved a greeting but shook his head, and returned to his conversation with Kate. Just a token appearance then, perhaps he didn't want to cramp their style. Phil gave the barman the fifty pounds, explaining the situation, checked that Kate was still talking to Southern, and then asked for a double gin and tonic for her and a low alcohol lager for himself.

Whilst he waited for the drinks to be served he studied the widescreen television behind the bar which displayed a rolling showing of the day's sports news. As the group were served their drinks they gravitated towards a long table with padded velour padded benches which would comfortably seat 8-10 people. Kate wondered what George would have made of the modern surroundings. The chain owned pub was in an old Victorian building which had been done up tastefully, complete with cast iron radiators and what may have been the original parquet floor. Couples lounged in comfortable leather covered armchairs enjoying food or just a cup of coffee.

Phil returned from the bar and handed Kate her drink, she took a sip, looking at him quizzically but was unable to comment as at that precise moment Chief Superintendent Southern rose from the seat he had taken at the head of the table. He used the plastic menu stand to rap smartly on the edge of the table and gain the group's attention. He needn't have bothered, as once he was on his feet everyone's eyes swivelled towards him expectantly, glasses half way to their mouths, and hush ensued.

"Ladies and gentlemen, if I could just have a few moments of your time? Unfortunately I am unable to stay and join in your celebrations, as I have a prior engagement this evening"

This announcement was greeted with a selection of half hearted mumbles of regret from the group.

"There are a couple of things that I would like to say. First of all I would like to congratulate all of you on the successful conclusion to the case and for all the hard work and extra hours that you've uncomplainingly put in. It's been an excellent result for the department and I'm very proud of you all"

Oh, very good. We've heard it all before. For goodness sake get on with it and clear off, Phil thought to himself.

"Secondly, I would just like to make another brief but no less important announcement. Phil, can you just come across here for a moment?"

Phil racked his brains frantically as he walked slowly to the end of the table. What could he have done wrong? He couldn't think of anything that he'd done to warrant this public singling out. Quickly he removed his hands from the pockets of his jacket, straightened his tie, and stood next Southern facing down the length of the table. All eyes were on them expectantly.

Southern turned to Phil and held out his hand.

Phil looked down at it as if it was some sort of trick.

"Phil, let me be the first to congratulate you"

"Er, Thank you Sir" replied Phil now shaking the proffered hand, still not sure exactly what the congratulations were for, but not wanting to look foolish.

Southern noticed Phil's obvious puzzlement. "Don't tell me Kate hasn't informed you?" said Southern smugly, enjoying Phil's discomfort.

He looked at Kate who didn't meet his eye, but instead smiled down into the glass of gin which she swirled and listened to the satisfactory 'plink' as the ice cubes connected with the glass.

"We've just had the excellent news that you've passed your Inspector's exam. Congratulations!" said Southern as he pumped Phil's hand enthusiastically.

Phil's thanks to Southern was lost in a rousing chorus of "For he's a jolly good fellow" which rapidly was drowned out by a duet from the rugby players, Chatten and Rayner who gave a lively rendition of "Beer, beer, we want more beer. Everybody's cheering, get the **ckin' beer in!"

It looked like it was going to be a good night. Southern gave them all a wave and left the building.

As Phil made his way slowly back through the group, pausing briefly to shake hands with his colleagues, or receive their congratulations, Kate watched a group of students at the next table who were tucking into the special offer burger meal. It was, the menu informed her £4.55 for a classic or vegetarian burger with chips and a beer and served all day. No wonder they were in here all day instead of going to lectures. She turned the menu over and noticed an invitation to the more adventurous to 'drink their way around the world' on it was listed a selection of imported beers, San Miguel, from Spain, Tiger beer from Singapore and Four Dogs from New Zealand. At the special price of £2.75 a bottle. No wonder the burger deal was so popular.

Youngsters lounged against the pillars clutching various bottles. The tempo of the music picked up as the number of younger customers outnumbered the older ones but as the drink continued to flow no one noticed or cared. In acknowledgement of his good news, Phil went and topped the kitty up, returning with another drink for Kate and himself. WPC Capstick having taken full advantage of the free drink, was beginning to look slightly the worse for wear. She wove her way between the tables, towards the 'Ladies,' clinging to the chair backs for support.

"I think I'd better just go with her and make sure she's OK" said Kate setting off across the room, too late, as Capstick missed her footing and landed in an ungainly heap at the bottom of the three steps down to the lavatories. She helped Capstick to her feet and they tried to make a dignified exit. In the coolness of the ladies toilet Kate inspected herself in the mirror over the hand basin, she appeared a little flushed, perhaps a combination of heat and the drinks. But at least she was still on her feet. "Are you Ok in there Capstick?" said Kate to the closed door.

"Fine, and it's Linda" came back the voice but she did not reappear.

Kate folded her arms and leaned back against the hand basin whilst she waited for Linda Capstick to come out of the cubicle. Looking round, she saw a poster encased behind plastic which advertised cut price DVD rentals, available by mail order. On the wall was a machine with various shapes and flavours of condom. And, a vending machine to her left which sold 'naughty toys for girls and boys' She averted her eyes, pondered for a moment, and then risked a closer look. The illustrations of the merchandise left her, she was ashamed to admit no wiser. Capstick was still in the loo. She peered again. The pictures looked like those intricate plastic puzzles that she could never solve, found in Christmas crackers.

Eventually Capstick emerged from the cubicle. Her face had a green tinge, but it could have been the lighting. After splashing her face in cold water they returned to their seats in the bar. Kate, gently steering Capstick by the elbow.

A young woman in tight blue jeans and with waist length black hair circulated between the groups, discreetly removing empty glasses. She was followed by cries of "Oh, you haven't got a drink, can I get you another?"

Phil handed Kate another glass of gin and tonic as she took her seat. She took it from him wordlessly, pretending not to notice, as she took a sip, that it was another double. To her surprise she was actually quite enjoying herself.

She could hear Dave Chatten saying to Paul Rayner in a puzzled tone,

"Yes, but what I still don't understand is why did Leon Edwards and Eliot Nelson get shot in the first place?"

"Well according to Alf White, Liam Nevin had said that Eliot Nelson had told Johnson he wanted out. It was as simple as that"

"What, and he wanted a big pay off to keep quiet about what Johnson was doing?"

"No. He just wanted out but he knew too much about what was going on. Johnson would never have felt safe while Nelson was walking the streets. And yes, I suppose that Johnson may have thought that there was always the danger that he could come back at some stage and blackmail him. He didn't want to take the risk. So he thought 'why not just get rid of him now'"

"So Leon Edwards wanted out as well did he?"

"No"

"What do you mean 'no'"

"What I mean is, I think Edwards probably knew what was going on. He shared Madeley Terrace with Nelson. Unless, of course, they were moving these people around when he wasn't there. I don't suppose we'll ever be sure about that. If he was involved, it was just as a bit player. Leon Edwards was in the wrong place at the wrong time. He just got in the way...literally"

"You mean he wasn't the target. He was shot by mistake?"

"Yep"

"Bloody hell!" They both stared morosely into their pint glasses.

At the back of the building a constantly changing procession of snooker players posed for the benefit of the prettily pouting young women drinking bottles of alco pops and leaning against the pillars and trying to look disinterested.

At the other end of the table Sergeant Smith held up Linda Capstick, and they broke into a hilarious and badly timed rendition of 'I got you, babe' accompanying Sonny and Cher, who warbled from the speakers.

In due course, one or two of the group said their goodbyes and began to drift away.

"Are you ready to make tracks Kate?" Phil asked her.

"Yes I think so" she looked at her watch, which swam in and out of focus, got to her feet, and wobbling slightly, sat down again "but I think I'd better ring for a taxi"

"I'll drop you off if you like. I think you might have a bit of a wait for a taxi at this time of night" said Phil diffidently "I've only had low alcohol lager, I'll be fine to drive"

Kate made her excuses to the remainder of the group and leaning fairly heavily but not too noticeably against Phil managed a respectable departure from the bar. The blast of fresh air as they walked out onto the street made her feel a little better, but she was enjoying his proximity and continued to lean on him.

In the car park of the police station Phil pulled the keys to the Astra from his pocket and they walked towards his car.

Abruptly Kate stopped.

"Are you alright, you don't feel sick or anything?"

"No, I'm fine. Look, I know this is a bit of a cheek Phil, but will you drive my car. I don't fancy leaving it here all night" She fumbled in the bottom of her bag for the keys and eventually held them up triumphantly.

Being a gambling man Phil did a quick calculation on the odds and decided it was least evens and it was worth taking a chance on leaving the old Astra behind. He took the keys from Kate and steered her gently into the passenger seat of the Audi.

Although the road was empty, Phil pulled out onto it cautiously from the police station car park, trying to get a feel for the handling of Kate's car. As he left the city centre and passed through the last set of traffic lights he was able to put the car through its paces. Yes, he thought he could get to like driving a car like this. It was certainly an improvement on his old car and he wondered if he'd be able to afford one when he got his inspector's posting. Probably not he thought ruefully. Kate's car was a couple of years old; perhaps if she was thinking of changing it he could make her an offer. He eased up on the accelerator as he took the sharp left hand bend of Harewood Bank just a shade too fast, he felt the car pull a little, but he needn't have worried, its road holding was good.

"We are going the right way aren't we?" he checked, as peered into the darkness.

Kate opened her eyes and looked out of the window into the inky night. A silhouette of the wind whipped trees was momentarily caught in the headlights. "Yes, take the next turning on the left, drive straight on through the village and bear left where the road forks at the church.

He followed her directions, and then crawled carefully along the winding single track lane up to the farmhouse. Thankfully there was no one coming the opposite way. He didn't fancy trying to reverse the car up onto the narrow verge alongside the very solid looking dry stone wall. With no small amount of relief he saw the open gateway loom up on his left and squeezing it in through the solid stone gateposts, he rolled the car to a standstill at the front door.

The farmhouse stood on high ground, and it was cold and blowy as they made a dash to the front door. There were lights at two of the downstairs windows. She must have them on timer switches thought Phil as he handed her the keys to open up.

Inside the central heating had been on, and it was warm and welcoming. Kate walked through into the living room, switched on a couple of table lamps and picked up the remote control to the Bose music system as she sank down onto the settee. The room was immediately filled with the powerful, resonant voice of a woman who was singing what Phil thought might be traditional Irish folk music "Is it Enya?" he asked.

"No, some one called Caroline Lavelle. They're similar, but I prefer Lavelle. I think she has more strength. She's also an amazing cellist"

"It's good" Phil admitted, but felt a little out of his depth.

"Pour yourself a wine Phil if you like. There's a bottle of white in the fridge, or some red in the rack, on top of the cupboard".

"No, it's OK, I'd better ring and see if I can get hold of a cab" he gambled

"There's no need. You can stay here, there's plenty of room, and I'll drive us both in tomorrow"

"Oh!" he tried to feign surprise at what he'd been hoping for. It was better than last time, even if was in the spare room "well, what are you having, red or white?"

"Just a small glass of white, please"

"That sounds good, I'll have the same. I'll be back in a second, and shall I feed Jasper while I'm in there?"

"You can if you like, he's never yet refused an extra meal, but he shouldn't need any more. Betty will have been in at tea time"

Phil rattled around in the kitchen, he found the glasses and the wine without difficulty but where the hell did she keep the cork screw? He was still madly opening and closing drawers when she came into the kitchen.

"Has the bar closed then?"

"No, service will be resumed a soon as possible. But I can't find the corkscrew"

Kate walked across to the wine rack and lifted a heavy, antique brass key down from a hook on the wall. She handed it to Phil.

"What's this then, the key to the wine cellar?"

"I wish. No what you see in the wine rack is all I have" She took the key back from him and holding on to the shaft gave it a sharp twist. The handle of the key came away, to reveal a corkscrew, which had been concealed in the hollow shaft of the key. The handle, she demonstrated could be used as a bottle opener.

"Very impressive. I suppose it stops people helping themselves to your wine if they can't get into it" He took the corkscrew back from her and deftly opening the bottle, poured them both a generous amount.

"By the way Phil, I don't think I congratulated you on passing your inspectors" she said, taking the glass from him.

"Thank you. It means I'll probably have to go back into uniform for a while, which I'm not really looking forward to. Although it's all a means to an end I suppose"

"Yes, I suppose. We'll really miss you though, especially if George doesn't come back"

"He'll come back Kate, don't worry. What else would he do with himself. He's not the type to start growing roses. This job is all he knows"

"I hope you're right" she sighed, suddenly sounding tired.

"There's no point worrying about it now Kate. These things always work out in the end" Phil placed his glass on the scrubbed pine table and put his hands on her shoulders.

Was it a gesture of comfort? He knew that she was exhausted by the events of the last twenty four hours, as he was himself. His hands moved slowly behind her shoulders, repositioning carefully so as not to pull her shiny brown hair.

She leaned into him resting her head against his chest. She was tall, but he was taller. Just the right height, in fact. 'For what?' She asked herself silently and stifled the urge to giggle. Well, for standing like this for one thing… her eyes were closed and she felt a bit unsteady. Either she was moving or the room was. Must have had one wine too many she thought. She turned her head slightly, she could hear his heart beating loudly, or perhaps it was just her close proximity.

He made no further move but held her firmly against him and inhaled the scent of her shampoo.

She mused for a second. The decision was obviously going to be hers. Should she lift her face to his and kiss him on the lips, or to make a jokey remark and move away from him. He was a good man and she knew he would allow her to do that without making things awkward.

He must have been reading her thoughts. Calmly and tenderly he whispered into her hair "So, …. What happens next Kate? It's your call"

Slowly she lifted her head and studied his face, and then kissed him gently on the lips.

Was it with a tinge of regret, he wondered.

She placed both hands against his shoulders and stepped back from him.

For an awful moment he thought she was going to tell him that she wasn't interested or that she didn't want to spoil a good friendship, but instead when she spoke all she said was "Wait"

He puzzled over the little word as he watched her walk through to the hallway. Was she going to return with his jacket which was hanging from the newel post? She'd said he could stay the night, but maybe she'd changed her mind and was going to call him a cab.

Instead she walked past the bottom of the stairs and to the front door of the farmhouse where she turned the key to lock the heavy oak door. She stood leaning against it, with both hands behind her back and faced him with a slow smile from the shadows of the hallway. Then she pushed herself forward from the door and set off towards the staircase. From the third tread she looked down at him, one hand poised lightly on the banister.

How beautiful she looked, he thought, the shadows accentuating the planes of her heart shaped face and the moonlight from the landing window burnishing her hair.

"Well Phil," she said so quietly, that he struggled to hear her "do I have to spell it out?" and continued walking slowly up the stairs whilst smiling down at him enigmatically.

He undid the top button of his crisp white shirt, loosened his tie, and followed her slowly up the creaking staircase.

*   *   *

When Kate woke up it was because she was chilly. The curtains were three quarters drawn and the moon partly illuminated the room. She could see that Phil lay on his front, one arm flung outwards and his lower legs covered by the one remaining triangle of sheet which was still on the bed. She took the opportunity to study the back view of his naked body. Broad shouldered, with a narrow waist, his torso was firm but not over muscled and not too hairy. A slight tan remained from his last holiday. Her gaze moved down. Yes it was all very pleasing.

She couldn't see the time on the clock as it was at his side of the bed, but it must be before six o'clock as the heating hadn't yet come on. Not wanting to disturb him she tip toed across and picked up a white terry robe put it on and lay down again on the bed. When she woke again it was broad daylight and the bed was empty. There was a note on the bedside table. Her heart lurched. Had he been disappointed? She rolled across the bed and picked it up. She unfolded it nervously. It read:

Walking the Dog.
Phil.x

Epilogue

The grey Group 4 lorry, known by the prison population as "The meat wagon" rolled gently to a stop outside the solid metal, double gates, obeying to the letter the notice which read "Do not exceed 5mph". The driver waited patiently until the officer on duty gave permission for the male Officer Support Grade to come out of the gatehouse and open the first set of gates. He grasped and lifted the handle to release the heavy gates and then pushed them slowly open one at a time. The lorry pulled into the lock area and sat with the engine idling whilst the first set of gates were secured with a clang behind it.

Devon Johnson sat handcuffed on the cold hard metal seat in the small cubicle, listening with distaste to the inmate in the next cubicle bawling for attention.

"Come on, boss. Get us out of here. I need a piss!" When no one took any notice he started kicking the door and hammering his fists on the metal partition.

Johnson leaned his head back against the wall of the lorry. What a burke, the guy was. He hoped he wasn't going to be padded up with him. Still, he could give him a quick pasting, act like a psycho. Tell them voices had told him to do it and he'd soon be shifted to a single cell for the safety of the other inmates. He had no intention of being stuck with an idiot like that.

The lorry lurched forward again as the second set of gates was opened and then parked sedately outside the reception building. The driver's assistant climbed down and went inside to hand over the prison records to the officers, and the medical records which were separately parcelled for each man. The yellow "Medical in Confidence" stickers over the flap of the envelope ensured the prisoners medical privacy. They were then escorted off the lorry one at a time. Next to the Reception building was an old single storey pre-fab hut, painted in a crisp cream colour. The sign outside proclaimed it to be the 'Staff Mess.' Immaculately edged flower beds set in a patch of carefully tended, lush green grass, and filled with a riot of colour, it had been planted for the staff to enjoy from the windows as they ate their meals. Johnson eyed them speculatively. That would be a good job if he could get it, working on the gardening party. Better than being inside all day. It was a sought after job though, apart from the obvious benefits of getting out in the fresh air, it was ideal for running an operation and collecting 'drops.' The sign on the prison gate reminded visitors about the penalty imposed if they were caught aiding a prisoner to escape or bringing in prohibited goods. It ranged from a £10,000 fine to a prison sentence. Although some attempted to bring drugs or other illicit goods into the prison on, or in their person, an equal amount was 'dropped' over the fence, and if the timing was right could easily be collected by a member of the gardening party before a patrol came round. An orange, or a rolled up pair of socks, concealing drugs, and thrown over the fence to land in the shrubbery could be picked up and smuggled back inside by a gardener.

Inside the reception building they were placed in a small smelly waiting area, being brought out in turn to be weighed, measured, photographed and entered on to the prison computer. They were then given a cursory medical assessment, being asked whether the had a history of self harm, or subject to fits and faints, before being led off to have their belongings examined, and if on the list of permitted items given back to them. If not, they would be locked away until they could be collected by a relative or given back to the inmate on discharge. You were only allowed so many sets of your own underwear. No wonder some of the lads had a shower in pants and socks. It was one way of getting them washed and ready to wear again. Finally, the paperwork completed they were escorted in single file down onto the wing.

*   *   *

At six feet eight inches tall, Devon Johnson was an impressive sight as he swaggered down the corridor accompanied by his minder Darren French. Eighteen stones of solid muscle strained against the confines of the prison issue clothing. He shook as he let out a deep guffaw, his glossy dread locks swinging half way down his back.

"Hi bro., what you doin' here man" he greeted the inmate standing in the line, waiting for his lunch to be served "didn't know you was coming'"

"Just landed this morning" said ferret-faced Mickey Phillips nervously, the silver stud in his tongue clicking against his teeth. "It's weird here, able to walk round on your own and all. Dunno if I can hack it"

"No worries bro., I'll show you round" Johnson smiled like a crocodile, his gold incisor glinted under the fluorescent strip lighting as he wrapped a beefy arm round Mickey's shoulder. Skinny Mickey shrank in the grip of the big man.

The supervising prison officer, looked briefly over the top of his metal framed glasses as the exchange took place but quickly returned to the more interesting material on page three of the daily newspaper. He'd extracted it from one of the newer inmates who had called to pick it up from the wing office only to be told, "You can have it when I've done with it lad" He could afford to be indifferent. There would be no arguments about who should be served first whilst Johnson was in the queue. At last Johnson released his grip on Mickey, who staggered slightly, relieved to find the wall behind him. The other men in the line melted back submissively as Johnson made his way to the front.

The prisoners behind the servery counter were frozen and watchful as this exchange between the two men took place. The first, holding two beef burgers in bread rolls, the second with a ladle of beans and the third with a huge scoop of chips all poised in mid air waiting for Johnson to hold out his plastic plate. The rest of the line shuffled and fidgeted but no one dared to hassle Johnson to get a move on.

Johnson held out his plate to the prisoners serving the food. Anxious to please, over-generous helpings were shovelled onto the big man's plate. He took it without comment as his due and strode back down the corridor to his cell. Darren French at a mere six feet four was a smaller, slimmer version of Devon Johnson, his father had been Jamaican and his mother a white girl born in Leeds. French had a startling appearance, his olive complexion, green eyes and shoulder length fair dreadlocks gave him a freakish look. Of slight build he didn't appear to pose much of a threat physically but a man known for supplying guns for a living doesn't need to. He took his meal and stepped out smartly after Johnson. The atmosphere relaxed and a nervous chatter began among the men as if to reassure themselves that everything was normal but they were all wondering who the poor sod was that Johnson had singled out. He certainly wasn't in for an easy visit.

*   *   *

That night after lock-up Mickey laid on his bed and stared at the ceiling. His fingernails were bitten to the quick. He froze, and listened, there was a noise outside his window. Swish, tap. Swish, tap. He listened carefully, there it was again. Quietly he got up and slid the glass panel in the window to one side. It screeched against the metal frame and a gust of wind blew a spattering of raindrops against Mickey's face. Outside a line of knotted boot laces with a piece of paper fastened to it swung backwards and forwards like a pendulum. The prisoner's communication system was simple but effective. Mickey reached out and pulled it back in between the bars. He unfastened the laces with fumbling fingers and carefully unfolded the sheet of paper. He smoothed it out on top of his locker.

"Got a job for you Mickey" it read "Jones owes me, I'm calling the debt in and you're the collector" Mickey's legs gave way and he sat down hard on the edge of the bed, putting his head between his hands. His face was wet with raindrops and tears. He stood and took three paces across to the door, resting his hot face against the cold metal. There was no signature on the note but he knew who it was from. Mickey had to think fast. Jones had supporters too. Was it worth letting them know what was going on? No, he didn't dare cross Devon Johnson. It was more than his life was worth. He was between a rock and a hard place for sure. What was he going to do? He knew he was in deep trouble either way.

*   *   *

The next morning in the Association Room Mickey patiently waited for his turn at the pool table. Across the room Johnson slouched against the doorframe, arms folded across his chest, eyes closed and his head nodding sleepily in time to some imagined rap music. Mickey wasn't fooled, he knew

Johnson was watching his every move, what he did and who he spoke to. He felt a film of sweat break out down his back, his head spun like the balls on the pool table.

At lunchtime, Johnson again made his way to the front of the queue, today unusually, he was unaccompanied. Where was French his protector, wondered Mickey? Johnson looked a little uneasy but no one there would even meet his eye let alone give him any trouble. He greeted Mickey, who merely nodded and cringed. Again he was served with extra portions and again swaggered back to his cell, plate piled high. Mickey breathed a sigh of relief and looking up and down the length of the queue saw Jones near the end. His wing must have been the last to be unlocked today. He needed to put the wind up Jones, scare him a bit and then when the time came to collect Johnson's debt perhaps Jones would pay up quickly. He knew he'd be punished for bullying Jones if he was caught but that was a comparatively small price to pay. If he didn't do what Johnson wanted he wouldn't be safe anywhere. He'd always have to be on the look out. Wouldn't dare use the showers… it was amazing what weapons could be made from a disposable razor and an old pencil. Wouldn't dare go to make a hot drink… he'd seen the result of a face full of boiling water with plenty of sugar dissolved to keep the heat in and make it difficult to clean off quickly. He was no oil painting but bloody hell, he didn't fancy that. No, he'd get further back in the queue, whisper in Jones's ear and see what the reaction was. Jones was standing with his back to Mickey talking to another inmate and slapping his plate against his thigh. He decided to sidle up, whisper his threat and continue to the back of the line. But as he drew level he was cut off from Jones by two big men who roughly elbowed him aside. One inmate punched Jones on the jaw, and the other thumped him in the stomach. Jones folded, buckled at the knees and dropped to the floor taking up a foetal position to protect himself from further attack.

"Jesus, what's going on?" shouted a shocked Mickey.

The Prison Officer hit the alarm. "Ok everyone back to your pads. Do you hear me? Back to the wing. Now!" The prisoners quickly dispersed, they didn't want to get involved in trouble of someone else's making. They didn't know what the incident was about, and didn't want to. Mickey sauntered back to his cell trying to make sense of what he'd just seen. The corridor rapidly filled with the white shirts of the prison officers who seemed to appear from nowhere.

"Sorry boss, Sorry boss" said the two attackers as they hung their heads in mock repentance and raised their arms tamely in the air. They were quickly marched from the corridor down to the segregation unit to await the Governor's punishment. They weren't worried they'd seen it all before. Loss of a few weeks pocket money maybe but someone was going to make it worth their while.

Just as calm seemed to have been restored on the wing, and the serving of lunches about to recommence, the alarm sounded again, and the tinny voice from the communications suite crackled over the officer's radios. "Assistance in Block F. Assistance in Block F" The Prison Officers set off at a brisk jog down the corridor.

$$*\qquad\qquad *\qquad\qquad *$$

The officers arrived on Block F, at the door of Devon Johnson's cell. It stood halfway open, his meal was untouched on top of his locker and a threadbare curtain blew in the breeze from his open window. A shaft of sunlight illuminated the scene. The big Jamaican was down. A blue-bottle buzzed above the thin trickle of already congealing blood which snaked across the concrete floor from his right ear. A dusty boot print was clear on his ruined face. Someone had decided they'd had enough. It was pay-back time.

$$*\qquad\qquad *\qquad\qquad *$$

Darren French, better known to his family as Daz, is currently serving a life sentence with a 21 year tariff in HMP Wakefield for the murder of Devon Johnson, whose DNA was found on the red nylon football sock, which, containing a couple of PP9 batteries had been swung with tremendous force against his skull. French considers it worthwhile to have avenged the death of his younger half brother, Leon Edwards.

Printed in the United Kingdom
by Lightning Source UK Ltd.
121009UK00001B/366